RISKY GAMBLE

Lord Egbert Norwoods's words echoed in Elizabeth's mind as Lord David Leighton entered the room to find her alone.

"Some women think they can reform a rake," Egbert had sneered. "I say, once a rake, always a rake. David can have his pick of the cream in London. Do you really think *you* could satisfy him?"

The sight of David's incredibly handsome face made Egbert's words seem all too true. How could she imagine that David's proposal of marriage was not a rake's ruse to make her his plaything?

There was but one way to test the honor of his intentions.

She swallowed hard and took the plunge.

"David. Kiss me," she said . . . shocked to discover she did not know what she wanted his answer to be . . .

ELIZABETH'S RAKE

by

Emily Hendrickson

A SIGNET BOOK

SIGNET
Published by the Penguin Group
Penguin Books USA Inc., 375 Hudson Street,
New York, New York 10014, U.S.A.
Penguin Books Ltd, 27 Wrights Lane,
London W8 5TZ, England
Penguin Books Australia Ltd, Ringwood,
Victoria, Australia
Penguin Books Canada Ltd, 10 Alcorn Avenue,
Toronto, Ontario, Canada M4V 3B2
Penguin Books (N.Z.) Ltd, 182–190 Wairau Road,
Auckland 10, New Zealand

Penguin Books Ltd, Registered Offices:
Harmondsworth, Middlesex, England

First published by Signet, an imprint of New American Library,
a division of Penguin Books USA Inc.

First Printing, January, 1993
10 9 8 7 6 5 4 3 2 1

To my dear Kirsten,
the finest assistant a writer could desire.

1

"I MET THE most divine gentlemen while at Emma Fenwick's for tea," Hyacinthe cooed, trailing her soft woolen scarf of peacock blue paisley behind her as she drifted across the room of her aunt's country home.

The small morning room at Montmorcy Hall was a favorite gathering place for Lady Montmorcy, her daughter Chloe, and two nieces who lived with her, cousins Elizabeth Dancy and Hyacinthe Dancy. They were daughters of her two brothers, and while quite unlike, she considered them charming additions to the household.

This February day proved no different. Outside, a strong breeze swept the Surrey countryside, and it looked to rain before long. Inside, a cozy fire warmed the air and cheered the eye.

Elizabeth Dancy gave her cousin an impatient glance from troubled blue-green eyes before returning to the difficult execution of a winter scene on the copper plate before her. "Lovely," she murmured, quite accustomed to Hyacinthe's transports of fancy after several months of her company. How Aunt Bel tolerated it was a mystery to Elizabeth.

"Well, and you ought to have been there." Hyacinthe preened before the mirror above the fireplace before making her next announcement.

Knowing what was expected of her, Elizabeth dutifully asked, "Why?"

"Well . . . the Marquess of Norwood, for one. And"—Hyacinthe darted a complacent look at her favorite cousin—"the Viscount Leighton as well."

The immediate stiffening of Elizabeth's spine gave the only clue of her reaction to this news. Drat and double drat, she fumed silently. She had escaped from London hoping never to see the man again. And here he popped up almost on her aunt's doorstep. She had avoided his calls, claiming the headache. What would the rake want with her, anyway? Their friendship in London had not flourished.

Fixing her dear cousin with the blandest of looks, Elizabeth said mildly, "How nice." She hoped her clenched jaw allowed her to be understood.

"Nice! That is all you can say to having two of Society's most desirable bachelors practically under our noses?" Hyacinthe ceased her posing and dropped into a chair close to where Elizabeth worked at her engraving.

"I am not interested, at least not in those gentlemen," Elizabeth said quietly. "You may have both of them with my blessing. I do not care for rakes," she added, thinking of Lord Leighton, "nor do I long for a title. A simple life in the country is all I desire." And, she added to herself, a man who does not stir up such scandalous yearnings within.

"Oh, mercy," Hyacinthe said in disgust. She looked at her dearest Aunt Bel for support, and received a cautioning nod.

Isobel, Lady Montmorcy, widow of the esteemed Marquess of Montmorcy, had welcomed her nieces into her Surrey home to keep her daughter company. Not yet out, Lady Chloe Maitland ached to rush to London to make her come-out and find a husband, not necessarily in that order. Lady Montmorcy hoped that her nieces would provide distraction.

"I think it is marvelous!" Chloe breathed, her eyes wide with the excitement which might be expected in a seventeen-year-old girl.

"They will scarcely bestow a look on a girl barely out of the schoolroom," Hyacinthe said in deprecating accents.

Elizabeth tossed her younger cousin a sympathetic glance, then added, "You would not wish to be thought *coming*, Chloe. I know you are impatient, but your time will arrive, and you had best savor every day, not wish it gone." Elizabeth spoke with the wisdom that comes with being nineteen and having a Season behind one.

"True," added Lady Montmorcy, looking thankful that her nieces were the ones to pour cold water on the impetuous Chloe's auburn head, and not herself.

"Elizabeth has had a Season, and she did not accept anyone. I do not see how you could pass up several proposals," Chloe said, giving her cousin a reproachful stare.

"I knew we should not suit." Elizabeth glanced up, then resumed her work with a somewhat faster heartbeat. How could she have accepted anyone when she nurtured a highly improper *tendre* for the most shocking rake in all of London?

"Well, I shall find someone, I can assure you of that," Chloe declared in ringing accents. "I have no wish to dwindle into a thornback." Then, giving Elizabeth a stricken look, she added, "Not that you fall into that group, for you are too young and beautiful. It will be years before you are past praying for." That these words were scarcely better was brought home to her by the frosty glare from her mama. It wouldn't do to be thought an old maid when one was nineteen.

"You met Viscount Leighton before, Elizabeth, didn't you?" Hyacinthe said. "I recall that he served as groomsman at Victoria's wedding. Since you were also an attendant, I fancy you first met him then? Or perhaps at one of those many parties you attended?"

"I cannot understand why you did not come to London yourself," Elizabeth said, hoping to change the subject.

"I detest the city. The air is injurious to the health and the atmosphere not to my liking. I far prefer life in the country." Hyacinthe tilted her pert nose a trifle, while staring off into the distance.

"Where she could be a queen bee," Chloe added, giggling at the scowl directed at her from her mother.

Ignoring her teasing, Hyacinthe returned to her original topic—the gentleman from London.

"But you did meet Lord Leighton? Did it have something to do with the daring deeds Victoria performed?"

"Yes," Elizabeth admitted.

Chloe frowned. "You have said nothing about it. Explain, if you please. I hate not knowing things."

"Victoria served as a government spy while doing her

sculpting,'' Elizabeth revealed. ''That is how she met Sir Edward. I fear I did no more than engrave banknotes for our spies to use in foreign countries. Only Julia did not join us. We all learned a bit about codes and ciphers, spy work in general. It is not as exciting as one might think.''

''I have a feeling there was a great more involved,'' Hyacinthe murmured, directing a curious look at her mild-mannered cousin.

''I believe we ought to invite both of the gentlemen to the Valentine's Day ball you are to give, Aunt Bel,'' Hyacinthe coaxed with demure propriety. '' 'Tis my understanding that while Lord Norwood is but visiting in this area, Lord Leighton is a resident.''

''He is the son of the Earl of Crompton,'' Lady Montmorcy said with a hint of curiosity in her voice. ''But he has not frequented his father's company for some time. Once a young man has a taste of London, he is seldom found languishing about the family estate . . . unless he has come to grief. Elizabeth?''

''If the gossips are to be believed, he is the worst rake in London, ma'am.''

''A rake!'' Hyacinthe uttered in ringing tones of horror and fascination.

''I wonder what has brought him home, then.'' Lady Montmorcy gave Elizabeth an expectant look, like an inquisitive robin listening for the sound of a meal.

''It was my impression that his father is ill, ma'am.''

''Ill? Oh, I do hope not.'' Lady Montmorcy subsided into solemn reflection that lasted some moments.

Elizabeth wondered at the wistful smile that lingered on her aunt's face, but said nothing, pleased to have the attention turned elsewhere.

''Well, perhaps he will not attend, but would it not be proper to send invitations to them both?'' Hyacinthe queried in dulcet tones that fooled only her aunt, who thought her the epitome of propriety and grace.

''I doubt they would wish to join in anything so terribly countrified,'' Elizabeth said in an offhand manner, as though it mattered not the least to her if the dashing beaux from London crossed the Montmorcy threshold to attend the annual Valentine Day's ball.

She had purposely avoided Lord Leighton from the

moment she had glimpsed his tall, handsome figure on the main street of the nearby town. Recalling he had left London to visit his father, she prayed that august gentleman had recovered, and that Lord Leighton was merely pausing nearby. It had meant some skillful dodging, paying a call or two she'd not intended, and shopping for things she'd not the least notion of buying as a means of evasion.

At last she decided to remain at home. It had not been easy. And now, to have him right in the house? At the ball? She knew her aunt and all the wild superstitions she believed. What did she think happened on Valentine's Day? Elizabeth knew enough to be extremely wary.

"Do as you wish, of course," she offered quietly. Then, deciding she had best be prepared, she continued, "What traditions do you hold for that day, Aunt Bel?"

"Oh, there are a number of delicious beliefs, my dear. Let me see . . . well, there is the matter of the first man you see on that day. The custom varies, but *I* believe that the very first man an unwed girl sees on that day will be her husband."

"I thought him merely to be her valentine for that day," Elizabeth objected in what she hoped was a reasonable manner.

"No, no," Aunt Bel denied firmly. "I have seen it work many times, although not for Chloe, but she is too young as yet." She gave her precious girl a fond look.

Hyacinthe sat up with a calculating expression on her face, but erased it when she caught Elizabeth watching her.

"I believe I shall remain in bed the entire day, if that is the case," Elizabeth said at last, giving up on guessing what might be going on in Hyacinthe's mind.

"I shan't," Hyacinthe said firmly. "I shall address the invitations right now, and hope they will not be offended at the lateness. The ball is almost upon us, and I think they ought to see that there are acceptable entertainments to be had in the country as well as in London."

Elizabeth repressed a sigh and bent to her work. It was a foolish dream for Hyacinthe to fancy they might compete with a London hostess, not to mention the extraordinary diversions found in the city. Elizabeth had missed

Lady Tichbourne's *conversaziones* and the other gay amusements she had known in London. But, she reminded herself, her expulsion from that mad whirl was voluntary. She had fled—for Lord Leighton had merely teased her when Elizabeth wanted something else entirely.

With Victoria on her way home from her wedding trip, and Julia at Viscount Temple's country estate, Aunt Bel's home proved just the right sort of haven. Or had.

Elizabeth could execute her engravings while deep in the country as well as in the heart of the city. The commission from Mr. Ackermann for a series on country life was a godsend. It gave her an excuse for doing something she enjoyed, and permitted her to refrain from going about with her cousins if she chose. Memory of Lord Leighton's stolen kisses had haunted many a night's sleep. The wretched man most likely had forgotten all about them. Not so Elizabeth.

"Is that a skating scene, Elizabeth?" Chloe said, frowning over Elizabeth's shoulder at the lines being cut into the copper sheet. "I do hope we can go skating this winter. Last winter was too mild. But if the cold weather continues, we just might."

"I think it would be lovely if we could have a skating party in that event," Hyacinthe said, folding her hands properly in her lap as she bestowed a demure look on her aunt.

"I suppose so," Aunt Bel said without a great deal of conviction.

"Is everything ready for the ball? What decorations do you plan this year, Aunt?" Elizabeth prompted, again hoping to change the subject.

"Nothing terribly unusual, I fear. I have had the footmen set up the cupids in the ballroom, and Hyacinthe and Chloe are nearly finished with the satin hearts. There will be flowers from the greenhouse, and the cook is making a confectionery heart from spun sugar."

"Ordinary, indeed. I vow it will look splendid. I'll have you know that the white and red satin hearts are quite exceptional," Chloe declared stoutly.

"I feel certain it will be the best yet," Hyacinthe added, throwing a significant look at Elizabeth.

Not misunderstanding the matter in the least, Elizabeth responded, "You know an invitation to your Valentine's Day ball is eagerly sought by everyone who is anyone, Aunt Bel. I venture to say this one will top them all."

"If only people are not too tardy," her aunt replied, taking note of the time on her locket watch. "I do not approve of this Town fashion, arriving late to functions." She rose, glanced at Chloe, then said, "I had best confer with Cook again," and marched out of the room with a militant expression on her face.

"I vow, Chloe, even if she is your mother, there are times when Aunt Bel positively gives me the shivers," Hyacinthe declared.

"I think we ought to write down a list of all her superstitions so we shall be prepared," Elizabeth said. "Chloe, my love, be an angel and find a paper and pen. You ought to know them nearly as well as your mother, and I would be aware of what to expect." Elizabeth fixed a compelling gaze on her cousin, who obediently rose to do as bidden.

"Pansies and verbena she believes to be love potions," Chloe began.

"Thank heaven it is February," Elizabeth declared.

"Well, you already know about the first man you see being your future husband. Are you really going to remain in your room, Elizabeth?" Hyacinthe said with an appraising gaze.

"Perhaps," Elizabeth replied in a noncommittal tone.

"When is your birthday?" Chloe inquired, while drawing little hearts around the edge of the paper.

"Mine comes in April, while Hyacinthe's is in March. Why?" Elizabeth knew that her aunt believed all sorts of things, and one could be entertained for hours listening to her ramble on. She appeared to believe in every one of her collection of superstitions.

"Mama says April has a precious stone, the diamond, which stands for innocence. March has a bloodstone, which means courage and presence of mind. I should say that fits Hyacinthe admirably. I have yet to meet anyone with more presence of mind."

"Chloe," the redheaded Hyacinthe cautioned. "That is nonsense, no matter how pretty it sounds. What else?"

"Mama says that two lovers can find out if they will suit by going out at night and picking a flower. If the stem is straight and smooth, their lives will be like that. But if the flower is crooked or spoiled, take caution." Chloe's eyes twinkled with delight. "And she also says that if you eat a piece of bride's cake before you go to sleep, you will see a vision of your future husband."

Hyacinthe and Elizabeth exchanged guarded looks. Elizabeth tried hard not to laugh; Hyacinthe appeared to reflect on the subject.

"Did you know that if you put a clover leaf in your right shoe, the first man you meet will be your love? Or at the very least someone who has that name," Chloe continued, aware that her cousins did not agree with their aunt's little notions. "Of course, you might recite a special verse first. It goes—"

"Spare us, Chloe. Since it is mid-winter, 'tis unlikely we shall find a clover leaf. And we have other things to concern us." Hyacinthe ruthlessly stopped Chloe with her words, and the younger girl subsided warily.

"Well, Mama may follow tradition and have each person draw names as they enter the ballroom, the girls to be paired with the young man whose name she's drawn."

"I think that might be horrid," Hyacinthe observed.

"Not if your valentine presents you with a lovely gift, as is custom here," Chloe replied. "Last year Mama received some very pretty gloves from her valentine, Mr. Smithers. He also sent her a very lovely valentine, embossed on paper from Dobbs, and very gallant it was, too. Although it was folded like a letter, it had hearts and cupids with love knots on it. I fancy I should like one like that, for it is superior to homemade ones, do you not think?"

"It is the message and intent that is most important, I suppose," Hyacinthe murmured.

"The homemade ones require talent as well," Elizabeth added. Relieved to find no other superstitions associated with Valentine's Day, she was only too willing to put aside her nearly finished engraving and join in completing the plans for the ball.

"Is it agreed that we shall extend invitations to Lord Norwood and Lord Leighton? Aunt Bel will be in alt if they accept, and surely they must, for anyone can tell them that her ball is most delightful." Hyacinthe cast a cautious glance at Elizabeth before proceeding to address two invitations in her flowing copperplate. "I shall send one of the footmen with these."

"You sound as though you will take no chances," Elizabeth joked.

"Indeed," Hyacinthe murmured as she gathered up a few papers with notes for the party before leaving the room. She paused at the door. "Is Norwood a rake as well?"

"I suspect he is." Weren't they all? Elizabeth could only hope that the illness that had affected Lord Crompton and had brought Lord Leighton on the run was serious enough to keep the young rake from attending the ball.

Excitement ran high the following day when formal acceptances were received from both gentlemen.

Aunt Bel studied Elizabeth before offering her thoughts. "I believe we shall have the cream of parties, my dears. There is not a mother around who will fail to see that her children attend. The young ladies should hope to catch the eye of the titled gentlemen, the young men would strive to learn the manners of a London beau."

"Even if he is a rake?" Elizabeth kept her eyes on her plate, pushing around the buttered eggs that had appealed to her a short time before.

"A titled, wealthy rake is always forgiven. Besides, everyone knows that a reformed rake makes the best husband," Aunt Bel said complacently.

"Another of your beliefs?" Elizabeth nudged her plate away, concentrating on the scrap of toast in her hand.

"I have seen it happen more than once." Lady Montmorcy finished the last of her chocolate, then consulted the locket watch she always wore. "Time to attend to the acceptances. I suspect others will quickly learn of our important guests. Word does spread. Not that our little affair would not be well attended all the same. I like to think the ball relieves the tedium of February. I only hope it does not snow.'' This last remark was said with a worried glance out of the window.

Elizabeth rose from the table to walk to the windows. Outside the gray skies did not hold the promise of fair weather. "It may wait, or possibly it will rain, and I doubt that will be any more welcome. The roads are bad enough as they are.''

"Are London streets better? Neatly cobbled and even?'' Chloe demanded to know.

"Cobbled, yes. Better? No. They smell, and are anything but even. One endures what one must, I expect.''

"How can you like the spring in London if it smells?''

"It is the company, love, not the condition of the streets,'' Elizabeth said, then chuckled as she recalled the many times she and Victoria had dashed madly about London while using their individual talents for the government. Did she miss the excitement, the daring subterfuge? She wasn't sure. She had welcomed the quiet haven at Aunt Bel's, but now sensed all was due to change.

She expressed as much to Hyacinthe when they went up to bed the evening before the ball.

"It is far and away the silliest thing I have ever heard,'' Hyacinthe scolded in her pretty manner.

"I cannot help it,'' Elizabeth replied slowly. "I have this feeling, a sensation of complete reordering.''

"Well, I am going to put up my hair in papers and retire for the night. I rather envy those chestnut curls of yours. You do not have to sleep with little knobs all over your head beneath a nightcap. Do you know that I have the prettiest collection of nightcaps? Mine are all embroidered and trimmed in lovely lace.''

Near Elizabeth's door they were confronted by the sight of Aunt Bel directing several maids. They were carrying Elizabeth's clothes from the green room, where she had been residing. Hyacinthe's maid was carefully transporting all of her belongings across the hall to the green room.

"What is this, Aunt Bel?'' Elizabeth demanded.

"I have decided that the pink room is to be yours, Elizabeth. The green one is more for Hyacinthe. Her unfortunate coloring, you see.''

"I see nothing unfortunate about lovely red hair and

beautiful white skin, even if she does have a freckle or two," Chloe stated in ringing terms as she joined the others.

"You do like pink, even if you wear aquamarine most of the time?" Aunt Bel said with an anxious look at Elizabeth now that the deed was done.

"Of course, Aunt, it will be fine, as long as Hyacinthe does not mind," Elizabeth said, trying to soothe her aunt.

"I had this vision, you see. It clearly told me to switch you girls." Aunt Bel stared off into space a moment before returning her attention to the maids.

"Who are we to argue with a vision?" Hyacinthe said with rare good humor.

Elizabeth suspected that as long as Hyacinthe's clothes were in order, and the bed comfortable, she really did not mind. "I fancy you will like the green room, Hyacinthe. The view is ever so pretty and the sun warms you in the morning."

Aware it would not be proper to make a fuss, Hyacinthe smiled and strolled into her new room.

Elizabeth watched until the door closed, then turned to her aunt. "Is that the real reason for the change? Not that I mind, for 'tis a lovely room. But it has been hers all these months."

"She misses her parents, it will keep her mind occupied."

"They have been gone over a year now, she is out of mourning. I suspect the advent of two qualified London beaux will more than keep her busy."

"She is exceedingly proper, and is not given to the ruses taken by other young ladies," Aunt Bel assured.

Elizabeth wondered how her aunt could be so blind, then shrugged off the feeling that Hyacinthe was being catered to while she, who'd lost her parents many years before, was not.

Actually, the pink peony room, as Aunt Bel delighted to call it, was more to Elizabeth's taste than the green jade room. Around her, the walls bloomed with luscious peonies amid oriental traceries of leaves and vines. The bed hangings were a deep peony pink that ought to have clashed with her hair but didn't. On the floor, a thick carpet with the same colors woven into peonies on a pale cream background looked lush and inviting.

The wardrobe doors stood open, revealing the rows of gowns in the aquamarine Elizabeth favored. The color matched her eyes, she'd been told often enough, and it was one of her few points of vanity. The aquamarine was also reflected in touches here and there about the room, much better than the conflicting jade.

The tap on her door some minutes later was not totally unexpected.

Hyacinthe stuck her head around the door, then slipped inside. "What do you make of this exchange?" She spread her arms out to encompass the room.

"One of Aunt's little oddities. I trust it does not upset you?" Elizabeth eyed her cousin with a few misgivings. Hyacinthe might not throw tantrums, but she could make life very unpleasant if she decided to be annoyed.

"Mercy, no. But it is strange. One never knows what Aunt Bel will do or say next." Hyacinthe prudently seated herself on a slipper chair of rich peony velvet.

"Which makes for a life that is never dull, at any rate." Elizabeth chuckled at the grimace that crossed her cousin's face.

"I know you were teasing when you said you intended to remain in bed all day tomorrow. But really, you do not fear that Aunt Bel truly believes in that nonsense?" Hyacinthe leaned forward, studying her cousin's expression intently.

"I believe she does, but what she might do at the ball, I cannot say. She is not predictable," Elizabeth concluded in a great understatement of the matter.

"I have noticed that you have behaved a bit peculiarly these past weeks. Even before I noticed that Lords Leighton and Norwood were in the vicinity." Hyacinthe studied the toe of her embroidered slipper, assuming a very nonchalant mien.

"I'll admit I was taken aback to discover Lord Leighton was in this area," Elizabeth confessed.

"Do I detect a romance?" said the ever romantic Hyacinthe, perking up to watch her cousin as she brushed her curls, preparing for the night.

"That is absolutely the most utter nonsense! He treated

me more like a sister. Lord Leighton is a monstrous tease. What a pity he did not have a string of siblings upon whom to vent his inclination—not that they would have enjoyed it any more than I did," she concluded acidly.

"You do not like him?"

"I loathe the man," Elizabeth declared, although quietly, and with less conviction than she ought.

"Fascinating."

"Do not tell me that hate is akin to love, for I'll not listen. Julia reminded me of that before I left London."

"Your sister is most likely right, having been married and all. Marriage makes a woman a woman, or so my mother always said," Hyacinthe murmured wistfully.

"Go to bed, Hyacinthe. I am worn to flinders what with the preparations for the ball. I should think you would be, too." Elizabeth made shooing motions with her hands, but wore an affectionate look on her face that belied any cross feelings.

"I shall see you in the morning. Be careful who you meet after midnight!" Hyacinthe giggled and fled to her room.

Alone, Elizabeth felt free to indulge in singing a little tune. As customary, she tucked her pistol beneath her pillow, something she had done for the past few years. A life in London that had been filled with spies and daring deeds had prompted her to keep the gun handy. Even though all that was behind her, old habits died hard.

She crossed to open the French window a crack, inhaling the crisp, cold air with relish. The windows led to a charming balcony. At least it likely seemed such in the summer, when the wisteria bloomed. There was no one out there now to hear her, for she was a dreadful singer, having what her family tolerantly referred to as a tin ear.

The melody was one she loved, and wished she could have done justice to, but alas, she couldn't. So she sang and hummed in the privacy of her room.

A glance in the looking glass told her that her nightgown draped quite nicely about her in sheer cambric folds, its tiny bodice covered in exquisite embroidery. Over her head she pulled a dainty nightcap of lace and

cambric, tying the ribbons neatly under her chin before
crawling beneath the covers.

She had barely drifted into a good sleep when she heard
it. A noise.

Suddenly alert, she stealthily sought the gun beneath
her pillow. Her fingers groped for the not-so-very-small
firearm. A crack shot, she knew how to handle the
weapon once she had it balanced in her hand.

She waited, scarcely daring to breathe.

Another sound, a scraping noise that one might make
while floundering about in the dark.

Elizabeth took aim at that noise, then cautiously waited
to see if the intruder would identify him or herself.

Silence. Then another soft bump and a muttered curse.

Elizabeth was correct. Danger lurked, even in the heart
of the country. She wavered in her resolve, reluctant to
shoot yet fearful of what might befall her if she called
for help. The intruder might attack her before help could
come! She had never thought to actually shoot *at* someone, only fixed targets, tame round objects stuffed with
straw. Too terrified to cry out a challenge, she knew she
must defend herself the best she could.

Taking a careful breath, she squeezed the trigger,
knowing she had but one chance to hit her target. A muf-
fled cry told her that her shot had struck its quarry. Another sound prompted her to believe the person had fallen
to the floor. With trembling fingers she placed the gun
on the table, lit her bedside lamp, then slid from beneath
the covers.

It was then she discovered the identity of her victim.
"Lord Leighton! Oh, jiminy!"

Elizabeth dropped to the floor, heedless of the impropriety of her dress or her isolation with the man she'd
assiduously avoided. Blood seeped from the wound on his
arm, and he looked to be in frightful pain. "Confound
it," she murmured as she rolled his lordship over to better examine the damage. What a pickle!

"All I wanted was a chance to talk with you," Leighton protested, his words slurred, to the apparition in
snowy white who hovered over him like an angel of
mercy. She missed the appreciative gleam that sparkled

in his eyes as he viewed the sheer cambric-veiled figure of the well-endowed Miss Dancy.

"You might have presented yourself in the drawing room, sirrah," Elizabeth snapped, albeit quietly. She could scarcely miss the alcoholic fumes that emanated from his lordship. The man was foxed!

"And be informed you were not at home? You have avoided me at every turn." He winced when she tugged the sleeve of his coat, pulling it from him with none-too-gentle jerks. "That hurts," he complained.

"And so it should. You have been shot," she reminded him, quite unpitying in her care. "And you are most improper, creeping like this into the bedroom of a young woman."

Then she remembered that this room had belonged to Hyacinthe until this evening. Her heart felt crushed as she considered the implications of that, even as she sought a pad with which to stanch his bleeding.

The door flew open and her aunt charged into the room, a poker in hand, her dressing gown flying about her. At the scene before her, she halted abruptly. "What's this?"

"It was an accident, ma'am," Elizabeth said, trying to figure out how she and Lord Leighton might extricate themselves from what she was rapidly coming to see might be a very tricky situation.

Her aunt consulted the mantel clock. "After midnight!'Tis Valentine's Day! You have just shot your future husband, my dear girl!"

2

PANDEMONIUM BROKE LOOSE.

A wide-eyed Chloe peeped around the door, Hyacinthe right behind her, both arrayed in voluminous white nightrobes with dainty caps tied neatly under their chins.

They were quickly followed by Gibbons, Aunt Bel's odd butler, clad in an awesome plaid flannel robe of generous proportions, and the first footman, James, attired in a hastily donned shirt and breeches. The latter two properly kept their curiosity under control.

Elizabeth threw Gibbons a wild glance, wondering if he would rise to the occasion. "Do find a doctor, or at the very least someone who knows more about medicine than I do."

"Here, here," murmured the injured Leighton. He shifted his position and placed his head on Elizabeth's lap. When she sent him a startled look, the one she received in return was limpid with innocence. "I am in great pain," he added sadly, then winced as she moved.

Elizabeth spared him a dark glance that told what she thought about his uttering a word one way or the other.

Before the plump, absentminded Gibbons could act, he was thrust aside by Purvis, Aunt Bel's formidable abigail. Her flowered chintz robe wound snugly about her spare frame, tied in place with a no-nonsense belt, and a lone braid of an odd shade of gray hung over one shoulder. Her nightcap was a prim muslin, with the barest frill, and tied precisely beneath her chin. She carried a neat basket from which she began to extract various dreadful-looking objects.

"All of you, out!" she declared in a brisk voice, seeming pleased to be in command. She placed a restraining hand on Elizabeth's arm, adding, ''Except you. You have sense.'' From Purvis, that was high praise.

The onlookers, disappointed that they had to wait for explanations, drifted away from the scene to confer in soft accents down the hall.

Feeling sorry for Lord Leighton, even if he had entered her room in a havey-cavey manner, Elizabeth deftly eased him from her lap, ignoring the look of reproach he bestowed on her. She tucked a pillow beneath his head, wondering aloud, ''Would it not be better to place him on the bed?''

Purvis surveyed that piece of furniture, then nodded. ''He ought to be able to manage that distance, surely.''

The patient made an inarticulate sound that both women ignored.

''Up with you,'' Purvis said to the unfortunate fellow, then firmly guided him to the bed with Elizabeth on his other side.

His right arm curved around her slim shoulders and pulled Elizabeth extremely close to his side. She considered giving him a sharp set-down, then chided herself for that unkind thought. The poor man could scarcely behave in an unseemly manner when he was in such pain, much less have amorous notions. As though to emphasize this, he groaned when Purvis nudged him against the edge of the bed. Elizabeth felt his body slump against her as Purvis threw back the covers. Those strange stirrings deep within her began to flicker again, and she ruthlessly thrust them aside, wondering how on earth she could feel like this at such a moment.

Instead she slipped her arms about him to offer support, pressing her slim body against his side to keep him from toppling over. To compensate for shooting the man, she tenderly helped him stretch out, noting how tall he was, how broad were his shoulders with his coat tossed aside. No padding needed in his coats.

With a speaking glance, Purvis thrust a robe into Elizabeth's hands. Impatiently she donned it, then returned to her duties.

Tucking her very own down pillow under his head, she then assisted Purvis in cutting away the left sleeve of his shirt, firmly nudging away any reactions to all that bare flesh. A young lady was rarely exposed to naked limbs.

With surprising skill Purvis set about examining the wound. She barked out an order for brandy, insisting Lord Leighton needed it. Elizabeth went to fetch it, glad to be away from the sight of all that blood for a moment. Wonder of wonders, James stood outside the door with a decanter of the late Lord Montmorcy's best on a tray. It took but moments to pour a glass for Lord Leighton, not that she felt he needed one.

Leighton drank deeply, then gave Purvis a grin. "Do your best," he said, his voice oddly faint to Elizabeth's ears, which made her feel even more wretched. She averted her eyes from the sight of Purvis cleaning the wound.

In the twinkling of a bedpost, Purvis completed her examination. Her self-satisfied grunt brought Elizabeth's gaze back to her. As though in response to an unasked question, Purvis glanced up to meet her eyes. "My previous mistress had a husband who liked to duel."

Elizabeth considered that statement in silence, assisting Purvis with what she required, while avoiding the sight of his injury. Taking the water pitcher from the dresser, she poured some of the cool liquid into a bowl. Then soft cloths, jars, and bottles were extracted from the depths of the basket, to be used and replaced in order.

When Elizabeth risked a glance at their patient, she met his eyes. His low moan of pain tore at her heart and she looked away.

The sight of all the bloody water and the stained cloths turned Elizabeth's stomach, and she felt utterly miserable. When he looked at her, she could have wept with vexation, for his gaze held no reproach, only appeal.

At last, Elizabeth surveyed the bandaged man who occupied her bed. That dark hair flopped in a frightfully endearing manner over his pale brow. She succumbed to the temptation to brush it off his forehead. To her consternation, she found her eyes caught in his steady gaze.

"I am sorry, sir. Never mind that you did ask for trouble, entering the house like that." She folded up the last of the bloodied cloths, placing it atop the stack.

ELIZABETH'S RAKE 25

Purvis gave a snort, adding, "Young men will do strange things around St. Valentine's Day, won't they?" She tidied the table and bed, then surveyed her patient.

"I doubt that had a thing to do with this nocturnal call, however," Elizabeth said in reply. Worry flooded her being as she continued to look at the silent man on her bed. "I shall sit up with him for what remains of the night. After all, it is my fault he is wounded." Her eyes added the rider that he would not be in her bed if he had gone about the call in a proper manner.

Aunt Bel materialized at her side, studying Lord Leighton with shrewd eyes. "I believe that would be permissible. You are betrothed as far as I am concerned." To his lordship she added, "You have fulfilled my vision, sir, but you might had arrived at a more proper hour."

She motioned James to her side, then watched as he removed Leighton's boots and settled the man more comfortably. Ignoring Elizabeth's sputtering, Lady Montmorcy organized the room, seeing that her niece had all she needed, then retired.

Once alone, Elizabeth met Lord Leighton's drowsy gaze with trepidation. Swallowing with care, she said, "We are not, you know. She fancies the notion tonight." She spared a glance at the mantel clock, then continued, "I shall convince her later that it is all a hum."

She paused by the side of the bed and admonished him, "What an exceedingly foolish thing to do, to be sure."

"It seemed like a good idea at the time. After all, Romeo tried it," he murmured groggily. "Didn't expect a gun."

"What with all that went on while I was in London, with those intruders, I find I have peace of mind with it under my pillow."

"I see."

"Besides, *I* was not the person you intended to see this night," Elizabeth observed primly, annoyed at the feeling of ill-usage that grew within her.

"And who did I plan to see?" he inquired.

"This was Hyacinthe's room until this evening. She is the woman you aimed to call upon."

"Rubbish." He stirred, then groaned. His sigh and

look of reproach brought Elizabeth to his side with a
cloth wrung out in cool water. She gently wiped his brow,
then offered him a drink of water.

"Hush, now. We can discuss this in the morning. You
are in no condition to make sense of anything at the moment."

She watched with a kind of satisfaction as the potion
Purvis had given Lord Leighton took effect. Those absurdly long lashes drifted down over ashen cheeks, and
in minutes he slept.

Three of the clock, and bitterly cold out. She wrapped
the robe Purvis had fetched her more tightly about her,
then strolled to the fireplace. She placed another scoop
of coal on the fire, stirring the blaze absently. The flames
leaped higher, and she relished the warmth. The French
windows were now shut tightly, and shut they would remain. She wanted no chill to injure his lordship.

Turning, she studied the man in her bed. He looked
different now as he slept beneath the prim white covers.
Innocent. Vulnerable. Odd, she had never associated
those words with the rake she considered him to be.
While in London he had teased her unmercifully, or at
least, she amended in all fairness, he had teased her with
the good-natured toleration of an older brother.

He had driven her quite mad with all those taunting
glances, the words meant to mock her. And as for those
kisses he had stolen while at the Fenwick's ball, well!

And now he sought her dear cousin, Hyacinthe. Regardless of his protests, she knew better. He must have
bribed one of the maids to reveal the location of her
cousin's room. Hyacinthe, with her glorious red hair and
green eyes and flawless skin—but for two or three freck-
les that only added to her appeal.

What would happen later this day at the ball? Elizabeth
wondered suddenly. She could scarcely attend, with a
wounded man in her bedroom, a man *she* had injured. If
word of this reached the local society, tongues would flap
like a flag in a stiff breeze. At least her sister Victoria
was still abroad and Julia off in the country.

What her brother Geoffrey might say didn't matter. As
far as she knew, he still remained on the continent with
Wellington. Her thoughts turned to where he served.

Elizabeth doubted for a minute that the peace negotiations with Napoleon at Châtillon would prove fruitful. She didn't trust the Corsican one bit, and hoped those who dealt with his generals didn't either. But Lord Castlereigh was no fool, and likely to see through any ruse the French might think up.

As to the rumors abounding that Napoleon was dead, Elizabeth doubted those as well. It would be too convenient for so evil a man to simply die just like that.

Leighton stirred, and Elizabeth immediately forgot her gloomy contemplations to check on him. He was slightly warm, but not alarmingly so. She wrung out the cloth and set to cooling his brow.

And so the hours passed with Elizabeth soothing his brow, keeping close watch over her rake.

When Purvis briskly entered the room to inspect her patient, she gave Elizabeth a grim smile of approval. "I told her ladyship you'd do just fine as a nurse, and so you did. You've learned well. She has decided he must be moved across the hall to the blue room. James is coming up, and we shall effect the transfer shortly."

A dismayed Elizabeth gave Lord Leighton a concerned look, wondering how he would stand such a move.

"It is not seemly that he be here in what is, after all, your room. The other is ready for him. Ah, here is James now." Purvis turned to greet him, giving softly voiced instructions that apparently met with his approval.

When Elizabeth glanced at the figure on her bed again, she met his bemused gaze with a fluttering heartbeat. Those eyes had such power to disturb her, even when he was half asleep. Aware he had needs that could not be cared for by herself, she greeted the news that his valet would be sent for with great relief.

"Until he arrives, James will stand as attendant for his lordship," Purvis declared.

With that bit of information, Lord Leighton was eased from the bed and assisted out of Elizabeth's bedroom and across the hall. It was not far, but she could see he leaned heavily against James as they shuffled to the blue room. How odd that such a small wound should be so utterly debilitating.

The door closed behind the men, and Elizabeth stood

uncertainly in her doorway, feeling somewhat foolish to be seen staring at the slab of wood, yet unable to move.

The rustle of skirts roused her from her abstraction. Chloe and Hyacinthe descended upon her with soft exclamations of concern, and unconcealed curiosity.

Determined to keep the matter as unromantic as she could, Elizabeth said, "It was all a hum, you know. I believe I mentioned he is the greatest tease in all of London. I daresay this prank will cause him to think before he tries such again." Elizabeth strolled back into her bedroom, glancing longingly at her pillow, wishing she might crawl beneath the covers and sleep for a week.

"A prank?" Hyacinthe said, looking puzzled. "He strikes me as being past that sort of thing. I cannot agree."

"Nor I," added Chloe, a dreamy expression on her sweet face. "It is far too romantic, the handsome nobleman who climbs the vines to see his true love." Her dramatic sigh caused Elizabeth to seethe. "And just to speak with you?"

"It is not romantic in the least. Oh, he is the most vexing creature alive!" Her eyes sparkled with indignation and something else neither of her cousins seemed to identify.

"Dear Elizabeth," cried Chloe, much affected by the thrilling event which had occurred in her dull life, "you are worn to flinders, and we stand here nattering on like a tea party. Forgive us, do."

Hyacinthe also recognized that her cousin needed sleep more than a coze and returned to the door. "We can discuss this later. I should like to know what it was like to nurse such a handsome man through the night."

That was precisely what Elizabeth wished to avoid until she had consulted her aunt, and possibly talked the problem over with the invalid in the room across the hall. She crawled beneath the covers of her bed, inhaling the oddly comforting scent of brandy and sandalwood that remained from the previous occupant.

Some hours later, feeling refreshed and well rested after her sleep, Elizabeth dressed herself in a warm gown of an unusual berry red color. Draping a cream wool shawl over her shoulders, she peered around her door; then seeing not a soul around, she ventured into the hall. Tiptoeing to the door of the blue room, she paused, listening.

Not a sound.

Depressing the door lever, she peeked inside to see his lordship propped up against several pillows. The snowy sheet was tucked neatly about him. He was now dressed in a proper nightshirt. And he looked bored to death.

"Come in," he whispered. "I trust you have satisfied yourself that I still live, no thanks to you."

"Good morning." She noted his wince and recalled the brandy, not to mention the pungent odor he had brought with him. Bristling with irritation, she thrust the door open wider, leaving it ajar, then stepped closer to him.

The blue silk hangings on the walls matched those draped over the bed. The carpet was a dull mixture of blues and tans, and added to the masculine appearance of the room. All this she ignored, concentrating on the man.

"You know full well that if you'd not had the harebrained notion to call upon Hyacinthe in the middle of the night, we should not be in this pickle now." There. It was out in the open. She waited to see what he would say in his defense.

His stare was quite disconcerting, she decided after a few moments had passed. "Well, have you nothing to say for yourself?"

"I have a better understanding of what a fellow who has been tried and judged before opening his mouth must feel like. You have it all wrong, you know," he said softly.

"Until last night, Hyacinthe occupied what is now my room. Aunt Bel had a vision, you see, and decided we must change rooms," Elizabeth added by way of explanation, although why it was needed, she wasn't sure. "Your informant could have no way of knowing of that change, surely?"

"I had no informant, other than the knowledge that you resided with your aunt in this house. You gave me the information yourself," he proclaimed with satisfaction.

"I have not seen you in months, sirrah." She had been unable to conceal a start of surprise at his words. "There is no way that you might have learned such from my lips."

When he shifted his gaze from her eyes to her mouth, Elizabeth groped about for a chair and sank down upon it, her knees feeling oddly weak.

"I have been trying to see you for an age, it seems. I need your help."

This pronouncement brought Elizabeth a feeling of alarm. "You *needed* to see me?"

"Indeed. And as for your location, I heard you singing in your room, and knew it could not be anyone else. I recalled your rather, ah, unique voice." He gave her a faint grin, and Elizabeth shifted back against the chair.

Nodding somewhat regretfully, she said, "That has the ring of truth, for I was singing before I went to bed. You ought not have been in the cold for so long. You must have waited a long time while I went to sleep."

Her scolding brought a wider grin. "That wisteria vine is handy. I managed to climb up and down with ease. Your aunt ought to have it cut back, for it makes it far too simple for a thief to enter the house."

"As you did," she reminded him.

"Quite so. Now that we have settled the matter of the not-mistaken identity or mixed-up rooms, shall I reveal why I was bound to see you?"

She gave him a judicious look. While dying to know what had prompted such drastic action on his part, she feared he would overdo, and subside into a decline. "If you are certain it will not make you tired, I should like to comprehend such outrageous behavior."

"Not going to make this easy, are you?"

"No." She clasped her hands in her lap, and waited with outward patience.

"I needed someone I could trust and depend upon. You know I came here because my father was unwell. Dr. Dibble has done what he could, but . . . It's all dashed peculiar. I need your help." He gave her a beseeching look, glancing pointedly at his wound as though to remind her that she owed him something. "He should be improving, yet he declines."

Any romantic notions Elizabeth might have harbored sank at once. "How can I help? I am not a nurse, although Purvis has tried to train me." She frowned at him, puzzled.

"My father has always had a constitution of iron, but lately he has failed badly. I fear something havey-cavey is going on. Pretend to nurse him, but I want you to keep your eyes open. I suspect everyone, but I can trust you."

She blinked at this encomium from a man who usually teased her to death.

"I knew you had aided the government before coming here. I have not forgotten your engraving banknotes. When Edward told me I was amazed at your daring. I figured that someone who knew how to hold her tongue and had a lively curiosity would be ideal."

"Ideal for what?" Elizabeth asked warily.

"I had hoped to take you over to Penhurst Place, to see what you might uncover," he repeated patiently.

Even as he spoke, Elizabeth realized that while she had conversed with him, he had abstained from his previous mocking manner in London. Rather, he treated her more like an equal, or at least like someone who possessed a particle of sense. Yet she wavered, aware others would deem her behavior improper.

Apparently mistaking her hesitation for a refusal, Lord Leighton continued his appeal: "Could you go to the house, bring the message to my valet, and inform my family I shall be gone for a bit? At least Sidthorp, our butler." He did not explain why the butler rated such attention. "I had thought you might tell your aunt that I have need of your nursing skills. You might come with me when I return home."

He glanced at his neatly bandaged arm and added, "I ought to send Purvis along. Perhaps she could determine what ails my father. Dr. Dibble certainly is puzzled, not that Father permits him around all that much. Detests the man. Calls him a quack."

Considering his request, Elizabeth found it impossible to deny. Not only had she been bored, she did not welcome the idea of attending the Valentine's Day ball and be subjected to the inevitable gossip that must be circulating by now, given the nature of things and the way servants talked.

"I shall be glad to do as you request. At least, I shall see that your valet brings what you wish, and I will inquire after your father." She felt dreadful about shooting Leighton, and felt she ought to make amends. She rose and walked to the door, pausing there to add, "I shall also attack Aunt Bel, to explain why we simply cannot be wed. This silly superstition about marrying the first man one sees on Valentine's Day is just that—silly. I doubt if you wish it either." Not wanting to hear him agree with her, she held up a finger for silence, then went on. "You had best rest now, for you must be fearfully tired after all that explanation."

Not waiting for a reply, she left the room, unaware of the sly grin on his face, closing the door quietly behind her before swishing down the stairs in search of her aunt. One thing at a time.

She ran her to ground in the room given over to the ball. Actually, it was three rooms that opened on to one another. Sliding panels could be pushed back into slots so that the area could become one huge room, as now. It was an eminently practical arrangement, offering flexibility without the problem of having an enormous room delegated to being a mere ballroom.

"Aunt, we must talk, if you please." Elizabeth did not have high hopes of making her aunt see sense. When Aunt Bel became convinced of something, that was usually it.

"Naturally, dear girl. You wish to establish a wedding date, one that will be good for a woman born in April. May is unlucky. Best consider June. Monday for wealth, but Wednesday is the finest of all days to be married."

"No," Elizabeth cried in frustration. "Not in the least. You must see that this entire situation is impossible. You cannot force his lordship to wed me merely because he stumbled into my room after midnight."

"I could do that even if he stumbled into your room *before* midnight.'Tis not the thing, you know." Her look of reproach brought Elizabeth to a halt. "Propriety!"

"I do not wish a forced wedding, Aunt Bel," Elizabeth replied through clenched teeth. While she might be compromised, just how many knew? Compromise be damned.

"Nonsense. You are of an age to be married; he is a handsome young man with a tidy fortune who needs a wife. What else is there to consider?"

"Why not try a different custom?" Elizabeth begged, bringing forth the one she'd gleaned from one of the maids. "Each girl may write the names of three beaux on slips of paper, wrap each in clay, then plop the clay balls in a bucket of water. The first to bob to the surface will be her valentine. It would be different," she concluded with hope in her voice.

Aunt Bel stared off into space for a time, evidently considering the custom from every angle. "Noooo, I think not. Besides, Leighton's name would likely be the one to pop up, anyway. I take these things seriously, you see."

Exasperated beyond belief, Elizabeth frowned, then replied, "I shall not marry the man, you know. Geoffrey has to give his consent, and he will listen to what I say." She actually didn't know that for a fact, since it had been a long time since she had talked with her brother. But she hoped he would pay heed to her reasoning, and have no more liking for a forced marriage than she did. If she could reach him before Aunt Bel acted.

"By the bye," Elizabeth said before she disgraced herself by losing her temper with her aunt, "Lord Leighton has requested that I check on his father, and also bring a note to his valet for certain things he wishes to have. His family needs to be told of this, and I am the most likely one to bear the news. Will that be acceptable, ma'am?"

"By all means. Be sure to take Rose with you."

Elizabeth welcomed the presence of her maid as a buffer against whatever might befall her at Penhurst Place. Although what that might be, she couldn't guess.

Leaving her aunt directing the placement of satin hearts, Elizabeth recalled she had yet to consume any food that day. She wandered to the breakfast room, where she found a selection of cold meats and rolls, a salad of sorts, and a torte set on the sideboard for anyone who wished a nuncheon. She filled a plate, then sat at the far end of the table by the window, where she could look out at the dreary scene. If it did not snow it would be a wonder, for the leaden skies looked ready to dump several feet of the stuff before nightfall.

"There you are!" Hyacinthe declared as she peeped into the room. She marched in, remarkably as her aunt was wont to do, then plumped herself down at the table. "I must hear all!"

"Precious little to tell," Elizabeth replied after a bite of cucumber pickle. She surveyed the assortment of food on her plate, and assembled a sandwich to facilitate the consumption of it.

"But what happened? That is, before the gun went off? Did he ravish you?" she concluded, having only a vague notion of what this meant.

"No," Elizabeth asserted, having a much better idea of things. "I heard a sound. I was afraid, so I withdrew my pistol from beneath my pillow. When I heard the third sound, I fired. And hit his lordship," she concluded with a grimace. "The dratted man ought not have been in my room."

"You seem rather unfeeling, cousin dear." Hyacinthe studied her cousin with an assessing gaze.

"Actually, it was utterly beastly. There was so much blood and his wound looked awful." The sandwich, at first eagerly contemplated, was placed on her plate and pushed away. "I cannot bear to think what he must have suffered, all because I avoided him at every turn. He was right, you know. I would have refused to see him if he had presented himself at the house. So, in effect, I drove him to climb up to my room."

"Mercy." Hyacinthe sighed at the drama that had unfolded in her mind's eye. "Now what?" she demanded impatiently.

"Now I shall do as I promised. I am traveling over to Penhurst to deliver a number of messages. His family must be told he will be away for a day or so. I dread informing them of the shooting. If his valet has not already left, I have instructions for him as well." Elizabeth glanced out of the window once more. "I only hope that the weather will hold until I return."

"And then?"

"Why, you shall be the belle of the ball, and I shall tend the invalid." It sounded about as appealing as a jail sentence. But, Elizabeth realized, she would have the rake in her power. And that thought was oddly pleasing.

3

ELIZABETH SLIPPED SURREPTITIOUSLY from her room, down the stairs, and out to the stables. The house had been at sixes and sevens between last-minute preparations for the ball—which Aunt Bel would not dream of canceling, even if Lord Leighton lay wounded on a guest room bed—and watching over his lordship. It must be admitted that the latter task fell to Purvis, who assumed the job with obvious relish.

The entire house knew of the shooting and subsequent betrothal of Elizabeth and Lord Leighton. Although not a word came directly to her, she could tell by expressions, the looks that followed her wherever she went.

At the thought that she might be forced to wed the rake, Elizabeth sighed. That was not what she wished. Not in the least. She would plot and scheme, and if worse came to worst, she'd run off. Julia and Victoria would understand.

Thankful her aunt was preoccupied, and that she need have no worry for Lord Leighton, for Purvis was the best possible nurse, Elizabeth urged Rose along to where the carriage ordered some time ago now awaited them.

"Hurry, Rose. I've no wish to be pressed into service by Aunt Bel with a last-minute commission."

"Yes, miss." The maid timidly climbed in beside her mistress, then settled uneasily in the corner of the gig as they set off smartly down the drive. "You plan to live at Penhurst after your weddin'?" Rose ventured to ask in a small voice.

"I fancy that Lord Leighton would wish me to remain there," Elizabeth replied, thinking that his rakish lordship would most likely consign her to the country forever if he was compelled to marry a slip of a girl like herself.

Then, realizing that Rose felt threatened, Elizabeth added kindly, "No matter where I am, you shall go with me if you wish."

The shy young maid, her eyes large with joy, murmured, "Oh, thank you, miss." She drew farther back against the cushion, her face rosy with relief.

The road that led to Penhurst Place was most impressive, Elizabeth decided as she drove the gig along the back roads. She studied the land they passed. Pretty cottages and farms revealed the excellent stewardship her sisters had mentioned when they scolded her for not enticing Lord Leighton into a parson's mousetrap. Since his lordship behaved well in their presence, they could scarcely be expected to understand how he teased her, or how she hated it.

At the rather plain but elegant brick gate, she paused while the caretaker opened it for her. Then, with a flick of her reins, she continued to proceed along the avenue to the front entrance.

The house was beautifully situated on the crest of a hill, with a fine view to the south of the Ranmer woods across a pretty valley. She considered the pleasant two-story building, built of mellow, saffron-hued stone. It seemed small for an earl. Perhaps it was but one of his residences, maybe a favorite? Come to think on it, the house looked very new, with no ancient ivy clinging to the walls, much less the sturdy wisteria vines her aunt's house wore.

With Rose trailing behind her, Elizabeth braved the front door, glancing back at the lad who walked her horse and carriage. Then the door opened silently, and a portly man appeared, a questioning look in his eyes.

"Sidthorp? I am Miss Dancy. I bring news that Lord Leighton was wounded last evening. He remains at Montmorcy Hall. I have brought a message for his valet, and wish to inform his family of the event." The terse description of his home had included the names of pertinent servants. "Is Hadlow about?"

"Lord Augustus and Mr. Percy are out at the moment. Hadlow is here. I trust his lordship is not seriously injured?"

"No." At least she hoped not.

Upon learning the valet had not departed for her aunt's home, Elizabeth asked to speak with him. She followed Sidthorp across the elegant, high-ceilinged hall, and along a paneled corridor that opened on one side onto a central courtyard. Sidthorp showed her in to a charming drawing room, leaving Rose behind to wait in a quiet alcove in the hall.

Left alone, Elizabeth surveyed the room where Lord Leighton must have spent some time as of late. It seemed odd to have the drawing room conveniently situated on the ground floor. French doors opened out onto a gallery that ran the length of the house, with a southern view of the pleasant valley.

Over her head carved and gilded paneling indicated that the earl had spared no expense in decorating his new house. Gilt lavishly adorned the pretty panels painted with cherubs. She was pleased to see that the furnishings were placed where they might be used, rather than lined stiffly against the wall, as had once been the custom. The crystal chandelier must be beautiful in the evening when lit for company, for even now, rainbows danced as the prisms caught the daylight.

A stir at the door brought her whirling about. Her first impression of the valet was that he would never get along with Purvis. He looked to be as strong-willed as the abigail, and twice as despotic.

"Hadlow, his lordship is anxiously awaiting your arrival. I brought a list of items he wishes to have you take him." She handed the slip of paper to the valet. "I trust the earl is well?"

The narrow glance from the valet did little to reassure her. "He is rather poorly at the moment." Then he left.

Deciding that her best course of action was to see for herself, Elizabeth crossed the room to make a stately progress along the corridor to the front hall. Sidthorp conducted her up the stairs to the bedchamber. Bowing, he left her standing before the door. She rapped gently. A thin face appeared when the door cracked open.

"I wish to see his lordship. Lord Leighton wants to know how he is."

"He sleeps now, miss. Tell his lordship he be unchanged."

Accepting his reluctance to permit a stranger inside, she nodded, then returned to the hall, where she found Rose.

Somehow the sight of her gig before the house did not surprise her in the least. With the earl ill, it was highly unlikely that any caller would remain for long.

While she and Rose jogged along back to Montmorcy Hall, she examined the situation from every angle and decided the entire matter was beyond her.

When she entered her aunt's house, the place was in a well-ordered hubbub. Footmen and maids bustled about, intent on their missions. Upstairs, she noted all the closed doors along the hall, and surmised that the occupants were either resting or preparing for the ball.

Elizabeth elected to do both. Her gown of coral silk was not new, but also not seen by anyone likely to attend this evening's function. And since she would most probably be required to dance attendance upon Lord Leighton, she really didn't care what she wore.

The dinner gong sounded precisely at six of the clock. After months of her aunt's company, Elizabeth rushed to gather her reticule and hurry down the stairs. There would be no dallying about, no waiting for a tardy guest. Aunt Bel would take a look at that locket watch she wore every waking hour of the day, and at five past the hour, head into the dining room. Woe betide a latecomer.

Outside the drawing room door, Elizabeth caught up with Lady Chloe and Hyacinthe, who appeared to be leisurely strolling into the room while deep in conversation. At the sight of Elizabeth, Hyacinthe broke off.

"I looked for you this afternoon. Wherever did you go? It was as if you vanished into thin air."

Gratified that her disappearance had proven so effective, and that not one of her aunt's capable servants had found her out, Elizabeth smiled, then murmured, "I had a brief errand to perform."

"For Lord Leighton?" demanded Lady Chloe in a breathless voice.

"More or less. Do you know, I do believe the weather is going to hold. Although the clouds are rather murky and look as though they might prove nasty, they won't."

"I wouldn't either, if it meant risking Mama's wrath,"

Lady Chloe retorted, then darted a glance at her formidable parent.

Elizabeth reflected that it was quite odd how that dainty woman, who looked as though she wouldn't harm a gnat, could have everyone quaking in their slippers at her merest frown. Perhaps it was her habit of checking her locket watch, demanding punctuality, and nicely getting her way in practically everything.

Which brought Elizabeth back to the riddle she'd been trying to solve all day—that ludicrous insistence that she wed Lord Leighton merely because he was the first man she had seen after midnight on St. Valentine's Day. Or did Aunt truly feel Elizabeth was compromised beyond redemption? That she must wed? Her aunt had uncommon persistence. What she wanted, she got, willy-nilly. And she wanted a wedding.

Perhaps later on, after dinner, Elizabeth could slip up to his lordship's room to discuss their counterattack. They needed to plan, put their heads together, and decide how best to change her aunt's mind. It could be done. Otherwise, it was a middle-of-the-night flight for Elizabeth Dancy!

He might be a viscount and wealthy and handsome as a hero in a novel, but he was a teasing rake, and she wasn't going to have him. Not as hers. If she decided to wed, it would be to someone who cherished her, whom she loved. The gossip she'd heard while in London about Lord Leighton's wild escapades and his bits o' muslin had scandalized her.

With her resolve firmly fixed, she sat down to dinner with an easier heart, ignoring those nigglings of disquiet that entered her mind whenever she glanced at her aunt's placid face. She knew that behind that amiable facade hid an implacable will. Still . . .

Hyacinthe was in alt to be seated beside the Marquess of Norwood. Lord Norwood's Brutus cut displayed his blond locks admirably. The black velvet coat he wore to such advantage complimented his fair looks. That his cravat was a trifle too high for Elizabeth's taste, or the blood red ruby set in the center of it a bit too large, did not matter. Hyacinthe seemed enthralled.

Down the table from where Elizabeth sat between

Squire Littledale and Mr. Beamish, Lady Chloe could be seen—when Mr. Beamish turned aside—happily chattering to the youngest of the Harlowe family, John. That connection would not be approved, since he had not a feather to fly with and would most likely be placed in the church. Since clergy were not known to be plump in the pocket, Aunt Bel would maneuver him to the outermost. Of course, had Harlowe sufficient connections so as to obtain several livings in prosperous churches, which naturally would be handled by an impecunious curate, John might do well enough. But Elizabeth suspected her aunt would look higher for Lady Chloe.

Leaving the gentlemen to their port, Elizabeth drifted after the ladies, Aunt Bel charging in the lead, to the drawing room. They congregated there for a short time before going on to the ballroom. Exclamations of delight at the lovely decorations were heard from all. It was there the gentlemen shortly joined them.

Two dances were all Elizabeth was to be allowed. Mr. Beamish requested one, John Harlowe the other. Aunt Bel summoned her with a faint nod, then ordered, "I would that you attend Lord Leighton. The poor man must be bored to death. He would be gracing our ball had you not acted so precipitously. I trust you have stored your gun in a more appropriate place by now?"

"Yes, I have, Aunt Bel. You wish me to entertain Lord Leighton? In his bedroom?" Elizabeth whispered the last sentences lest someone overhear and make the worst of it.

"Indeed."

Taking an irate breath, for she hated to leave the gaiety for the sick room, yet knowing she must do as her aunt thought best, Elizabeth left. Never mind that she had originally intended to do just this. She disliked being ordered about.

The upper floor was silent, the rooms deserted, with only faint strains of music creeping up the stairs and down the hall. One could hear a wisp of laughter, a snatch of melody, the murmur of conversation, but all muted, as though from a great distance.

His door stood ajar, and Elizabeth paused after touch-

ing the lever, wondering if she might sneak away and
later pretend he had been asleep.

"Come in, whoever you are. I vow, the veriest tweenie
would be welcome" came an irritated voice Elizabeth
had grown to recognize.

"Aunt Bel sent me up here to look after you. Where
is Purvis? Or Hadlow?" Elizabeth had hoped the abigail
would be there, to keep him from his teasing worst. His
valet was another matter, and she could not like the man.

"Ah, the treasure. Purvis decided I may be left alone
for the nonce, and has taken herself off to the kitchen. I
suspect she intends to brew up some more vile concoctions to pour down my throat. Hadlow returned to Penhurst for the moment. He decided I required a change of
clothing."

"You look well enough, sir."

"So timid? Is this indeed the fearless woman who shot
the intruder who dared to enter her holy of holies, her
bedchamber?" His voice mocked her, while those unusual hazel eyes looked almost black in the dim light.
They had a slight tilt to them, which added to that rakish
image. Quite devilish he was, and his glance turned her
legs to mush.

Elizabeth favored him with a narrow-eyed glare as she
groped for a straight-backed chair to ease down upon.
"It could have been an intruder, a thief . . . or worse."
She could feel her cheeks grown warm at his speculative
look.

"Worse you definitely do not want."

"Aunt Bel insisted I spend time comforting you, as I
am responsible for your being here, instead of gracing
the ballroom." Her tone clearly revealed that she, at any
rate, doubted his ability to grace any place well.

"Hm."

She considered him a few moments, then said, "If we
were smart, we would be figuring how to spike Aunt
Bel's guns, instead of sparring like this. I mean, you
cannot wish to marry me and, as I have stated several
times, I do not wish to marry you."

He looked affronted.

Elizabeth repressed a smile. "I did not tell anybody
that you were, er, disguised when you entered my bed-

chamber. Perhaps I ought to have revealed that in aid of our release.''

"Foxed? No. Well, perhaps just a trifle in my cups. Dutch courage.''

"You? I do not believe that taradiddle for a minute. I rather suspect this piece of mischief popped into your mind, and you blundered into my room on the spur of the moment. I trust that in the future you will be less impetuous.''

His silent perusal of her unsettled her considerably, but she kept her chin up, returning his look with what she hoped was cool detachment.

"Actually, I have been doing a good bit of thinking about that. Goodness knows, I have had more than enough time to solve any number of problems.''

"And?'' she replied with a great deal of hope in her voice. If only Lord Leighton were not quite so handsome, or possessed of so many other admirable qualities that would likely be thrown in her face again and again when she broke off with him.

"I have an idea.'' He flashed a grin at her that made her wonder at her resolve, and her ability to keep it.

"Please do go on. I cannot bear the suspense.''

"You won't like it,'' he prophesied. "I propose that for the time being we allow this foolish arrangement to stand.'' He held up a hand when he saw that her bosom swelled with indignation. "Allow me, please, to finish? I came here to obtain your help, and your help I shall get—you owe me, remember?'' When she subsided, he continued. "If we are engaged, no one will think the least of it if you go to Penhurst, spend time inspecting the house, becoming acquainted with the place where you will live someday. Correct?'' He ignored the fact that she'd been compromised by him.

Elizabeth nodded slowly. "I must agree your scheme has merits.'' Her guilt ate at her conscience.

"You needn't be so reluctant with your praise. I haven't heard anything better from you. While you are at Penhurst you can keep a weather eye on my father. I cannot fathom what has struck him down like this. Bloody mysterious. Never known him to cast up his accounts for so long, or be so dazed.''

"Filpot said there was no change in his condition. Hadlow said very little. I trust he told you more?" She raised delicate, inquiring brows, while folding her hands in her lap.

"Dash it all, I want to be there instead of languishing in this confounded bed." He balled his hand into a fist, gently pounding the bed in his frustration.

It seemed he truly cared for his father, and Elizabeth felt her heart soften, for she had precious memories of her own papa that she treasured. Any man who could reveal his affection for a parent in this day, when it was fashionable to act as though you somehow were created without benefit of such, must get her respect.

Then Elizabeth realized that all this talking had not been good for him. He could become feverish. Rather than ask him, for she well remembered how annoying it could be when ill to be constantly nagged about how one felt, she rose to do something about it. Crossing to the dresser, she found a basin filled with cool, lavender-scented water. Wringing out a small towel, she walked to his bedside, perching on the very edge of it.

His suspicious look cut her. With a deal of patience she softly said, "You are wearing yourself out with all this nattering. Hush now, while I talk for a bit." She stroked his brow with the scented liquid, soothing him, almost caressing him, if she'd but thought of it.

She concentrated on their joint dilemma. "I believe your plan might work. Aunt Bel muttered something about going to call on your father. I expect she will demand to see how he does, and I would not be surprised were she to gain entrance to the sickroom. Would you wish Purvis to have a look at him as well?"

"Your eyes are turquoise in this light," he said in a thoughtful voice. "Your skin is remarkably creamy, my dear."

"Except when you put me to the blush by absurd compliments, sir." She flashed him a look of reproof.

"I could do worse than marry you, I suppose. I doubt if any of my cronies would raise an eyebrow at the connection." He peered at her, a twinkle in his eyes, looking as rakishly fetching as any man she'd ever seen.

Elizabeth was utterly incensed. She allowed a few

drops of cold water to fall on his cambric-covered chest, the sheet somehow having slid downward. "I shall fulfill my share of the bargain and look after your father. But nothing more. I shan't marry you, sir. Not for anything."

"I'm such a good catch, how can you turn down marriage to me?" He affected a pout, and for an instant she had a glimpse of what he must have looked like as a boy. It took great resolve to resist his appeal, but he was most provoking.

She scowled at the plaintive note in his voice. She ought to pour the entire contents of the basin over his head. How dare the man propose marriage so casually? He was impossible. Rather than brush aside that appealing curl that had fallen over his brow, she rose and walked to the door, after dropping the cloth back into the basin.

"I shall pay my respects to Aunt and consign myself to bed. It will be a penance of sorts. On the morrow I will begin our plan."

"Before you leave, I have something for you. A Valentine's Day gift, if you like. I hope it pleases you. Over there, on the dresser. Open that package." He turned his head to watch her.

Disregarding his offhand presentation, she hastened to the dresser to pick up the rather large parcel. Sitting back down on the chair, she proceeded to undo the wrapping, exclaiming softly when she beheld what was inside.

"Good gracious! You ought not, you know. This is frightfully valuable." Perched in the tissue reposed an enameled gold singing-bird music box. The base, sides, and top were blue enamel. Wide gold bands trimmed the corners and the oval upon which the bird sat. Unable to resist, she wound up the music box and listened, utterly enchanted, to the sweet melody. "How lovely!" The smile beamed at his lordship was quite, quite bemused and delighted.

"I thought that since you are plagued with that infirmity of the voice, you might like a song sung on key."

Only the delicacy and great cost of the music box kept her from throwing it at him then and there. How like him to tease her about her lack of musical ability. Unwilling to let him know she was hurt, she smiled serenely at him.

"It is truly a marvelous gift, and I shall treasure it always. Would you mind if I conceal it from Aunt Bel for the nonce? We scarcely wish to add fuel to her determination to see us wed." At his nod she rose. "Thank you, Lord Leighton, for the valentine gift."

"I knew you'd be pleased, and so I sent a request to Hadlow to bring it along. Been in the family awhile."

His triumphant smile almost made her take back her words. What a devious man, to be sure. She turned to leave the room, the music box clutched tightly in her arms.

"And the name is David, you know. I think you had best learn to use it."

Compressing her lips and taking a deep breath, she nodded her good night to him. After first hiding the music box in her room, she sailed down the stairs to find her aunt. David, indeed.

The next morning Elizabeth discovered her aunt in the breakfast room, staring out of the window with a frown on her face. Beyond the panes of glass a few lazy flakes of snow sifted to the ground. Elizabeth believed that if her aunt frowned hard enough, the snow would cease, afraid to fall and vex that formidable lady.

"Good morning, Aunt."

"Bad weather to travel to Penhurst Place."

"You plan to go with me, then?"

Aunt Bel nodded. "I wish to see what Herold has done with that house. He was secretive about his plans, and with him not having a proper hostess, I've not had the chance to see it." She shot a sharp look at Elizabeth. "What did you think of the place?"

"Well, I saw nothing other than the hall and the drawing room. But it seems charming. The stone exterior is such a lovely hue of saffron, and the French windows in the drawing room seem most pleasing. Did you know the drawing room is on the ground floor? With doors that open out onto a very nice gallery with a delightful view?" Elizabeth reflected on the charming aspect of the room.

"Good thing you like the place. You'll live there soon enough." Aunt Bel consulted her locket watch, then stared out of the window again.

Elizabeth prudently refrained from disputing this statement. If she roused her aunt's suspicions, her plans could come to naught.

"We shall depart as soon as you have broken your fast. Hurry up, girl. We do not have all day. I fancy my drawing room will be full of callers this afternoon, paying respects after the ball."

"It was such a lovely affair."

"What do you know about it? You danced twice, then retired. Eat." After consulting her locket watch, Aunt Bel rose from her chair and sailed from the room in august dignity.

Elizabeth flashed a look of dismay after her closest relative of the older generation. There really was no one else she could live with, and Aunt Bel had a heart of gold. If only she did not also harbor such strange superstitions.

Having little taste for a meal, Elizabeth shortly left the room. In the entryway, she discovered her aunt attired in an attractive pelisse of dove gray trimmed in deep blue. A confection of blue feathers and gray ribands sat on her head, and made Aunt Bel look years younger.

"I requested that Rose bring down your pretty aquamarine pelisse and bonnet. No sense in going up just to come down again. Wastes time."

Rose timidly offered the articles, while Elizabeth reflected that it was as well she didn't care if she made an impression on the people at Penhurst or not. She'd not be given a chance to primp before leaving.

"I trust the household will be astir, Aunt? With a person as ill as the earl, they may be taking things quiet."

"We shall be ushered in," replied her aunt.

Of Lady Chloe and Hyacinthe, not a speck could be seen. Elizabeth suspected they still slept, relishing that delightful feeling after a ball at which one has been smashing and had masses of partners.

"I am pleased you have agreed to perform this nursing. Purvis declares you have been a fine pupil. You set a good example to the girls not only in this, but your acceptance of your lot. Your marriage to Lord Leighton will turn out quite well, I believe."

Elizabeth shot her a dismayed look. Why did she have the sensation of being trapped?

Before they could exit, a stir above stairs brought them to a halt. Both ladies paused in their steps as a polished gentleman slowly made his way with the aid of James down the stairs to join them. His wounded arm was cradled in one of Aunt Bel's less colorful scarves.

"Leighton! What's the meaning of this?" demanded Aunt Bel of her guest.

"Why, my carriage awaits us, my lady. I intend to go with you."

Elizabeth detected the faint bulge of his bandage beneath his superbly cut coat that indicated where his arm had been shot. Otherwise, he looked complete to a shade, and not the least in need of pampering. His color looked remarkably well for one who had suffered grievous injury.

"Good. That is, if you are in shape to travel," Aunt added. "The more you and Elizabeth are seen together, the better."

"But of course. May I call you Aunt Bel?" He bowed over her hand, smiling lazily down into her soft blue eyes.

Repressing a snort of disgust, Elizabeth eyed him with a jaundiced eye, then said, "Come, *David*, we had best be going. There is such a lot to be done, and no time to lose."

"I shall agree to that, my love." With that, he gestured her before him, and they hurried through the cold to the waiting carriage.

Once in the carriage, her feet on a hot brick, Elizabeth fumed in silence. Did he always have to get the best of her?

4

"YOU OUGHT NOT have left your bed, sir," she began. 'I fear you are not strong enough." He sat opposite her in the closed carriage, next to her aunt. His wicked flash of a grin ought to have warned her.

"Why, after you cooled my fevered brow last evening, I slept like an infant. I feel certain that your ministrations did more than that vile brew Purvis poured down my throat." He behaved as though he had bested her again, with an odious grin on his face.

Elizabeth firmed her mouth, thinking of the dire things she would like to do to his lordship—like boiling him in oil, or something equally lovely. Her mind flashed to the nasty little comment he made the night before, saying that he could do worse than to marry her. Ohhhh, that abominable male conceit of his. It was not enough that he had to be the most handsome man about, but he must tease her into a muddled heap of sensibilities.

What a lowering reflection to be considered as nothing more than a passable connection. Well, she would just keep that lovely music box he gave her last evening. If she must end up on the shelf, the lovely tinkling music would serve to remind her how she got there. She surveyed the gentleman across from her coolly.

"Forgive me for my concern. You seemed a bit pulled this morning, and I naturally believed you to be suffering from the effects of your wound. 'Tis unlike you to look so weak and worried." She bestowed a sugary smile on him, demurely folding her hands in her lap. It was as well, for she dearly wished to punch him on the jaw, as her brother had taught her years before.

Leighton's gaze narrowed, and that devilish smile disappeared. Uncertainty flared in his hazel eyes for a moment, much to her satisfaction. Oh, to strike a blow against all gentlemen who delighted in teasing poor defenseless girls! She quite forgot her lethal little gun that had wreaked such disaster on his lordship two nights ago.

"I declare, sir," she continued sweetly, "I hope you intend to go straight to your bed when we arrive at your home. It would be dreadful if you took a turn for the worse, what with being your father's only heir and all."

He frowned at her, and Elizabeth repressed a smile.

"I believe there are a number of hopefuls in the offing, in the event I go aloft without an heir of my own," he replied in a repressive tone.

It would serve him right if—after she gave him the mitten quite properly—he was unable to find a woman who'd accept him. For that matter, could he ever be serious long enough to make a suitable offer? Casting a doubtful look at him, she decided he would most likely tease his way into marriage, as he did other things. Providing, of course, that he ever got around to it. She'd wager that marriage was not high on his list of things to do.

"Children," began Lady Montmorcy in her most quelling manner, "I believe you had best cease this sparring. Lord Leighton, I should like to know more about this illness that has struck your father."

"Dashed odd thing," Leighton replied. "My father has always been healthy, never sick a day. And then, little by little he became ill, and before long he was in bed, feeling wretched."

Elizabeth noted his apparently sincere worry, and reflected that there definitely seemed to be a serious side to Lord Leighton, or David, as he had insisted she call him. She was skeptical as to how deeply it ran.

"I recall Crompton as being fit as a fiddle," Aunt Bel commented as she stared off into space. "Always on the go with the goers, and never one to malinger." She shook her head in dismay. "Puzzling."

"Quite so, Lady Montmorcy," Leighton said in that persuasive manner he possessed in such abundance. "That is why I hoped to enlist Elizabeth's help. There appears to be a mystery here. She performed noteworthy assistance to the government, and may still be engaged in helping their efforts, for all I know. At any rate, since we are betrothed, it would be acceptable for her to spend time at Penhurst Place assisting me, would it not?''

Aunt Bel frowned slightly, then her brow cleared. "I believe it would be most proper. After all, she did you an injustice, shooting you like that."

"Aunt Bel," Elizabeth protested, "he broke into my room in the dead of night. For all I knew he might have been a robber . . . or worse! What was I to do? Meekly permit him to do as he pleased?''

"Elizabeth Dancy" came a scandalized retort.

His lordship's grin was quite the most odious one yet. Elizabeth knew she blushed, most likely a fiery red, and contained her anger just barely. Trust the two of them to put the worst possible construction on her words.

The two younger people avoided further quibbling by their providential arrival at Penhurst Place. Aunt Bel surveyed the neat brick gate with a shrewd eye, then scanned the orderly avenue to the house with an astute knowledge of what it took to keep an estate in such excellent repair.

"You have a good steward, Lord Leighton," she commented.

"A cousin, Jeremy Vane. My father took him in some years ago, training him in estate management with the hope that some day Jeremy would have experience enough to command a good position."

"Admirable," Aunt Bel said. "Difficult thing for younger sons to find a niche for themselves." She sighed. "I worry about my John. As an only son, he must assume his place before long. I trust his traveling will bring him home safe and sound soon."

Lord Leighton gave her an inquiring look.

"John decided he wished to duplicate the journey his father had made years ago, haring across the Alps down to Italy. How he avoided the Frenchies, I don't know." She checked her watch, then added, "Ought to have been home long ago." As though Aunt Bel thought her John would arrange his trip to her timetable.

"I feel certain cousin John is fine, Aunt Bel. He is as practical as even you might wish, and always manages to land on his feet no matter what happens," Elizabeth assured her.

The topic of the missing heir to the Montmorcy fortune was dismissed as the carriage drew up before the charming home of the Percy family. Or at least one of their homes.

Sidthorp ushered them in with a good deal more propriety than he had Elizabeth the day before. She surmised that Aunt Bel made all the difference.

"We are pleased to see you home, sir," he said to the Percy heir.

Lord Leighton gave him a lopsided smile, then removed his hat, handing it to the waiting butler. His gloves offered a problem his valet would solve later. "My father awake, do you know?"

"As to that, sir, you would have to see Filpot, his lordship's valet," he added for Aunt Bel's edification.

With an apprehensive glance at Lady Montmorcy, Lord Leighton said, "Shall you wish to go with me, my lady?"

"Most definitely," she declared firmly. Turning to Elizabeth, she added, "Wait for us in the library. We do not wish to overwhelm his lordship."

"Yes, do," Leighton inserted.

"Very well," Elizabeth said with resignation.

She watched the pair slowly make their way up the stairs until they reached the open gallery. They walked along the corridor leading to the south bedroom wing until they disappeared. She found the sight of Lord Leighton bending to listen solicitously to her aunt's conversation unsettling. Who knew what her dearest aunt poured into his ears!

Elizabeth turned to Sidthorp. "I believe I shall wish tea, if you please. I feel sure that Lady Montmorcy will as well once she has investigated Lord Crompton's condition."

The butler nodded, then ushered Elizabeth around the corner and down the corridor to the library. Just beyond an elaborate long-case clock, he showed her into an elegant room with book-lined walls.

The air of somber comfort must reflect the personality of the earl, for it certainly didn't his son. Elizabeth liked the neoclassical decor of the pleasantly airy room very much. She trailed a finger along the back of one of the many armchairs scattered about the room, casting an eye at the exquisite needlepoint covers with approval. She'd wager Leighton's mother had worked those. Or perhaps they had come from another estate, for one didn't often buy such delightful treasures that so well fitted the decor.

A writing table of the very latest design stood in the center of the room. Papers were strewn over the top, with a letter knife, a large seal, and red sealing wax in a clutter next to the inkstand. A tray with a pen and a knife for sharpening the quill sat by a silver-rimmed jar of sand. Quite evidently someone had been working here until a short time before. The pen point looked to need sharpening, and Elizabeth immediately decided that whoever used this desk seemed a trifle messy, and not as careful as he might be. Shouldn't those papers have been stored away from prying eyes? Not that she would snoop.

Dismissing the desk, she strolled to the first of the many bookcases set into the walls of the room. The latest works were found on the shelves at eye level. Above, she could see volumes in Latin and German. Walking on, she found a great number of books in French and a few in Italian. Evidently the Percys were a family well taught in many languages.

It did not help her to understand David any better, however. He remained as much an enigma as ever.

A pair of wing chairs flanked the fireplace, offering a cozy spot for reading or quiet conversation. The white marble fireplace was all classical elegance with fluted Ionic columns to either side. The portrait above the fireplace undoubtedly was a Percy, for he wore the faintly amused expression she saw so frequently upon Lord Leighton, not to mention the same brown hair and rich hazel eyes.

At that moment the door opened. She turned around, expecting to see Sidthorp with a tea tray. Instead she found a young man of moderate height, certainly shorter than David, Lord Leighton, who seemed to tower above everyone around. As matter of fact, this man seemed very much like David, only a faded shadow, not as handsome, or as personable. Confused, she raised her brows in inquiry.

"Miss Elizabeth Dancy? Sidthorp told me that we had guests. I am Jeremy Vane, cousin to Lord Leighton."

Elizabeth bestowed a welcoming smile on the gentleman. "How charming to meet you, sir. When we drove up to the house, we were much impressed by the landscape, giving evidence of your care."

His modest shrug could only be commended, she decided. He did not assume airs and graces unfitting a person so removed from the title.

"I appreciate all his lordship has done for me—the earl, that is. He has treated me like a son, and I do all I can to repay his faith."

"Praiseworthy, indeed, sir." She was at a loss as to what to discuss next.

Sidthorp solved the dilemma by entering the room with the tea tray. In addition to the generous pot of Bohea tea with the usual milk, sugar, and lemon slices, there were delicate lemon biscuits and treacle tarts.

"Lovely," Elizabeth said, recalling her slight meal before leaving Montmorcy Hall. In the process of arranging cups and saucers, she glanced up as the door opened once again.

"Jeremy! So you found our guest," Leighton said with a distinctly cool look at the steward.

"Not often we are treated to such a pleasantry nowadays," Jeremy replied evenly.

"Good," Lady Montmorcy said as she marched in behind Leighton. "We can refresh ourselves while we decide what to do. May I say that I find that man Filpot to be a nodcock of the first order, Lord Leighton?"

"You may," he said, sighing with apparent resignation. "Father refuses to part with the man, and indeed, he has been here a good many years. I'd prefer a reliable nurse, but that is not to be."

Aunt Bel exchanged a look with Elizabeth, one full of meaning.

"Would he perhaps permit me to look after him? Aunt Bel? What do you think?" Elizabeth ventured to say. "After all, if David and I are to be wed, I am like one of the family. How could he take exception to that?" She gathered, from the hard look directed at her by her dearest aunt, that Aunt Bel's efforts had come to nothing.

"Filpot would most likely be upset," Jeremy commented.

"Hang Filpot, the old fussbudget," David answered with a distinct lack of his usual charm. Indeed, he looked harassed and troubled, if Elizabeth was any judge. Perhaps his wound pained him. At least he had been able to obtain help with his gloves, and now was draped with a neat nankeen sling for his arm.

"I believe that keeping the room in utter darkness a bit rash," Aunt Bel declared. "Not to mention that potion he gives him. Seemed exceedingly nasty."

"That is the housekeeper's special remedy, my lady," Jeremy stated, looking as though he thought Lady Montmorcy might bite him. But then, she tended to have that effect on people, especially those of the lower orders.

"Hmpf," Lady Montmorcy replied, highly indignant that she had not been permitted to take charge as she longed to do.

Elizabeth had seen that look before, and decided she had best step in before her aunt said something utterly outrageous.

"If there is no other objection, I believe I would like to tend his lordship. Does that please you, David?" she inquired in dulcet tones for the benefit of his cousin.

She couldn't deduce what his reaction would be, for his face was in the shadows. However, he ultimately nodded his agreement. "As long as the arrangement meets with your aunt's approval." He turned to that lady to add, "Mind you, if the weather turns foul, she may not be able to return to the Hall for a brief time. Her maid will be with her, but outside the housekeeper and the maids, there are no other women living here."

"Lord Percy and his son ought to suffice. Neither cousin Egbert nor his father are precisely what you might call top-drawer, Lady Montmorcy, but they do well enough, I should think," Jeremy added, sharing an apologetic smile with Elizabeth.

"Fine. I shall return to the Hall and gather what I will need." Elizabeth resolved to consult with Purvis as well, once she had questioned Aunt Bel as to what she knew of the earl's condition.

Aunt Bel settled on one of the embroidered high-backed chairs to partake of her tea. Nothing could dissuade her from that important task. Sampling a tart, she

daintily wrinkled her nose. "You will doubtlessly wish
to find a new cook, Elizabeth, once you assume your
position here. I believe this tart to be a bit off."

Elizabeth thought the milk a trifle sour as well, but
didn't dream of complaining about it. Elderly ladies could
get by with murder.

Once they finished tea, Elizabeth rose when her aunt
decided to depart the house, following her from the library with a backward glance at Jeremy Vane. Perhaps
she would enjoy his company while here. At least he did
not intimidate her like his cousin. Nor did he appear to
be the teasing sort.

"While you are in this house, you will please remember at all times that you are betrothed to me," David
murmured in her ear, well out of her aunt's hearing.

"Whatever would I do that might call that into question?"

"I saw that languishing look at Jeremy. He doesn't
have a feather to fly with, and is definitely not for you,
my dear," David said rather close to her ear.

Elizabeth bristled at the tone of his voice. Of all the
odious insinuations! As though she would set up a flirt
with his steward. She had considered it might be nice to
find a friend. Nothing more. Before she could reply to
this insulting innuendo, the front door opened.

Two men entered the front hall. Both wore riding
clothes and carried whips in their hands. They appeared
to be amiably arguing about something. Upon seeing
there were guests, and ladies at that, both halted in their
tracks, the argument set aside.

Introductions were made, with Egbert appraising Elizabeth but thankfully not flirting with her. Aunt Bel studied Lord Augustus, as though searching for a hint of the
man she had once known while in London years ago.

"Uncle Augustus, Egbert, I see you are enjoying the
stables," Lord Leighton said in a voice that made Elizabeth glad she wasn't one of the men.

"Dashed fine lot of horseflesh, my boy. Dashed fine,"
replied the older man. He had the look of the Percys, but
his skin was raddled, most likely from too much port, and
his eyes above sagging pouches of skin looked cyn-
ical. While his clothing was spotless, the coat was sev-

eral years behind the current styles and his vest amazingly plain.

Egbert glanced at his father and said, "That new mare appears to be an excellent addition, cousin."

"See that she remains that way, Egbert," David replied, giving his cousin a steady look.

With that, Lord Leighton ushered his guests to the closed carriage awaiting them in front of the house.

"You have done well, David," Aunt Bel praised, "in spite of that man Filpot. I shall feel better, however, when Elizabeth takes up her nursing duties. A pity your father would not allow Purvis to attend him."

"We have yet to see how he takes to Elizabeth," Lord Leighton reminded her.

"Everyone adores Elizabeth. Girl can charm a bird from a bush. I do not foresee any difficulty in *that* quarter. Perhaps she can succeed where the doctor has failed. However, I cannot say I have ever had much faith in Dr. Dibble." She glanced fondly at Elizabeth. "Just keep her safe, my boy."

Elizabeth shared a shocked look with Lord Leighton. What did her aunt think might happen?

"I had believed we would do rather better than that, my lady," his lordship declared.

"Fools frequently do. See that you remember that." She glanced at her locket watch, then turned to leave.

Elizabeth followed her aunt into the carriage, pausing only to inform Lord Leighton when she would return.

David watched the carriage roll down the drive with misgivings. Keep Elizabeth Dancy safe? The girl who so intrepidly shot at an intruder in the dark? He'd rather nurse a keg of blasting powder.

When he reentered the house, his relatives were nowhere to be seen. Trusting his memory, he ambled to the library door, where he found them inside. The remains of tea lay ignored while they sipped excellent port and discussed the morning's ride. He watched them for a moment before joining them. He took care to preserve his invalidish appearance.

"Pretty little gel. Pretty," Lord Augustus stated firmly, a twinkle lighting his rheumy eyes.

"Odd time of day to be paying a call, wouldn't you

say?'' Egbert added, unable to keep the curiosity from
his voice.

"Lady Montmorcy is a dear friend of my father's. Did
you chance to know her years ago, before she wed and
moved to the country, Uncle?'' David strolled over to
stand by the fire, warming himself, and wishing he might
rest. Although the injury was not as serious as he led
Elizabeth to believe, it did pain him some.

"Believe I did. Bound to. Knew everyone in those
days,'' his uncle replied, looking deeply into his glass of
port. "Am sure I did. Believe your father rather fancied
her at one time.''

"And you, Egbert? I vow I am surprised you had not
met Miss Elizabeth. She was everywhere to be seen in
Society last Season. Or do you prefer other company
while in the city?'' David suggested in an even tone.

An angry redness crept up on Egbert's face as he stared
at his cousin.

"Lightskirts. The boy enjoys his fun, David. Pity you
are not more inclined that way. Been Friday-faced ever
since you came home. Can't think why you stay. Ought
to find a good lightskirt to keep you company. Yes, sir,
a good lightskirt.'' Lord Augustus pounded his left fist
on the arm of the high-backed chair to emphasize his
point.

"I do well enough while in Town, Uncle, as you would
know if you ever went there. And you well know that I
am here because of the summons from Filpot. My father
is ill. Or had you forgotten?'' He studied the trio who
sat by the fireplace, the glow of the flames reflected in
their now sober faces. Jeremy had remained prudently
silent throughout their conversation, having nothing to
contribute, it seemed.

"He forgets now and again, David,'' Egbert said.

"We all do,'' David replied wearily. He began to leave
the room, then paused by the door. "Miss Elizabeth is
coming over later today. She will be looking after my
father. I want the three of you to keep out of her way. Is
that clear?''

They all nodded. David noted that Egbert looked exceedingly worried. Good.

* * *

At Montmorcy Hall, Elizabeth fended off questions from her cousins.

"I cannot see how Aunt Bel will allow you to visit a gentlemen's establishment, Elizabeth," Hyacinthe scolded.

"Somehow I doubt if I shall encounter them in the sickroom, cousin," Elizabeth said dryly.

"It sounds vastly romantic to me," Lady Chloe said in a breathy voice. "Fancy, nursing the father of the man you are to marry." A conscious look came over her face. "I do hope he does not die while you tend him. That would be dreadful."

"Indeed," Elizabeth replied with a wry twist of her mouth, rising from her chair by the fireplace. "I wish to consult with Purvis before I leave. Rose shall pack a small portmanteau for me, just in case the weather turns nasty and I cannot make my way home."

Lady Chloe dashed to the window to search the leaden skies. She shivered. "Oh, it looks bad to me. Purvis says she cannot recall a more vile February. I should say it is very likely you will spend at least one night there."

"I think it is all highly improper," Hyacinthe stated in the primmest of manners. "Nothing good will come of breaking Society's rules, mark my words."

"Do you intend to broadcast it to all and sundry, then?" Elizabeth inquired before leaving the sitting room.

"Hyacinthe," Lady Chloe rebuked, "they are betrothed now. I fancy that if Aunt Bel gives permission, it must be acceptable. And Elizabeth is a most agreeable girl."

"Perhaps too agreeable?" Hyacinthe suggested.

"I'll have you know that I have no desire to go to Penhurst Place, Hyacinthe. First, Lord Leighton requested that I assist him, then Aunt Bel as good as ordered me there. Since I am dependent upon her kind mercies, I shan't say no to her express wishes. Is that clear?"

"You met his cousin?" Hyacinthe said, her eyes calculating.

"Egbert Percy? Yes. Not a very prepossessing young man. An incipient fop, I'd say from what I saw. He cannot hold a candle to his cousin, Lord Leighton. Nor, for that matter, can his other cousin, Jeremy Vane.''

"My, what a lot of men!" Lady Chloe declared, her shocked eyes round with amazement.

"I believe I once read there is safety in numbers. His uncle, Lord Augustus Percy, lives there as well. I trust they will all behave like gentlemen. I doubt if Lord Leighton will do more than tease me. He seems to enjoy that a great deal.''

"How curious," Lady Chloe said in a wondering voice. "That does not sound the least lover-like.''

"Quite," Elizabeth replied, closing the door behind her as she left her cousins. Mercy, what an ordeal. Getting Purvis to share her knowledge of healing ought to be a snap compared to escaping from her cousins.

When Purvis was found at last in the still room, Elizabeth expressed her wish for healing potions. After explaining what she had learned about Lord Crompton from Aunt Bel, Purvis nodded sagely.

"Most peculiar. Can't say I could pinpoint the illness. If I could see the man. . . ?''

"Aunt Bel and Lord Leighton say that Lord Crompton will not have anyone else about. And Aunt Bel says the concoction that the cook makes him is a vile potion. Aunt said the smell made her feel ill. I'll wager you could do much better than that woman. Do you know her treacle tarts were off and the milk a trifle sour?''

"No!" Purvis declared in horror. "Well, and I shall do my best, Miss Elizabeth.''

With the honor of Montmorcy Hall at stake, Purvis set to work compounding her best restorative tonic. Once that was completed, she set to stir up other, more interesting potions. By the time two hours had elapsed, Elizabeth felt as though she might dabble in this sort of thing herself, for it fascinated her.

"Finished," Purvis declared, setting the last glass vial into the basket Elizabeth had placed on the table in the still room. "Remember, give him the tonic twice a day. And open the curtains. Poor man." Purvis tsk-tsked at the thought of a gloomy room, even if some of the best doctors urged such. She'd found a cheerful room to be better for health.

"Anything else?" Elizabeth began to fold a crisp white napkin over the contents of the basket, then paused as Purvis handed her a bottle of a brown substance. Frowning, she gave Purvis a questioning look.

"For Lord Leighton. I fancy his arm will be giving his a bit of bother. I showed that Hadlow how to dress the wound, but the man looks none too bright. You best see to it yourself."

Elizabeth meekly agreed, while wondering how in the world she was to get Lord Leighton to bare his arm so she might check his dressing, much less pour down his throat some of the stuff he declared to be utterly vile.

5

ON THE RIDE BACK to Penhurst Place, Elizabeth reflected on how life had changed for her since arriving to live with Aunt Bel. In the past Elizabeth had literally burst into a room, questions tripping off her tongue. A short time with her aunt had cured her of the habit. That, and having the correct and proper Hyacinthe around.

What with her aunt's penchant for punctuality, Elizabeth's habitual tardiness at meals had also been changed. She quickly learned that unless she arrived at the table promptly, she might not eat. Since that was also a habit she'd acquired over the years, she soon adjusted.

But now her punctual and proper aunt wanted her to violate all the dictates of society to tend a gentleman Elizabeth had never even met. To make it worse, she entered a household composed entirely of men, three of them close to her own age and eligible one way or another. Before leaving the house, she had turned to face Aunt Bel just inside the front door.

"How do you know I shall do the right thing? Or for that matter, how do you know I *can* do the correct thing?" Elizabeth inquired while being shuffled out of the door to the waiting carriage that would return her to Penhurst Place.

"You have become quite a sensible girl in the months since you came to live with me," Aunt Bel replied, patting Elizabeth's arm, while handing her the basket of herbal preparations Purvis had mixed for the earl and Lord Leighton. "I trust you to use your brains. You possess compassion along with your common sense. But keep your wits about you, for if that Filpot person is around, you shall have need of it." She watched as Elizabeth climbed into the carriage and the door was shut before scurrying back into the house out of the cold.

Not convinced her aunt was in the least correct in her assessment, but comforted by her words, Elizabeth settled back on the seat for her brief journey, tucking the rug across her lap for warmth.

How ironic it was that the one man in the world that she most wished to avoid should turn up, not on her doorstep, but in her bedchamber! She well knew that marriages often were compelled when a couple were found in a compromising situation. And with her in her nightgown . . . Mercy, he had looked straight at her! Perhaps he wouldn't recall the sheer cambric that permitted a shockingly intimate view of her person. And pigs might fly.

And . . . Aunt Bel still acted as though Elizabeth intended to marry Lord Leighton in due time.

When she sighed, Rose asked, "Be you troubled, miss?"

"Just a bit. I shall want you by me while at Penhurst Place. I cannot imagine what I shall encounter there. If nothing more, I want you to keep a watch on those valets. I do not like Hadlow, and I agree with my aunt that Filpot is missing something in his upper story."

"That Hadlow was right proper when he came to the Hall, miss. Treated us all with fittin' manners for a valet to a viscount, he did. Might not seem like a friendly fellow, but that wouldna' be right, you see. One must respect his position, he must." Rose nodded her head in a virtuous way, the single feather adorning her neat straw bonnet bobbing up and down in emphasis.

"Curious." Elizabeth found little comfort in this commendation, although she well knew that servants were not easy to fool, and that they were severe judges of character.

Sidthorp ushered her into the saffron-hued house with a much improved manner. Of course, he did not go so far as to actually smile, but at least he didn't look quite so forbidding. She handed her pelisse to Rose along with her bonnet and gloves. The basket she retained.

"This way, miss. Lord Leighton is in his room, but

he left instructions that you were to go directly to his father's room when you arrived."

With Rose trailing behind, she followed the portly butler up the stairs and along the hall where her aunt and Lord Leighton had gone earlier.

"Is Lord Leighton's room in this wing?" she inquired in what she hoped was a disinterested manner.

"Yes, miss. Last room on the left." The butler paused, rapped gently, then opened the door before them, quite some distance from Leighton's.

Elizabeth stood in her tracks, trying to adjust to the dark. For in spite of it being afternoon, it might have been night in there. "That will be all, Sidthorp."

She must have sounded accustomed to giving orders, for Sidthorp left her immediately, even bowing. Elizabeth crossed to the windows and gently pulled the draperies aside to allow the winter light, such as it was, to enter. Then she turned to study the room while tying an apron about her waist. Although vast in size, it was simply yet elegantly furnished.

The enormous bed drew her attention. Nestled in the middle of the magnificent structure hung with royal blue silk that was embroidered with delicate gold threads lay a man. A very still man. Then he stirred.

Elizabeth hurried to the side of the bed, placing the basket atop the night table. "Sir? Is there anything I can do for you?"

It seemed to her that he fought to open his eyes. When he succeeded, Elizabeth suffered a shock, for David, Lord Leighton's hazel eyes stared at her from a lined face. Only there wasn't that familiar teasing present in them. They merely looked tired and ill.

Swiftly hunting through the basket, she found the tonic Purvis had prepared. In a trice Elizabeth had opened the bottle and poured a dose into a glass.

"Now, let me ease you up a bit. I shall have you feeling better in no time." He obediently drank the liquid, then studied Elizabeth with puzzlement.

"Who are you?" he managed to whisper.

"Elizabeth Dancy. Lady Montmorcy's niece. I have come to nurse you. My aunt wishes you to be well, as does your son. For some peculiar reason they believe I can manage to persuade you to get better.'' She twinkled down at him, sharing the absurdity of a young woman convincing an old man he ought to live.

A ghost of a smile fluttered across his mouth, then was gone. "Amusing. Must know I like pretty gels."

The effort of that little speech exhausted the earl, and he closed his eyes to sleep once again.

She turned to share a concerned look with Rose, who set about tidying the room, muttering beneath her breath at the shortcomings of the Penhurst Place staff.

Elizabeth inspected the room. Aunt Bel had told her to dispose of anything that had come from the Penhurst kitchens or the valet. Elizabeth was inclined to agree after her own experience with both. She scooped up various evil-looking potions and proceeded to pour the contents out the window—after first checking to see that she wouldn't be dumping them on someone's head. She pulled the window shut quickly, grateful for the brief breath of fresh air.

That accomplished, she went about the room to check what else might be done, wishing she could give the place a thorough airing, for the stale atmosphere felt stifling to her, and it must to the invalid as well.

At last there was nothing left to do.

"Rose, I must also tend to Lord Leighton." The maid glanced with incurious eyes and nodded, accustomed by now to Elizabeth's ways.

She studied the potion Purvis had ordered her to give Lord Leighton with great misgivings. How could she dare to command his lordship to do anything? Then, recalling that she was responsible for his condition, she squared her shoulders and marched down the hall, bottle and spoon in hand, the ointment for his wound in her apron pocket.

At the last door on the left of the hall, she paused, then gently rapped.

"Enter."

Taking a deep breath—for she had never in her life gone into a gentleman's bedroom, except for her brother's and he didn't count—Elizabeth gingerly opened the door and peered in. He was alone.

She swallowed carefully, then stepped across the

threshold. She was inside. Holding the bottle and spoon before her as though to ward off any demons that might linger in a bachelor's bedroom, she moved forward.

"What the devil are you doing in my room? Elizabeth, you know you ought not be in here. Out!" he ordered, and not in a kindly manner.

His odious attitude, when she had come to administer medicine to him, and that not her own idea, firmed her resolve. "I have something for you."

"I have no doubt as to that, sweetheart. But I fear it will have to wait until this arm is better. You see, I'm a bit hampered in my movements." He gave her a caustic grin.

She knew she must be blushing. And it angered her even more. The dratted man could do it every time—disconcert her into a feminine flutter.

Annoyed, she did what she might not have had the nerve to do ordinarily. She marched to the side of his bed, poured out a spoonful of the "vile stuff," as he called it, then aimed the spoon at his mouth.

"If you think for a mo—" He was halted mid-speech when the spoon was deftly thrust into his mouth. She poured another and waited.

He glared at her. "You'll do it again, won't you? I pity our children."

Refusing to allow him to overset her again, she nodded. "Right you are. Open wide . . . sir."

He meekly obeyed, to her surprise. Finished with that task, she pulled the jar of ointment from her apron pocket. "Now to your wound."

"Hadlow will not like this," Lord Leighton prophesied.

"Oh, bother Hadlow," she said crisply, beginning to enjoy her authority in the sickroom. It did have merits after all. She could quite see how Purvis had become such a dictator. She rolled up the cambric sleeve of his nightshirt to a point above the wound, trying to be impersonal in her attentions.

The bandages unwrapped, she sucked in her breath when she saw the wound. While not actually nasty, it was scarcely a pretty thing either. She ignored his probing look and set about gently cleaning off the concoction

Hadlow had smeared over the injury, then replacing it with the mixture Purvis stirred up. In minutes she efficiently had his arm neatly wrapped. All that tending to the tenants at Montmorcy Hall had proven beneficial after all. She'd had training of a sort from a master, Purvis.

"Now then, you shall feel more the thing before you know it," she said as soothingly as she could. Then she recalled where she was and with whom. She took a step back.

He groaned.

Elizabeth immediately dropped the jar of ointment into her apron pocket and rushed to feel his brow. Staring down at his face, the closed lashes, she wondered what had happened. Purvis had not warned her that the "vile stuff" might affect him like this.

Wondering what she ought to do, she stretched out a hand to check his forehead for a fever.

His eyes flashed open. Before she realized what he was about, she found herself pulled down on the bed, falling against his body in a most scandalous way. Worse yet, his good arm snaked about her waist. In a trice she found herself being thoroughly and most adequately kissed. Warm little pulses went dancing up her spine, flittering along her nerves, until she was quite certain she would end up in a spineless heap on the elegant carpet.

Even though he had the full use of but one hand, he appeared to make good use of it, caressing her in delectable ways in improper places. Never had she dreamed anything could feel like this. And this was called lovemaking, she had no doubt. That seemed a rather prosaic word for such delightful passions.

This was *not* like the kiss at the Fenwicks' ball. There was no question in her mind he was an expert at this business. And she completely enjoyed being the recipient of his mastery. He smelled delicious, of sandalwood and something spicy. And he felt delicious, firm and muscular and somehow oddly comforting. She didn't care if she ever left this room.

He withdrew first, to her chagrin. She ought to have fought him, pounded at him, protested in some way, instead of meekly submitting. No, that wasn't true. She had not submitted. She had enthusiastically cooperated!

His satisfied smile was almost too much to endure.

"You, sirrah, are a cad and a bounder."

"You forgot scoundrel and rascal, not to mention rake."

"Those too."

She hardened her heart at the sight of the lopsided smile, the curl that flopped so endearingly over his forehead. "I had best leave. *Now.*" She slipped from his light clasp, rising to unsteady feet. She positioned the bottle that Purvis had sent on his bedside table, then turned away, hoping to calm her flip-flopping heart to normal.

"No. I want to give you something. Over there on the dresser. See the box? Fetch it . . . please?"

Unable to restrain her curiosity, Elizabeth did as bidden, telling herself that if she didn't, he might suffer a relapse. Returning warily to his side, she held it out to him.

He took the box, opened it, to extract a ring. An incredibly lovely diamond winked up at her from his fingers. A delicate gold setting surrounded it, and it was quite the most beautiful ring she had ever seen.

"You wish me to wear that?" she inquired with a mixture of horror and delight. "I daresay it's extremely valuable. I do not think I should," she said with an air of propriety.

"I found out your birthday is in April, and you are most assuredly an innocent. I believe this to be appropriate." He smiled a trifle grimly, then added, "Your presence here will be more readily accepted if you are seen wearing the family betrothal ring."

Her heart sank to her toes, although she knew that neither of them wished for the marriage. What a silly fool she was, to think for a moment that something else existed. This man was an experienced rake, a polished man about Town, certainly not interested in unsophisticated girls.

She accepted the ring, surprised to find that it fit her well. "How amazing. It fits."

His chuckle further unnerved her, and she backed away from his bed, glaring at him, lest she succumb to temptation. The trouble with resisting temptation is that it might not ever come again.

"I shall see you tomorrow?"

And then it might. Elizabeth nodded, totally unable to speak after her outrageous thought. She turned and fled the room, fuming at the faint chuckle that drifted after her.

Back in the earl's room, she found Rose standing at the foot of his lordship's bed, studying the man who lay so quietly.

"He be awful still, miss. Not natural-like."

"I know. I doubt if the tonic Purvis used is supposed to have that effect." Elizabeth walked closer to the bed, staring down at the earl with a frown pleating her brow.

"Reminds me of the time my brother got too much laudanum, miss. He lay just like that, in a stupor he was."

Elizabeth froze. Could it be possible that someone had drugged his lordship? But why? And who? She shook her head. Most unlikely. And yet, as she watched the spare frame, the barely rising chest, and flaccid countenance, she could not help but wonder.

A glance at the mantel clock revealed it to be time for dinner. She checked the earl's pulse and forehead, then slowly went from the room, leaving Rose in charge for the time being.

Once outside she encountered Filpot. His hair was neatly parted in the center and dangled about his ears, and his long legs were encased in modest black hose, with everything else he wore also in funereal black. The lanky valet glared at her.

"I shall return later to check on his lordship and give him his tonic. Nothing from the kitchen is to enter this room without my approval." Elizabeth folded her hands before her, hoping she could manage that quelling look her aunt did so well. "You may close the draperies this evening, but I want them open come morning. I shall be coming in to tend him then." Giving him a hard stare, Elizabeth calmly walked down the hall, then down the stairs to the ground floor.

Sidthorp stepped forward to offer his assistance.

"Going so soon, Miss Elizabeth?" Egbert emerged from the shadows of the corridor to her left.

"Mr. Percy. No, I remain for the time being."

"I see." He made her feel most uneasy, reminding her this was a predominantly male household.

"Come, have a glass of sherry with us. My father wishes to speak with you."

Recalling David's suspicions, she agreed, hoping to discover something useful about both of the Percys. Could there actually be someone in this house who wished the earl ill? Dead?

As preposterous as it seemed, she knew the expression "waiting for dead men's shoes" had valid grounds, and as well, arsenic was not called "inheritance powder" for no reason.

Darting surreptitious glances at Egbert while they walked down the corridor to the drawing room, she wondered about him and his ambitions. Did he desire a title? Wealth? Being a dandy could be vastly expensive. He certainly looked the fop this afternoon with his lilac pantaloons, primrose vest, and pale gray coat.

"My dear Miss Elizabeth," he said in a mocking manner as he ushered her through the drawing room door.

"Sirrah?" She raised what she hoped was an imperious brow at him, reminding him that he took a familiarity not granted.

He shrugged, not seeming the least affected by her words or expression. Apparently quelling took practice.

"Ah, so there you are." Lord Augustus Percy rose from his chair with a faint creaking of his corset. "Knew you'd come. How's my brother doing? Better, I hope. Rummy thing, getting poorly like that. Do the ticket, having you to look after him. Yes, sir, do the ticket."

"Stands to reason, Papa. A pretty girl by one's bed is sufficient to make one want to get well." Egbert cocked his head to one side, leering at Elizabeth in such a knowing way that she wondered if he had been in the hall while she attended to Lord Leighton. And kissed him.

"Right, my boy. Did you say m'brother is still among us?" Lord Augustus dropped back into the large high-backed chair near the fireplace, and peered at Elizabeth curiously.

"Yes, sir," Elizabeth said respectfully.

"Pretty behaved lass."

It was then Egbert spotted the engagement ring. He sauntered over to pick up her hand, ogling it most odiously, then displayed her hand to his father. "Well, well, dear cuz has not wasted a minute. Trotted out the family ring, no less. I trust you are honored, my dear."

"I am, indeed, sir."

"We are practically family. I insist we not stand on formality, and I claim the right to kiss the future bride." Egbert did more than leer at her, he stepped closer to her side, lifting a hand toward her face.

Elizabeth backed away from him, alarmed by his look of intent. A glance at his father told her to expect no help from that quarter, as the older man wore an amused and quite benevolent smile.

"I thought I told you to keep clear, Egbert," came a deep voice from the doorway. "Put one hand on Elizabeth, and you will suddenly find yourself in need of a new place to lay your head this evening."

Elizabeth relaxed. Although the words were spoken in a casual way, there was no mistaking the seriousness of the person who uttered them.

"Are you all right, my sweet?" David walked over to stand close to her. He effectively forced Egbert to retreat, to Elizabeth's relief.

"Quite. I believe Mr. Percy was merely teasing. It is a trait that must run in the family." She turned then, and saw at what cost he had come to her rescue. He looked pale, and she could detect the strain in his face.

"I shall join you." He drew her aside while Egbert replied to comments from Lord Augustus.

"You ought not be out of bed," she scolded.

"Hadlow informed me that he had seen Egbert, my most detestable cousin, hauling you off to the drawing room. I came to save you from a fate worse than death."

"Egbert?" she said, horrified at her escape.

"Any time spent in his company is regrettable."

"I can see there is no love lost between the two of you."

"Did you see my father?"

"Indeed, before I tended to you. If you hadn't put me so out of countenance, I'd have told you all about it," she couldn't resist saying. Then she grew serious. "I gave him the tonic, tossed all the other potions out of the window.'' At his amused expression she added, ''I first checked to see if someone chanced to be outside.''

''Any observations?''

''Rose made a peculiar comment. She said he reminded her of her brother when he had taken too much laudanum.'' Elizabeth studied the viscount, then gently nudged him onto one of the comfortable chairs on the far side of the room.

''Drugged?'' He sounded as appalled as he looked. ''But who? Or ought I say, which one?'' he finished grimly, glancing at his relatives.

''It may simply be his illness. Perhaps after a good night's sleep, you will think of something. Or someone.''

Before she could urge him to take better care of himself, and make a fool of herself by revealing her concern over him, Jeremy Vane entered the room.

''Miss Elizabeth. How charming to see you on this dreary day. I vow, it is like having the sun come out.''

Elizabeth smiled at the modestly attired man, such an agreeable contrast to Egbert.

Not so Lord Leighton. He rose to his full height, frowned at Jeremy, then said, ''No need to dump the butter boat over her, Vane. She is not only spoken for, but her fortune is only modest.''

Jeremy drew himself up, nodded to Elizabeth, then joined the others, seeming unaffected by the snub.

''That was not kind of you,'' Elizabeth admonished quietly.

''I am not a kind man. Haven't you learned that by now?''

Not trusting that gleam in his eyes in the least, Elizabeth turned in a whirl to march up to her room. She would request a tray and avoid the entire Percy family.

She looked down when she reached the top of the stairs, and was surprised to find Lord Leighton standing in the entry hall, watching her.

''Oh, do get up to bed before you truly take ill.''

''You care.'' He grinned at her, lazily walking toward the bottom of the stairs.

Elizabeth hurried to her room, closed the door behind her, then shut her eyes, totally exasperated with herself, not to mention that wretched man. Would she never learn to guard her tongue when near him?

"You prefer a tray up here, Miss Elizabeth?" Rose inquired at long last, seeing her mistress made no move to return downstairs. She had been put out of the earl's room by that Filpot, she explained when Elizabeth inquired.

"Indeed."

Crossing to the window, she studied the sky. Bleak gray skies were to be preferred to snow, she decided.

In the drawing room, David sank down upon a nearby chair, relieved to be off his feet. Not that his arm pained him as much as he implied to Elizabeth. He suspected that she would hightail it out of this house and back to Montmorcy Hall if she knew just how lightly he was injured. Oh, it looked rather bad, but in actuality it was amazingly mild. How fortunate Elizabeth had hit his arm, and with a gun not fully loaded. Hadlow assured him that the wound ought to heal nicely, with scarcely any scar.

"Had us worried, my boy," said his uncle when he realized David had rejoined them. Shifting in his chair drawn close to the fire, he studied his nephew from beneath his brows. "Dashed odd business, if you ask me."

"Perhaps a bit foolish. I have been trying to see Miss Elizabeth for weeks, and with the fortification of some excellent brandy I decided to beard the lioness in her den, or bedchamber if you will."

"Egad," Lord Augustus muttered while Egbert chuckled.

"As you know, I received a shot for my trouble."

"What the devil did you want to see her about that was so urgent you couldn't wait?" Egbert demanded when he could stop chuckling.

"It seemed like a good idea at the time. I wanted her to come nurse Father. That woman and her gin bottle was the final straw as far as a hired nurse. You must admit that Filpot has done poorly."

"Cannot abide that man," Lord Augustus grumbled.

"Nor can I," David replied. "However, he has been

with my father for ages, and so he remains. Perhaps Elizabeth will be able to counteract his influence.''

''The wound very disagreeable?'' Jeremy inquired from his chair to one side.

David looked down at the neat sling that covered his arm. Something told him that he had best be careful what he said about the injury. ''So-so.''

''Can only hope it doesn't turn putrid,'' Lord Augustus added in lugubrious tones.

''Amen to that, Uncle,'' David replied before rising. It was best he go to his room to keep up the appearance that his wound truly pained him.

''I always told you that your pranks would get you in trouble one day,'' Egbert said as a parting shot.

David considered the lingering kiss he had shared with the delightful Elizabeth and grinned.

6

ALL WAS SILENT the next morning when Elizabeth came down to break her fast. In the dining room, usually a pleasant place, the gloom outside seemed to have crept in through the windows and seeped beneath the doors.

"And a good morning to you," Elizabeth said to the sole occupant with determined sprightliness, although some of it was forced.

Lord Augustus surveyed the sky, then turned from the window. "Not good, not good at all," he said with a dejected shake of his head. "Weather turning miserable again. Best to remain inside." As if he jaunted about. "Known people to stray off the road in a snowstorm and freeze to death before help arrived. If one cannot see, one can hardly find the way."

He turned again to scan the clouds, speaking loud enough to be clearly heard although he was turned from her. "Good of you to stay. Proper gel. Worry about m'brother. You'll see to him right enough." There was a hint of a question in his voice she couldn't ignore.

Elizabeth buttered her toast, considering the previous day. In a mere few hours she had antagonized Egbert Percy, caused poor Jeremy to receive a tongue-lashing, and tumbled into Lord Leighton's arms. No, that was one arm, and she had assisted him, more's the pity. Proper girl? Hardly.

"I shall do all possible for the earl, you may be certain. It is a pity you are not as close as you once were. I wonder if a visit from you might not cheer him up."

"No. Not from me," he said with a trace of sadness.

She wondered about Lord Augustus. Why did he stay here when it seemed he and his brother had become estranged? It seemed most peculiar to her.

She would need to keep a sharp eye on all the inhabitants of this house. Could there actually be someone who would use poison on the earl? Was that why Lord Augustus persisted in staying? She stared at the man, lost in his unhappy reflections. What really went on in his mind? Poison? Her appetite suddenly fled, and she abandoned all pretense of eating, resorting to her teacup for a bit of warm comfort.

"Least he don't seem contagious. Bad to have you in any danger, proper gel like you," Lord Augustus said at long last.

A wry smile touched her lips. There was danger, and there was . . . danger. It seemed to her that Lord Leighton presented a peril of a serious sort. Or did he merely seek to provoke her once again? Exasperating, maddening man.

"Have you been at Penhurst Place very long, sir?"

"Dun territory, y'know. Some time ago. Just need a bit of time to come about. I will one of these days." His corset creaked as he joined her at the table. "M'home is lonely, don't you see? Wish things were different." He subsided into morose reflection again.

Elizabeth made a show of brushing crumbs from her fingers, then pushed away from the table. "I shall go up to see your brother now. Could I bring a message from you to him perhaps?"

"You are going now?" Jeremy Vane said in a dismayed voice. He stood poised uncertainly in the doorway.

"Only upstairs to stay with the earl."

He gave her a hesitant smile, then stood aside to allow her to leave the dining room.

She briskly walked to the central hall and up the stairs. Seeing Rose, she requested that she heat up a bit of the special broth for his lordship. Then Elizabeth marched down the south corridor to the earl's room.

She wondered what her reception would be today. If her suspicions proved true, and that repulsive Filpot was trying to do in his master, her attentions could save the earl's life. Feeling immeasurably better, she resigned herself to whatever came her way.

Sidthorp approached her. He had just come from the

earl's room, and she wondered if she dared to ask him what the mood was today.

"I trust that all is to your liking, Miss Elizabeth?" Sidthorp inquired. "You suffered no disturbance in your wing of the house?"

"Lovely," she assured him, a smile touching her lips as she considered her aunt's hopes. "A good sleep does much to restore one's spirits." It seemed Sidthorp was on the side of virtue. "May I go in to see the earl now?"

The butler rubbed his chin, then glanced about them. Nodding, he said, "Filpot went down to the kitchen not too long ago. I shall find some manner of delaying him, so you may investigate his lordship's condition without that, er, man about you."

Pausing, Elizabeth did something she normally would not have considered. She quizzed a servant. "Sidthorp, it seems that Filpot is not well liked. How odd the earl should be so devoted to the man."

"As to that, miss, his lordship is not one to make changes. Detests a deviation from the customary, you see."

That did not auger well for her assuming control of the sickroom. "Thank you, Sidthorp. I can only hope that I shan't find myself on the doorstep in a few minutes."

"Oh, he likes a pretty face, miss. Fact is, I believe I heard Filpot muttering a complaint to that effect when the staff ate their morning meal."

"Undoubtedly that is why I am here rather than my aunt." She made a rueful grimace at the thought.

"His lordship has avoided any attentions from ladies his own age." The butler shared a look of understanding with Elizabeth, then recalled the impropriety of the conversation about the same time she did. He turned and walked toward the stairs, while Elizabeth continued on to the earl's room.

She was to nurse an elderly man who was set in his ways and liked a pretty face, while avoiding entanglements with women his own age. A difficult task at best. Perhaps that was where Lord Leighton came by his inclinations? Like father, like son? She could just have well been describing David, Lord Leighton, come to think about it. He too seemed set in his ways, and he certainly liked a pretty face, if the gossips in London were to be believed. He was yet a bachelor, having eluded every matchmaking mama in Town. Only to be caught of his own doing.

Elizabeth giggled to herself.

"What a lovely sound so early in the morning."

She looked around from where she now paused before Lord Crompton's door to find Lord Leighton bearing down upon her.

"How are you this morning?" she inquired. "I trust you did not come down with a putrid throat, or something equally dismal, after your outing yesterday."

"Strange, whatever that vile stuff is that your Purvis concocted seems to work. I do feel more the thing today."

"Good, as there will be no repetition of yesterday." At his devilish grin she hurried on to say, "You shan't require my attentions."

He shifted his gaze to the door behind her, then reached around her to open the door. "Come, we had best have a look at the old boy."

She noted his face assumed a serious mien as they entered the bedchamber. Once inside he fixed a more cheerful look on his countenance, walking close to the bedside.

"At least the curtains have been opened, and the fire is not excessive. Quite pleasant, in fact." While she spoke she checked about the room, then walked over to join Lord Leighton at the side of the bed.

Reaching out her hand, she placed it against Lord Crompton's forehead, relieved to find there was no fever. A clean spoon lay on the table by the tonic Purvis had created. Elizabeth met the viscount's gaze before she picked up the spoon and turned her attention to his father. She measured the tonic into a glass, then leaned over the bed.

"Good morning, my lord."

He opened his eyes. "Ah, the pretty face," he said in a barely audible voice.

"I believe you are on the mend, sir." Elizabeth chuckled, then held the glass to his lips, urging him to swallow the tonic. He obeyed her, then sank back onto the pillows with a more alert expression on his face.

"About time."

"Good morning, Father," Lord Leighton offered. "Glad to see you look better."

"Odd that. Feel like I've slept a year."

Lord Leighton shared a look of consternation with Elizabeth. "Dr. Dibble found nothing amiss with you."

"Bah. Then why do I feel as weak as a new kitten, I ask you? I missed you—have you been ill?"

"Er, no. I ran into a slight complication."

Elizabeth decided to insert a comment. "He sought my help. I mistook him for a burglar and shot him in the arm."

"Good Lord!"

"It was a bit of a surprise." Lord Leighton cleared his throat before proceeding. "Also, Miss Elizabeth and I are betrothed, Father."

Surprisingly shrewd eyes surveyed Elizabeth from beneath a pair of shaggy brows. "Fell into a bumblebath, did he? Knew he would someday. Bound to. I believe it runs in the family."

"Something like that, sir. You see," Elizabeth said, deciding to confess all while the earl seemed in a good mood, "he happened to be in my bedchamber at two of the clock when I shot him. In the morning, that is," she added for clarification.

A ghost of a smile flitted across his lordship's face as he turned his gaze to his son. "Did it right and proper, eh?"

"Yes, sir. But my arm is better today." He gestured to the neat nankeen sling which supported his arm. Of Aunt Bel's print shawl there was no sign. Apparently seeing what Elizabeth noticed, that the earl showed signs of fatigue, Lord Leighton said, "Best get down to eat something before Elizabeth offers me some of your tonic."

Once he had left, Elizabeth set about smoothing the bed and checking the room as she had done the day before. She wanted to make certain that nothing from the kitchen had entered the room. No matter who might be trying to poison—if that was the case—it was better not to take any chances.

Rose slipped silently into the room with the broth. She handed the tray with the covered bowl to Elizabeth, then stepped back. "I'll just tidy up some, miss," she whispered.

"Care for a little broth, sir?" Elizabeth coaxed. "I should like to see you continue to improve. It does a nurse's heart good."

"I should like something more substantial, if you please," he insisted. But his voice was weak, and Elizabeth suspected he was putting on a good show for her benefit.

"Try this first. I promise you that I shall bring you hearty roast beef as soon as you may not take ill from it. Now, let me tempt you." She proffered a spoon, leaning over the bed to feed him.

A twinkle lit his eyes, reminiscent of the one she so frequently saw in David's. "That you might do, my dear."

"What a naughty man you are, sir," she whispered, so as not to shock Rose. She grinned back at him, then continued to feed him the contents of the bowl until all was gone. "There now, you shall feel better soon."

"Um," he replied, already drowsy.

"Sleep well." It wasn't necessary to speak in an undertone, as his lordship had returned to the world of sleep.

Elizabeth strolled to the fireplace, absorbing heat while indulging in a bit of reflection.

There were several prime suspects here. Lord Augustus, Egbert Percy, Filpot, Hadlow. Even the cook was not free from suspicion, Elizabeth thought with a grim smile, considering the deplorable meals at this house. She supposed she must include the innocuous Jeremy Vane, although she thought him unlikely. What could he possibly gain? Could there be anyone she had missed? Probably not. Egbert seemed the most likely, especially given David's aversion to him. But then, David did not care for Jeremy Vane either. She sighed with vexation. Was there ever such a coil?

One thing she needed to do was to find a book to read to his lordship. Now that he remained alert for longer periods of time, she hoped to entertain him with suitable material. What would he like?

The door opened, and Egbert Percy stepped into the room.

Elizabeth gave the earl a worried glance before walking across the room to meet his nephew. She intended to prevent him, or anyone else, from disturbing the earl.

"May I assist you in some way, Mr. Percy?" She made certain to keep him standing close by the door.

"I wondered how my uncle did this morning." He gave Elizabeth an uncomfortable look, and she wondered if that was the only reason he sought this room.

"Better, I think. He seems more alert, for one thing." She glanced at Rose, hoping the maid received the message she silently conveyed. "I was about to go down for a cup of tea. Rose will keep watch here. Shall you join me?" She bestowed an inquiring look on Egbert, then gestured to the door.

"Of course," he said politely.

It seemed that Egbert was not averse to playing the gallant. He placed her hand on his arm, chatting about the weather as they strolled down the stairs. Elizabeth felt quite in charity with him by the time they reached the vaulted corridor.

"Is there a garden out there in the summer?" Elizabeth inquired, studying the courtyard that was enclosed by the many-windowed corridor.

"Once there was. Lady Crompton had a fondness for flowers, I believe. Now there is naught but grass and a few bits of shrubbery."

"What a pity. I fancy that a bed of colorful blooms would look quite cheerful on a warm summer day."

Elizabeth guided him in the direction of the morning room in the back of the house, where Sidthorp had confided the earl's late wife had enjoyed spending her time.

Catching sight of one of the maids, Elizabeth sweetly commanded her to bring tea into the morning room.

"Avoiding your betrothed this morning? I thought newly engaged women couldn't wait to spend time with their sweethearts. It all seems dashed sudden to me." Young Mr. Percy stationed himself by the fireplace, watching Elizabeth with a narrowed, and somewhat hostile, gaze.

Sensing she skirted dangerous ground, Elizabeth pretended to examine a lovely painted screen near the window before replying to his comment.

"But we are sweethearts," she said, searching for a plausible reply. "We met in London, you know, at the Fenwick ball. I suspect it was love at first sight for both of us, at least it was for me. And I confess David seemed most enamored. Wherever I went after that, I seemed to discover him. He found me here in Surrey after I joined my aunt. How fortunate that she lives so close to his father. Most convenient for David and me."

She neglected to mention the vast amount of time before he had again sought her company. After all, she was embroidering the truth a great deal, so what did it matter if she did it royally?

"I still say there is something dashed peculiar about the entire business. I had not the least notion he'd formed an attachment."

"But then, you have never been in love, cousin," came a rich, smooth voice from the doorway.

Lord Leighton entered the room, crossing to where Elizabeth stood. He surprised her by touching her on the chin with one finger, then placing a gentle kiss on her lips. It was like a whisper of fire on her skin, singeing her lips with danger.

She knew he sought to prove the validity of their connection to his cousin, but she wished he hadn't kissed her. It stirred things best left alone.

"Good morning," she said, deciding to pretend they hadn't met earlier. "I trust it is agreeable that I have ordered tea. It is such a wretched day outside, and somehow tea always makes things better."

"Most acceptable. After all, my dearest, you will reign here one day." He settled down far too close to where she had sought a place on the settee. When he stretched his good arm out behind her, touching her back, she just barely refrained from jumping. That would never do—a proper bride to be did not flinch from the touch of her beloved.

"How do you feel? I notice you still use a sling." She

worried his arm was not improving. "Does Hadlow dress your wound properly as he ought?" She had a dim view of the valet's nursing abilities.

"I do well enough. He does not have your delicate touch, however." He shared a smile with her that sent tremors to her toes.

She noted the teasing twinkle in his eyes before he turned his gaze toward his cousin. Would she never remember that much of his behavior was due to his delight in teasing her? He could not be serious.

"Lingering about the house, Egbert? Thought you would be out on that new mare."

"Too cold by far."

"Ah, yes, the precarious health of the town beau."

Elizabeth decided to interfere. "Your father does seem to be doing better today, does he not?" She hoped her voice didn't squeak, but she feared it might, making her sound like a ninny.

"What's that? Crompton better? By Jove, that is good news." Accompanied by a creaking corset, Lord Augustus ambled into the morning room, seeking a chair next to the warmth of the fire. "Excellent, excellent. Best news I've had all day." He wheezed as he settled down onto the depths of the high-backed chair, giving Elizabeth a beetle-browed stare. When she tensed, David dropped his hand on her shoulder, bestowing a slight pressure on her.

" 'Tis the *only* news you've had this day, Father," Egbert said impatiently.

"What? Quite so, quite so. Nasty weather. Can't think but what it snows before the day is out, what?" Augustus frowned as he moved his stare to the window.

"Miss Elizabeth will grace Penhurst Place with her presence for more than a day if that is the case. These roads become impassable at the least bit of snow, you know," Egbert said, rather snidely, Elizabeth thought.

Jeremy paused in the doorway, a sheaf of papers in his hand. He gave David a hesitant look, then said most apologetically, "I'm afraid I need your signature on these, Leighton. With your father unable to run the estate, it dumps rather a lot on your shoulders."

Elizabeth smiled warmly at the young man, liking his shy manners. "Will you not join us in a cup of tea, sir?"

The maid entered at that moment, apparently having anticipated the gathering, for there were sufficient cups and a plate of macaroons as well.

At a slight nod from David, Elizabeth poured the tea, added milk and sugar as wished, then thankfully sipped her own, after noting that David had to remove that disturbing arm from her shoulders in order to consume his brew.

"He is feeling much better this morning, you will be pleased to know."

"How is that, Miss Elizabeth? From what I had heard, his lordship was sinking," Jeremy said awkwardly, shifting from foot to foot. He sipped his tea, watching Lord Leighton with a wary eye. The batch of papers was tucked beneath one arm, and Elizabeth wondered how long they would remain there.

How ill at ease he was, to be sure, she thought. Poor fellow, he must feel overshadowed just to be in the same room with Lord Leighton. She believed she had detected a faint family resemblance, however. His eyes were a rather insipid hazel, not the rich, deep tone she saw when she chanced to be entrapped by Lord Leighton's eyes. And Jeremy's hair was straight as an arrow, rather than possessing the charming curl his cousin owned, but it was a shade of brown not too unlike his cousin's.

"It is snowing out," announced Lord Leighton to no one in particular.

Desiring to put some distance between herself and the man who disturbed her, Elizabeth rose from the settee and walked to the window to watch large white flakes drifting down from the sky.

Jeremy Vane dropped all the papers to the floor, and they scattered about the room.

"Oh, dear," murmured Elizabeth. Quickly she placed her cup and saucer on a table, then assisted Jeremy in gathering them up. The poor fellow's face had flamed with embarrassment at the accident.

"Here you are. Such a tedious matter on a pretty, if cold, day. Leases and settlements. Victoria has tended to those while my brother has been away." She sighed, then caught an odd expression on Leighton's face that stopped her speech.

"Give me the papers, and I shall go over them in the library. It wouldn't do to get macaroon crumbs on them, would it?" Lord Leighton bestowed his lazy smile on all, then added, "Join me shortly, will you, Elizabeth? We have a small matter to discuss, if you please."

"Of course, David." She recaptured her cup, pouring a bit more tea for something to do with her hands while she thought. Jeremy had merely requested that David sign the papers, an administrative thing. Why was he placing the young man in an awkward spot by going over those papers? Surely he trusted his cousin to do his best.

Then she recalled how her aunt checked every piece of paperwork before signing anything, claiming she felt it best to know what went on under her nose. Elizabeth relaxed. David was trying to learn more about the estate, nothing more. But the very idea that he would treat his cousin like a mere employee bothered her.

Leaving Lord Augustus and Egbert to argue about how long the snow might continue, Elizabeth left the room. At the door to the library, she paused, then rapped sharply. The door opened before she could drop her hand.

"Good, you came promptly."

Elizabeth followed David over to the desk, wondering what this was all about.

"That young fool ought to know that I cannot sanction the authorization of these leases. It would be illegal. What kind of a spot is he trying to place me in, anyway?"

"I do not understand."

"Although I am the heir, it is not my privilege to approve these—according to my settlement—unless my father specifically allows it. He has not to this date. And I will not approach him about it at this time." David gave her a warning look lest she urge him to do just that.

"Perhaps you should talk with him about it?" she said anyway.

"And make him feel as though I believe he is about to snuff it?"

"I see." But she didn't, actually. She wondered if David was just trying to get at his cousin, whom he appeared to dislike excessively.

Seeking to change the subject, she said, "Do you have a copy of a good herbal in the house? Culpeppers perhaps? Or that new one, the *Family Herbal* by John Thornton? Aunt Bel has a copy and I think it quite good, for it deals with the medical properties of our English plants. Bewick has done excellent engravings which I very much admire," she concluded, wishing she might do such a volume herself someday.

He gave her an arrested look. "You believe there might be a clue in such a book?"

" 'Tis possible," she admitted.

David rose from the chair by the fire to wander along the shelves, touching a volume now and again.

Elizabeth joined in the search, hunting for either volume or anything like them.

He was awkward with only one hand and couldn't easily pull out books. She thought she could be of help if there was one he wanted to see, so she remained at his side.

Elizabeth noted various interesting volumes and pulled one out, thinking it might be good to read to the earl. As she did, another book fell to the floor. It proved to be a slim little volume.

"An Essay into the Operation of Poisonous Agents upon the Living Body," they read in soft unison, both horrified at the implications that began to hit them.

A chill crept over Elizabeth, and she shivered.

"Quite new, isn't it? Was your father interested in such as this?"

"Not that I know," David replied, meeting her eyes in an apprehensive frown. The teasing lights were gone now.

Egbert popped his head in to see what kept Elizabeth. "It's time for nuncheon, you two. Had a lover's spat?" His face wore a maliciously gleeful look, and Elizabeth longed to toss the book at his head.

"Merely looking for something to read later on. If I must spend the night here, I would enjoy a novel," she said instead.

He looked unconvinced, but could say nothing in the face of her declaration.

"Time we had some nourishment, my love," David

added. He unobtrusively tucked the slim volume in his sling. Then he drew Elizabeth along with him by the simple means of placing his arm protectively around her shoulder.

She supposed he said that for Egbert's benefit, although what possible difference it made whether his cousin accepted their betrothal or not, she didn't know.

"I believe I shall look in on your father first, if you do not mind. After all, I am here to nurse, not chat with you two. Rose will need a moment to herself as well. Please go ahead without me, for I might be awhile."

Elizabeth slipped from the room, leaving David and Egbert staring after her as she hurried down the hall and around the corner. With any luck, she could avoid the meal entirely.

The earl's bedchamber looked pleasant and warm, with the soft light flooding the room. Outside, a white world made it seem as though the room floated in space. It looked rather eerie, and Elizabeth rushed into speech.

"You had best get something to eat, Rose. But first, could you fetch me a shawl from my room? It is not precisely chilly, but the very thought of snow makes me cold."

"So, you return."

Whirling about, Elizabeth discovered the earl watching her. "You are awake!"

"For my sins, yes. What is that potion you poured down my throat?" His voice seemed stronger, and his color not quite so ashen.

"You sound like David. He loathes the potion Purvis sent for him." She lingered by the bed, watching him as much as he eyed her.

The earl chuckled, though it was faint and brief.

"Aunt Bel's abigail, Purvis, is marvelous when it comes to mixing up healing concoctions. I believe she is a frustrated apothecary."

The door opened and Rose entered with the shawl. Elizabeth thanked her maid, then requested that she heat more of the broth brought from Montmorcy Hall. "Best see to it yourself, then bring it up directly."

Rose darted an awed look at the figure lying in state

on the bed, then bobbed a hasty curtsy. "Yes, miss," she murmured before disappearing from sight.

It might annoy David were she to remain here, tending his father rather than joining them, but it gave her time to think.

While they waited for Rose, she held up the novel she had found just before the little poison book tumbled to the floor. "Why do I not read to you? This is a delightful book I feel certain you will like." She commenced to read at his nod. " 'It is a truth universally acknowledged that a single man in possession of a good fortune must be in want of a wife.' " His lordship nodded, and Elizabeth took them both into the world of Jane Austen's Miss Bennet.

When the soup arrived, Elizabeth reluctantly set aside the lovely book. She spoonfed his lordship the delicately flavored chicken broth. Once he had consumed what he could, she replaced the cover over the bowl, then set the bed to rights. She was about ready to go to her own lunch when Filpot entered.

The earl had shut his eyes, and there was nothing, other than the covered bowl on the tray Elizabeth now held, to indicate that he had been fed—or been awake, for that matter. She noted the valet's darting perusal of the room, and she hated to leave, but knew she must.

"I shall be back as soon as I can," she said quietly to the valet, hoping the earl caught her words as well.

Filpot frowned but could say nothing.

Nuncheon was over when she paused at the dining room door. In the kitchen she poured the broth into its jar. Then she supervised a light repast to her taste, and quickly ate it before returning to the library to seek out David. While hardly earth-shaking news, he would be pleased to know his father had consumed a bit of broth and enjoyed her reading.

"Where the devil have you been?" he snapped as she entered the library.

Her pleasure in the earl's progress dissolved at the cold expression on Lord Leighton's face.

"You will be pleased to know I fed your father a tidy amount of broth and read to him for a bit. We enjoyed our time enormously." She whirled about and marched to the door. A hand latched onto her arm, and she halted, waiting.

Heart beating madly, she turned to look at David. What did he want of her?

7

"PLEASE STAY. You may as well know I've a wretched temper when I have to deal with my uncle and cousins, particularly my cousin Jeremy." He stared down at her with an odd expression on his face, one she certainly could not fathom.

She eased herself from his clasp and slowly moved so that a table stood between them. "He seems most innocuous to me."

"He does, does he not?" David rubbed his chin with a speculative gesture.

"Why do they remain? Oh, I know Mr. Vane is your father's steward, but why your uncle and his son? Surely they could go home? If I am not being presumptuous," she added as an afterthought.

He strolled around the table, then drew her with him to the cozy arrangement of chairs before the fireplace.

"You know, I can see merits in marriage if it offers an arrangement like this, where a fellow may discuss problems with his wife." His eyes developed that familiar glimmer of teasing, and Elizabeth doubted his sincerity.

"I shan't comment on that, I believe," she replied.

He urged her down on the high-backed chair, then sat opposite, staring moodily at the fire. "My Uncle Augustus is really not such a bad sort of chap, a bit of a hanger-on, but he once he got along famously with my father. His son is another matter entirely. Father ordered Egbert to take himself off to London, or anywhere, rather than sponge on our estate. Quite created a chasm between the two families, or what is left of us. When Father became ill, Jeremy stayed on, claiming he could not leave at such a time when families must pull together. I suspect he lingers about waiting for the will to be read."

"What a ghastly thing to say." She reflected a moment, then continued, "But I believe I can see why you might feel that way." She thought a moment, then said, "Have you looked through that book we found? Is it of any value? Would it help someone who wished to poison another?"

"I should say a clever person could apply the lessons learned without difficulty."

"So all we must do now is figure out who bought that book, then plotted to murder your father."

"I knew you were a girl of uncommon good sense." He paused. "I really do not understand my antagonism to Jeremy. Perhaps it has something to do with all the time my father has lavished on him." He gave her a searching glance.

"And not you?" Elizabeth inquired with intuition. She could appreciate that David might resent the hours his father spent teaching estate management to Jeremy while ignoring his son.

"I did mention you are most perceptive."

"My father always favored Geoffrey over us girls. Although he is the heir, I suspect it had more to do with Geoffrey's amazing ability with languages. I do well enough with French and have a smattering of Italian, Julia about the same, while Victoria is close to my brother in her abilities, yet he favored his son." Elizabeth shrugged, then went on, "We all tried our best to please him, each of us perfecting a proficiency in some craft, and Mother seemed proud of us."

"But you craved a word of praise from your father?"

"Since you understand how I feel, then you know how I am able to sympathize with you." She gave him a dry look, then clasped her hands in her lap. "What do we do now?"

"I shall continue searching the house for evidence of the poison, and I should appreciate it if you would do the same. When you are not with my father, that is. I just wish I knew what I was looking for—precisely." He exchanged a rueful look with her and they both sighed.

"Which reminds me, why did you tell him that we are betrothed? You know it is not the truth, even if Aunt Bel insists we are to wed." Her annoyance had dissipated with time, but she was curious as to why a man who had so assiduously fought being leg-shackled was informing one and all about their bogus engagement.

"You are a remarkably pretty woman, my dear. And my father would wonder about your presence here, in a household of men, if I did not offer a plausible explanation." His grin was as devilish as his smooth words were prosaic. Those hazel eyes danced with an aggravating gleam.

Her pleasure at his compliment dimmed as she considered the practicality of his words. Speculating on what might lie behind that grin was something else.

"I wonder how long it will snow." Oddly enough, she wasn't worried about it. And she supposed she ought to be, had she an ounce of brains in her head.

"Regardless of when it stops, I doubt if the roads will be passable. Even London streets are a frightful mess when it snows."

"True enough." She rose, strangely reluctant to end their little interchange, yet knowing she must check on his father again. "You ought to find a reputable nurse, you know. I may do my best, but what if that is insufficient?"

"We *had* a nurse before you came. I found her raiding the gin bottle during the night and sent her packing." He had also risen and now stood close to her, looking faintly amused as she backed toward the door and bumped into the table instead.

"I understand that is not unusual." I ought to go, she reminded herself, yet she lingered, and she could not understand why.

"I shall attempt to keep my cousins out of your way." He fiddled with a leather bookmark that he'd found on the table, watching her face intently.

What was on his mind? Maybe he merely missed his London society, and perhaps his mistress? That thought so distressed Elizabeth that she turned to flee the room.

A hasty glance behind her revealed his lordship standing where she had left him with a thoughtful expression on his face. Face aflame, she hurried up the stairs and across to the south wing, where she could check on his father and be safe.

Rose met her breathless entrance with raised brows. "How is he?"

"Fine, miss. He's been restless, but I gave him some of the tonic, and he seemed to perk up, like."

Elizabeth walked over to the bed to study her patient. It was challenging to know what to do for someone who slept so much, especially when she was not skilled in nursing. Her lessons from Purvis had been too brief, she could see that now. But then, she was doubtlessly better than a nurse who indulged in gin.

With that thought as comfort, she sent Rose off to have something to eat.

Elizabeth was most curious who might have used that book on poisons. Perhaps the cook took it to prepare herbal potions in the still room, since Lady Crompton no longer was there to take charge.

"It surely cannot be as bad as all that."

She whirled about to face the gentleman who gazed at her from the depths of the enormous bed.

"I fear it is, sir. What with snow and trying to get you on your feet, I have my hands full." She held up her slim hands and smiled at his expression.

"I believe I feel better this afternoon. Shall you read me some more of Miss Austen's book?" His eyes had that appealing gleam so noticeable in his son's.

She promptly seated herself, opened the book to the marked page, and began. " 'But it must very materially lessen their chance of marrying men of any consideration in the world,'' replied Darcy.' " She raised her eyes to meet those of his lordship, sharing an amused look, then continued with the story. When it became necessary to light a lamp, he gave a sigh.

"Is it time for dinner?" he asked in a vexed tone.

Encouraged at what she took to be a sign of improvement, Elizabeth glanced at the mantel clock and agreed. "I believe it is. Goodness, the hours fly past when one has a good book." She placed the bookmark at where she had stopped, then rose. "I shall order some more of that special broth to be heated for you, and Purvis said you might have some of her special herb biscuits." Elizabeth turned to give the bell pull a tug.

"I only said that because I want to see you dressed for dinner."

She shook her head in dismay. "You are a wag, sir. I believe you are malingering here, and not the least under the weather." She tilted her head and flashed one of the Dancy smiles at him. She crossed to the bed and smoothed his covers, plumping a pillow to tuck beside him while bestowing a fond look on the gentleman.

"I think my son a very lucky man."

Elizabeth blushed, thanking her stars that Lord Leighton was not present.

"Never say that I do not have the best of taste, Father."

The sound of that rich voice came as a distinct shock to Elizabeth, and she found herself quite shaken.

"I am all agreement, son."

While Elizabeth went to the door to explain to Rose what was wished, she could hear quiet conversation between father and son.

It bothered her that David could slip into the room without her hearing a sound. After a spy had crept into their house in London, Elizabeth had slept with a gun beneath her pillow, but the gun was not here for tonight. And she wondered if she should have brought it.

"I am feeling so much more the thing that I believe Elizabeth ought to join you for dinner, David. Leave that shy little maid in here with me."

Unwilling to argue, Elizabeth instructed Rose on what to do. After explaining that the maid ought to consider his lordship like her father, it seemed she felt more at ease. By the time Elizabeth left the bedchamber Rose had proceeded to bully his lordship into consuming the broth and herb biscuits.

"Can you bear to join us for dinner this evening? I'll not like the notion of you hiding in your room just because my relatives put you in a quake. Or is it me you fear?"

"Neither, sir," she denied bravely. "I shall join you. Have you found any evidence of a poisonous substance?"

They continued to the head of the stairs in speculation. David had found nothing at all, to his frustration.

"I shall be down directly, when I freshen up." She took her leave, wondering how she was to manage her dress with Rose attending Lord Crompton.

Her gown lay neatly on the bed in the room Sidthorp had assigned to her. An open door revealed a small dressing room that also held a pretty cot suitable for Rose.

The decor of the bedroom looked to be the very latest designs, directly from London. Simple, almost austere, after Aunt Bel's rather ornate interior. Fluid curves and lovely woods graced the few pieces. The blue and cream with touches of gold on the walls and fabrics pleased Elizabeth very much.

The thought entered her mind that if she held Lord Leighton to his oft repeated declaration of betrothal, she would be mistress of this house. Then, as quickly as it had come, that idea was dismissed. But she had to admit that David did not appear the rake while under his father's roof. Although those hazel eyes did mock and tease her most dreadfully.

Even as she stripped her day gown off, then put on the evening dress suitable for a winter dinner with friends, she wondered how accurate the London gossips were. Her sisters had scolded her roundly for accepting the prattle of the London ladies as truth.

She had pinned her bodice in place and draped a modest string of pearls about her neck when the sound of the dinner gong reached her ears. Alone in this wing, she felt oddly shy walking along the broad corridor to the head of the stairs.

Below, she could hear voices, and once downstairs she drifted along to the drawing room whence they came. They were standing about, quite obviously waiting for her.

"Ah, Elizabeth. I have the good fortune to escort you to dinner. One of the times I appreciate my rank," David joked as he offered his arm.

"My lord, you do like to tease."

"You have mentioned that before. I know you have a sense of humor. Could it be *my* wit that you fail to appreciate?" He arched a wicked brow in mock dismay.

"My, the chit does have taste," Egbert murmured just loud enough for Elizabeth to overhear.

Dinner proved singularly uneventful. Seated at David's side, Elizabeth managed to do the food credit, although she felt the dishes lacked originality or taste. Several were overdone, others tasted most peculiar. Overcooked roast beef and bland apple pie, with other equally ordinary fare, must be to their liking, she thought, for all ate without complaint.

Following the meal, David excused them from the others, saying they wished to check on his father. Once up the flight of stairs, he paused before the door to the first of the rooms.

"This is not your father's room."

"Filpot just brought word that Father is sleeping nicely. I thought we might search this room while the others are below."

Suspicion flared up. "Whose room is this?"

"Jeremy's."

"Of all the foolish things to do, this is prime. If you *must* search here, do so when he is away from home. He could decide to come up at any moment."

"Quite so. Stand by the door and listen, I'll do a quick check." He placed his hand on the lever.

"I shall do no such thing. Come." She tugged his arm, to his obvious amusement.

He quickly walked with her from the room, then on down the hall to the end.

"This is your room, sirrah. I hardly think we need look here."

"More's the pity. I wondered if you needed to have a look at my wound."

She pursed her mouth in speculation, then chided herself for a suspicious mind. Of course his wound needed inspection. She ought to have thought of it without his prompting.

He whisked her inside even as he pulled off his coat.

Elizabeth sighed inwardly when she observed how well formed Lord Leighton was. He certainly stripped to advantage, as Geoffrey would say.

Once David's shirt lay discarded on the chair, she efficiently removed the bandage to study the injury. Thank heaven she had only put in three-quarters of the powder normally used in the gun. Not only had it lessened the force of the bullet, but it meant that the wound had healed better, with less tearing of the skin.

It took but a short time to make her examination, gently smear some of Purvis's compound on his arm, then bind the wound once again. She concentrated on her task, determined to ignore his proximity and the feelings he stirred within her. She glanced at the open door. Why that ought to make her more assured, she didn't know. She felt quite certain that if he wished to make improper advances to her, whether the door stood ajar or not wouldn't affect him in the least.

She gave the finished bandage a light touch. "There, now, it looks much better today. You heal well, my lord. In time the scar will scarcely be noticeable."

"I trust my wife will not mind it, then." He pulled his fine cambric shirt over his head, wincing at the strain on his arm. He managed the three buttons concealed beneath a modest frill. Fortunately, his collar points were not as high as Egbert favored.

Elizabeth knew she ought to leave the room, but she had never been privileged to observe a gentleman in the process of dressing before, and it fascinated her. He fumbled with his cravat, then gave up, tossing it aside.

"Shall I call Hadlow?" she offered.

He nodded regretfully. "I cannot manage yet. But soon." His eyes held a message, but it was one she was reluctant to read. "I shall see you downstairs."

Put totally out of countenance by his quite proper observation, Elizabeth blushingly escaped, pausing to check on the earl. Leaving Rose capably standing guard over his lordship, she returned to the library. Her face burned with embarrassment at her behavior. Why, a lady simply did not stand by while a gentleman restored his attire. She knew better.

While she waited, she perused the shelves again for some sort of herbal. She wanted to help if she could.

By the time David joined her, Elizabeth's equanimity was somewhat restored, and it improved by the simple matter that he did not tease her about her folly.

When David entered, he closed the door carefully behind him. The familiar twinkle returned to his eyes as he surveyed Elizabeth perched precariously on the library steps.

"I am discouraged," she admitted, wiping a stray hair from her forehead while surveying the area she had managed to cover. She reached to replace a book, offering him a scandalous view of a neat pair of ankles. When she realized what she had done, she moved suddenly, and the library steps tilted to a perilous degree.

David left his place by the door and rushed to steady her, both arms reaching for her lest she tumble.

Embarrassed at her silly display, she averted her face. Fortunately, he said nothing about her impropriety.

"After studying that book you found, I have been over most of the rooms in the house," he said. "I hoped to find evidence, but all I find are cobwebs and dust."

"It must be very discouraging for you." She felt her face lose some of its heat as he ignored her display of ankles.

"However, since he appears to respond well to the tonic Purvis sent and the broth you brought, I am convinced we are on the right track. If we can just keep the would-be poisoner from finding out that Father is well on the mend. Let him think the progress is nil, or very slow. What do you think?"

"I am not skilled in dissembling, but I could try. This cannot help but worry you."

"Indeed," he said wearily. "I believe we owe ourselves a respite, since he improves. Tomorrow, providing the cold weather holds, we ought to try a bit of skating. Do you indulge in that sort of thing?" He ran his fingers through his hair, the baffled expression replaced by one she thought calculating.

"I cannot say I have," she replied cautiously. "Hyacinthe and Lady Chloe spoke of a skating party."

"Then, by all means I shall teach you. I am reckoned to be a dab hand at skates," he said with modest pride.

"Even with one hand?" she teased. Let him have a taste of what he did so well.

"Still at it, you two?" Egbert's sneering voice cut between them like a knife. "I should like to know what attracts you to this particular room." He gazed about as though searching for the clue. "Although I have heard a library is a favorite place for lovemaking among betrothed couples. So much can be conveyed across the pages of an open book, don't you know?"

Utterly outraged at his assumptions, although she knew she invited such by her behavior, Elizabeth straightened and prepared to give him a blistering set-down. A nudge in her back stopped her.

"We have been merely looking through the books. Did you find something to read, Miss Elizabeth?"

She smiled. "As a matter of fact, I did. 'Tis a book I have long wished to read, *Self-Control* by Mary Brunton. It is reputed to be a good tale of the triumph of virtue over passion." With that crisp statement she whirled about and pulled the volume in question from the shelf where she had seen it earlier. Then she marched from the room, head up, chin firm, and a saucy gleam in her eyes.

The soft chuckle that followed her departure brought a grin to her lips. His lordship appreciated her ridicule of Egbert's pompous attitude. Not but what he was right.

Morning saw a light sifting of snow, but Elizabeth believed the weather looked as though it might change for the better later on, and she grew hopeful.

Rose entered bearing a cup of chocolate, full of news of the day.

"His lordship's ever so much better, miss. Purvis will be that puffed up when she learns how effective her tonic is, and that's the truth." Rose set about drawing back the curtains and shaking out the warm kerseymere gown Elizabeth had brought to wear.

"What a relief. You and Filpot managed to come to terms over the night nursing, I gather." Elizabeth downed her chocolate in a rush, then slid from the warmth of her bed with reluctance.

"His lordship said that if it pleased you, he would take you skating after breakfast." Rose looked round-eyed at her mistress. "What do you wear to skate?"

"Something warm and sensible, I gather from what I have heard of it. I shall put on my stout half-boots. And do not forget my fur muff." She exchanged a look with her maid, one that said she doubted the outcome as much as Rose.

When she met Lord Leighton in the large hall, she still held doubts but thought she hid them successfully. In her favorite aquamarine pelisse and bonnet, she braved the day.

"Come, the wind is down and 'tis a fine day for skating, as the temperature looks to rise. I tested the ice, and it seems to be fine."

Tucking her hands inside her muff, Elizabeth walked with him along the path leading down the hill. Below, she could make out a pond, one with little inlets and pretty knolls above upon which to view the scene.

"I believe I ought to stand there to watch you, sir," she said primly.

"And not skate?" he replied, scandalized.

"I shall fall, most likely."

"But I will be at your side to assist you."

She darted a dubious look at him then, wondering if this was some sort of ruse to tease her.

Placed close to the pond was a stone bench, and it was here that Lord Leighton urged Elizabeth to put on her skates. Or rather, to allow him to fit them on her boots.

"Your footwear is most practical for skates. I heartily approve." That he also could not miss a glimpse of her shapely calves while adjusting those skates didn't escape Elizabeth, and she thought him outrageous.

The iron-bladed runners were fixed to sturdy brass plates. He brought the leather straps about her boots to tightly fasten with a knot just over the instep. He screwed the heel peg into the sole of her boot and proclaimed her ready. He affixed his blades to his Hessians, and she thought he appeared smart in his blue tailcoat buttoned up with large brass buttons and a dark round hat set jauntily on his head.

"You are not wearing your sling. Dare you use your arm? I would not have you expose yourself to further injury just to amuse me."

"I am not concerned," he said in a typically masculine disdain for pampering.

When it came time to venture on the ice, Elizabeth put a tentative foot on the slippery stuff, then withdrew.

"What? Are you such a timid creature? Allow me."

The wickedly handsome Lord Leighton proceeded to introduce Elizabeth to the delights of ice skating. Placing his arm firmly about her waist, with a look that told her not to quibble about his closeness, he led her forth. At first hesitant, she began to relax, and soon found herself able to perform simple gliding steps.

"I really believe you ought to permit me to guide you a bit longer," he admonished as Elizabeth sailed past him toward the far end of the pond.

"Nonsense. I cannot see that this is so difficult after all," she sang back gaily, enjoying the crisp air and faint sun that peeked through the clouds.

"It is possible to dance on ice with a partner," he said in an aggravatingly appealing manner.

Absorbing this intriguing notion, Elizabeth returned to his side, tilting her head as she decided whether he was serious or not.

"Willing to try?" he dared her.

"On my headstone you may carve that here lies one who dared anything," she quipped, even as she offered him her hand.

This time one of his strong arms went about her waist in a tantalizing way, and his other hand, of the arm that had been shot, firmly captured hers, letting her know he would not allow her to fall.

Had she paused to consider, she would have thought it most peculiar that he used that wounded limb so well. However, Elizabeth was lost in transports of delight, and far from reality.

With a taunting side glance, reminding her that he well recalled her inability to do the same, he hummed a gay waltz, then slowly guided them away from the bank.

She decided it lovely to be spinning around and around on the ice. Then it occurred to her, "The surface is remarkably smooth, my lord. I had always thought ice to be a bit bumpy when it formed."

He actually looked chagrined at her words. "As to that, I went out last night with three of the men, and we sloshed water over much of it. Not that we covered it all, mind you."

"I see." But she didn't, not really. That he should go

to such lengths to please her seemed unlike him. Tease, yes. Please, no.

"You are a very clever pupil, Miss Elizabeth," he said with approval.

His provoking grin and dancing eyes brought warmth to her cheeks. "I wonder that your cousins do not indulge in this delightful pastime."

"Egbert might, if he ever gets out of bed in time. But Jeremy said he does not care for skating, or ice, for that matter. He insists he has business to attend." He added as an afterthought, "I should like to see his account books."

"Now," she reproved, "do not be putting the poor man in a quake. You are rather good at disconcerting him." And Jeremy was not the only one who found Lord Leighton intimidating at times.

"But not you, I think. Why, I could kiss you here, and you would not bat one of those delightful lashes at me."

She pulled free of him, darting away with surprising speed for a novice. Although she wobbled a bit, she chuckled to herself. Kiss her, indeed.

"Elizabeth, wait!"

"Oh, no, I will not." He had teased her once too often. Foolish man, he must learn that a lady has limits to her tolerance. Elizabeth wished for sensible conversation, not trifling.

"Elizabeth!"

Ignoring his call, she turned again to look ahead of her. Unfamiliar with the pond and skating, she really should have been paying attention to what she did.

An ominous creaking reached her ears, and she came to an uncertain stop. Little lines radiated out from where she stood. Not sure what it meant, she turned, her face serious, to gaze back at Lord Leighton. He approached warily, and even from here she could see his concern.

"I suspect you had best keep your distance."

"Little fool, you could get hurt. All you have to do is say no. And mean it."

"No, and I mean it."

"I am wounded . . . again."

"I do not believe a kiss will make it all better."

"My mother told me that, however. She was a great believer." He offered a cautious hand to draw her away.

"I daresay she was, if you say so," Elizabeth said with a composure she didn't actually feel. He was fast, she decided, and the tattlemongers of London had the right of it.

The creaking increased, and Elizabeth wondered aloud, "Is that something to be worried about, that funny sort of noise?"

When he looked down, a comically dismayed look was quickly replaced by one of concern. "I would have sworn the ice to be more solid here." He took her hand, tugging her to follow him.

But it was far too late for departure. The cracks rapidly spread, and in seconds Elizabeth first, then David, plunged through the surface into the icy water.

She clutched at the pieces of ice, trying to obtain purchase so she might pull herself from the water. Fortunately, the pond seemed shallow at this end, for as she went under the water, she found her toes just touched the bottom. Or something solid.

Heavy clothing and rapidly numbing fingers prevented success, however. David dragged her up, then instructed her, "Hang onto me if you can. I shall get us out."

She had flung her muff across the ice as she fell, and now she longed for its warmth. "I do not see how," she confessed.

"Oh, ye of little faith," he muttered, attempting to pull himself from the pond, then deliberately breaking the ice some more in order to reach a branch that poked up through the ice.

This proved an effective means of leverage, and in short order he crawled from the icy water, inching his way across the cracked ice to firm ground, leaving Elizabeth to cling to the ice. Here, he soon located a stout limb, then extended this to her, pulling her free with a great effort.

She stood with her arms tightly about her, shivering in the slight breeze. "I do believe I prefer a fire at the moment, my lord."

"For once, I cannot help but agree."

She bent over to pick up her muff, then thrust her hands inside, hoping for warmth.

They skirted the edge of the pond, clumping through the snow in their skates even though it meant a longer route. Eventually they made their way up the hill to the house.

A horrified Sidthorp ushered them in, while Lord Leighton barked out orders one after another. "Hot baths for us both, and a posset to warm our insides. The brandy one I think best. Send Hadlow to me, and Rose to Miss Elizabeth. Immediately." He pulled off his boots, then fumbled with the straps that held Elizabeth's skates on her half-boots.

He was seized by a fit of shivering, and Elizabeth realized that the cold plunge augured far worse for him than for her.

She had always been a healthy sort, not prone to colds and megrims. But Lord Leighton was still recovering from that bullet she had shot him with and could be in grave danger.

After a very hot soaking bath, Elizabeth dried her hair by the fire wrapped in a black velvet robe. Her long curls hung down in a chestnut fan of waving silk as she brushed.

A knock at the door gave warning, but barely. She hastily composed herself, withdrawing bare toes beneath the wealth of velvet just in time. As she suspected, Leighton entered, barging in without an apology.

"I sent Hadlow out to inspect the pond. He and one of the stable lads found what we missed. Elizabeth, that was no accident! Someone wished us ill. He hoped we would fall into the frigid water. The ice on the deep end of the pond was thin, so a sign had been posted. That warning sign was found hidden behind a bush."

8

"How TERRIBLE, to endanger your life like that!" Elizabeth cried, rising to commiserate with David as best she could. "How is your arm? Have you had the bandage changed? I hope you do not develop an inflammation of the lungs, or some dreadful infection of your wound." She studied his face for signs of incipient debility. "Oh, *who* could have done such a horrid deed?"

"Your concern is welcome," he said hesitantly. "We must consider that you were with me, and that you were as much the intended victim as I, however." He stuffed the hand of his wounded arm into the pocket of his velvet banyan that he had donned over a blessedly dry cambric shirt, buff pantaloons, and shoes.

"I, a victim?" she said in amazement. Then she smiled at the absurdity of that idea. "Nonsense." She paused a moment, then admitted, "Now, if I truly intended to marry you, there might be an heir who wished me out of the way. Tell me, who is next in line in the event that you fail to marry and produce the required heir to the title?"

Elizabeth drew closer to the fire, still a trifle chilled from their wetting. She played with the hair brush in her hands, while studying the flames that danced, such a contrast to the frozen cold beyond the window.

"Augustus." David watched her, the black velvet clinging to her slender form, so enchanting, so desirable. Her beautiful hair curled delicately about her face, a veil of finest silk. It was unthinkable that someone wish her ill, but he didn't trust anyone at this point, and however silly it might seem, it must be considered.

"I want you to be careful when you go about here,"

he insisted. "Remember, the others believe our betrothal is genuine. You could be wished out of the way."

"Oh, pooh, what a poor honey you must think me. I refuse to jump at every shadow. Although," she admitted, "there is the problem of your father's condition. I still say that whatever ill will abounds is directed toward him, for some obscure reason."

Rose entered with a tray of posset for them. She gave her mistress a bland look as she offered her a steaming cup of the brew, then his lordship.

"Now we shall be warmed on the inside as well as the outer being." David sipped the herbal potion mixed with his favorite brandy. He smiled as Elizabeth took a taste, then made a face at him.

"I hope I am not required to drink this often. I fancy this is an excellent way to keep one well, if for no other reason than to avoid drinking it." She grimaced, then sipped some more.

Rose hovered in the background. David turned abruptly to her. "You may leave us."

When the maid had scurried from the room without a backward glance, Elizabeth gave him a look of reproof. "That was not well done of you, sir."

"I do not like to think of her tittle-tattling to others about our private conversation. Not even accidentally. However good she might be, what she does not hear she cannot repeat. We have much to discuss." He crossed to firmly close the door after first checking the hall to see that no one lingered along the corridor. He was alone with Elizabeth in her room—in the entire wing, for that matter.

He drew up a chair to the fireplace for her, then found one for himself. "These may not appear comfortable, but I have found them tolerable." He gestured to the fashionable chairs with their graceful arms curving under and curved legs. "As to the maid, we are past caring about what she thinks.

She sank down, looking suddenly uncomfortable, as though she had just realized that she entertained him in her private quarters dressed in her velvet robe and with bare feet. An adorable expression of confusion that warred with annoyance sat on her lovely face. He longed to caress her, but knew he must be wary in his dealings with the attractive Elizabeth Dancy.

"I must return to Aunt Bel's as soon as the weather permits," she announced abruptly. Then, meeting his eyes, she added, "It is not because of the ridiculous assumption you have made. Not for a moment do I believe that someone wishes me ill. But," she continued, "your father seems much improved. You have no further need of me."

He cradled his cup of posset in his hand, staring at the flames much as she had done earlier. He needed to find an excuse for her to remain. He said suddenly, "But I need you here. You see, I can trust no one, other than my father, and I would not burden him with all my suspicions. I need a fellow confederate, as it were. Someone I can discuss my problems with and confide in and feel comfortable with, if you follow my thoughts. Also, if you leave, he might take a turn for the worse," he concluded, throwing himself on her mercy and relying on her sense of duty to do as he wished.

"I . . . I do not know quite what to say. I admit I am flattered that you feel able to confide in me, trust me to such a degree. But what about the others? Do you not worry about what they will say? This is a highly irregular plan, you must agree."

She took what he felt to be a resolute sip of the posset, and he prayed she would suffer no ill effects from the wetting she'd had in that freezing water. A cousin of his had died under similar circumstances, succumbing to an inflammation of the lungs.

"I have no regard for what others say," he said. "They have been gossiping over me for years, ever since I went to London to acquire that patina of Town Bronze so desperately wanted by all young sprouts." He watched the play of emotions over her expressive face, but could not figure out what went on in her mind.

"I see. You are a sad rattle, I fear," she replied with a flash of amusement.

"What about you? I place you in an unpardonable position with my request. Your aunt is of the opinion that we will wed, and so it may not be reprehensible to her if you at least spend your days assisting me. My father's condition provides the excuse, if you will.''

"My aunt is inclined to be rather silly, but she is none-theless a formidable lady. Should she take the notion that we must wed immediately, I fear you would find yourself waiting at the altar for a bride you do not wish. I feel you must be warned of the danger you face.''

Her face wore a speculative expression, but her voice reflected serious concern. He would be ill advised to ignore her warning. He reflected on her words, then shook his head. "My need of you, your assistance, is greater than my fear of your aunt.''

Elizabeth rose from her chair before the fire, and walked across the thick carpet to look out the window. "The sun is out, however weak it might appear. The roads ought to be passable before long.''

"Another day, I beg you. Then I shall return you to your Aunt Bel.''

"Could we send a groom to her with a message? Not but what she knows the weather forbids my return just yet.''

He marveled that she should fall in with his wishes so easily, then reminded himself that he must not trespass on her kind nature with the sort of attention he would like to bestow on her, those inviting lips. It was the first time he had ever placed his scruples ahead of his desires for a woman who responded as she did to his advances. Not one of his London acquaintances would believe it possible. His friends knew differently.

"Certainly." He had risen when she did, and now followed her to the window. "I want to know who was out there. Everyone knew we planned to skate today after you invited them to join us.''

"I scarcely wished it to be a secret. Now, that *would* have looked odd.'' She picked up a drapery cord, playing with it in seeming nervousness.

"Nevertheless.''

"I expect I ought to make myself respectable, then meet you downstairs.'' She smoothed a hand over her dressing gown. It covered her from neck to toe and concealed her in an enticing manner.

"I am sorry for the ruin of your lovely pelisse. That

aquamarine color well becomes you.'' He decided she had the most attractive blush he had ever seen, a delicate bloom that suffused her cheeks like a lovely peach rose.

''It can be replaced, thank you. I have a great many items of that color in my wardrobe. Vanity, I imagine.''

Her rueful laugh pleased him. 'Not vanity in the least,'' he refuted, ''merely common sense—to wear what is becoming.''

She strolled to the door, drawing him along with her. ''I shall join you below before long. My hair is nearly dry, and I feel much more the thing.'' She held the nearly empty cup of posset up for him to see.

Unable to stop himself, he pulled his hand from the pocket, reaching out to run his fingers through that fall of silken hair. ''You look startled. You must know that your hair is a lovely feature.''

''Sir, you make me feel the temptress. I protest.''

Her blush had deepened and he cursed himself for a fool. ''Later, then.''

She closed the door behind his rapidly disappearing figure, and wondered if she had completely lost her mind. Swallowing the last of the posset, she allowed it to heat her insides while returning to the window again.

Curious how she was so terribly willing to fall in with Lord Leighton's plans. Of course, she knew why in the innermost part of her mind. But she refused to accept that reason, for it was utter folly. No, she had best lay it to her quite reasonable desire to see the solution to this puzzle.

Cup in hand, she paced back to the fireplace, ruefully recalling the state of her feet as she felt the lush thickness of the carpet. How unspeakably foolish to permit his lordship to enter her room, make himself at ease, then listen to him tell her that he needed her! Utter stupidity.

With that thought she briskly rang for Rose, then strode to her dressing room, undoing the velvet robe as she went. In short order, her hair was properly dressed, as was the rest of her.

The corridor appeared deserted as she peeped from her room. Not surprising, she supposed. But one never knew. Unable to contain her curiosity any longer, she peered into each room as she proceeded along the hall. Since no one occupied this wing save herself, she felt quite safe in doing so.

The earl, or whoever had assisted him in the decoration of the house, had excellent taste. A lovely sleigh bed graced one room, a four-poster from an earlier time another. That every room was tastefully arranged, with no thought spared for economy, brought home to her precisely the temptation that might exist for a man who wanted all this, plus the remainder of the estate. If this was merely a small residence, what must the others be like?

On that depressing thought she marched down the stairs, then sought the drawing room.

Lord Augustus turned from his contemplation of the fire to greet her. "Heard about your dip in the pond, dear girl. Really, not quite the thing to do on a February day, what? Now, come July . . ." He subsided a moment, apparently contemplating a lovely summer day. "Shan't leave here today. Roads bound to be nasty. Always are," he reflected gloomily.

"Ah, the intrepid Miss Elizabeth." Young Mr. Percy sauntered into the drawing room, raising his quizzing glass to inspect her person, as though anticipating a drapery of pond weed or some such nonsense.

Elizabeth was hard put not to laugh at his pretensions. "Indeed, sir. Not altogether as intrepid as you might believe. I fear I wholly disliked plunging into that frigid water, then being trapped by my heavy skirts, unable to climb free. It is a good thing that Lord Leighton found it possible to pull himself out, and thus drag me free of the pond's icy grip." Had he used both hands to do so? She worried that he had harmed himself and was too heroic to complain. Oh, if he had reopened his wound, she'd not forgive herself.

"Ah, dear cuz, ever the champion," Egbert said with a sneer.

"My maid informed me that Lord Crompton is improved," Elizabeth said to Lord Augustus rather than reply to his son's graceless remark.

"Good to hear," offered Lord Augustus, shifting about in his chair accompanied by the usual creaking of his corset.

"Pity David couldn't have kept you from ruining that admirable pelisse I saw you wearing earlier," Egbert added in a snide undertone.

She tensed, wondering how Mr. Percy had seen what she wore if he had remained in bed at that hour. "I fear it is a total loss, in spite of Rose's attempt to restore it. I shall wear it home and hope that not a soul sees me."

He affected a look of horror. "My dear Miss Elizabeth, that would indeed be unfortunate."

Firmly repressing a strong desire to laugh, she calmly replied, "At least my fur muff escaped a watery grave. I tossed it toward the shoreline when we plunged into the water."

"Indubitably fortuitous." He raised his quizzing glass to his eye again, offering Elizabeth a highly magnified view of that slightly reddened object.

She turned aside, choking back the laugh that longed to escape. "How true," she managed to say. Then she considered the foppish gentleman. The notion had occurred to her before that he must spend an inordinate amount of money on those elaborate clothes, not to mention the seals and fobs—discreet but of the highest quality.

Shifting about, she attempted to study him without his being unduly aware of her scrutiny. Would he? Could he? Everyone in the house knew that Egbert slept late of a morning, that he detested ice skating. What better cover than to slip from his room when all expected him to be inside? He could have made his way to the pond, removed the warning sign that had been posted, then returned to his bed with none the wiser. If Lord Augustus inherited, Egbert would have access to all the funds he desired, for his parent seemed most indulgent.

"I say, Miss Elizabeth, you are inspecting me as though I was a worm that had turned up in your apple."

"I do beg your pardon, I was deep in reflection." She added, "I hope that Lord Leighton has not taken ill from his immersion in that frigid water. It is not long since he was injured."

"You ought to tell me more about that particular event. I find I am most curious." Egbert strolled closer to where she stood, peering at her with intent curiosity.

She had done the foolish now, Elizabeth decided. Not knowing what Lord Leighton had revealed to his family about his injury, or her part in it, she hadn't the vaguest idea what to say.

"Ought not pry," Lord Augustus growled from his chair by the fire.

"Pry?" queried Lord Leighton as he strode into the room, looking for all the world as though he never heard of such a thing as falling through thin ice or a February wetting. He had exchanged his banyan for an elegant corbeau coat which covered a rose waistcoat of fine marcella. His buff pantaloons blended nicely and created an impression of refinement.

"Questions," Lord Augustus said abruptly, staring at Elizabeth from beneath those shaggy brows as though she were responsible for his son's behavior. He brushed a bit of snuff from his dark brown coat as he happened to catch sight of it.

" 'Tis all very vague, you know," Egbert continued, ignoring his father.

"Did you enjoy the novel by Miss Brunton last evening?" David turned to inquire of Elizabeth, just as though he had not seen her in her sitting room but an hour past.

Guessing that he did not wish to have the subject of his injury brought up for discussion, Elizabeth searched for an intelligent reply.

"Well, she has a charming manner, but I fear I fell asleep before I could get very far into the story."

"I trust that virtue will be rewarded?" he said with a lift of that devilish brow.

"Ought to replace her pelisse," Lord Augustus volunteered, totally ignoring their conversation. "Poor gel. Not the thing to be falling into ponds in the middle of February. Not the thing at all," he scolded.

David tugged at his earlobe while he considered this comment.

Unable to repress a smile at his obvious surprise at this attack from his uncle, Elizabeth picked up a dainty statue from the table, ostensibly to study it.

"No worry, Papa. Once David and the lovely Elizabeth are wed, she'll have no end of pelisses—and other interesting things as well, no doubt." Egbert's smile was excessively crafty.

"Forgot," Lord Augustus mumbled, studying the fire once again.

Hoping the sound she heard in the hall was that of Sidthorp coming to inform them that it was time to march across to the dining room, she was dumbfounded when the portly butler ushered in her cousin Hyacinthe.

The pretty redhead rushed to Elizabeth's side, then flung her arms about her in a tender show of sensibilities.

"I vow, when his lordship's footman brought news of your catastrophe, I simply had to come. It was not easy to persuade John Coachman to make the trip, for the poor man feared for the horses all the way over, but I knew there would be no peace in my heart until I assured myself that you were safe. You *must* need more of the tonic Purvis made." She thrust a basket at Elizabeth, cast a calculating glance at Lord Leighton, then shifted her attention to Mr. Percy.

"I believe I may set your heart at rest, Miss Dancy," Lord Leighton quietly replied, his very calm making Hyacinthe seem silly and affected. "Your cousin is quite all right, and there is no cause for alarm in the least."

He met Sidthorp's inquiring look with a nod, then said to Hyacinthe, "I do hope that you will join us for dinner. Uncle Augustus prefers to keep country hours, and so we dine early here."

She fluttered her hands in the air, looking fragile, lovely, and frightfully vulnerable. "I should adore it, if it does not discommode you?"

"I should think that anyone who has the temerity to charge into another's home at this hour of the day might expect to find them at the dinner table," Elizabeth could not resist saying, her tone as dry as a desert.

Hyacinthe's pretty chin trembled, and from the depths of her reticule she fetched up a scrap of lace and cambric to dab her eyes. A flash of what Elizabeth believed resentment appeared for a moment when Hyacinthe looked at her. It disappeared when she turned her splendid green eyes toward Lord Leighton.

"I merely grew concerned, and I fear I am never practical," she added with a helpless shrug of her slim shoul-

ders incased in sheer, buttery velvet. She seemed like a
delicate flame, all red and gold, glowing with her inner
fire on this cold, snowy February day. Elizabeth felt like
a frump in yesterday's gown that was not quite unwrink-
led, in spite of Rosc's valiant attempt to restore it.

Hyacinthe gave the sort of performance, Elizabeth decided, that brought out every chivalrous instinct in any
living, breathing male. Lord Leighton appeared stricken,
Lord Augustus lumbered to his feet, intent upon assuring
the fragile creature of who knew what, while Egbert
sauntered to Hyacinthe's side, offering his arm.

"This is all frightfully tedious. Let us set aside reasons
and all that dreadful nonsense. Join us for dinner, for
you will perk up the dining room no end."

Blinking in surprise at the assertion of the dandy into
what had been a conversation between herself and Lord
Leighton, Hyacinthe nonetheless placed a dainty hand on
Egbert's arm. A triumphant glance at Elizabeth told her
that Hyacinthe had planned and hoped for, well, not precisely this event, but near enough.

"I do apologize for my cousin's sad want of manners,
my lord," Elizabeth whispered as she walked with Lord
Leighton some distance behind Hyacinthe and Percy.

"I dimly recall another young lady who was used to
be thought a bit of a hoyden." Although she could not
see his face, she could hear the laughter in his voice.

"No names, please," begged a chagrined Elizabeth.

When they were seated at the hastily rearranged table,
she considered the order admirable. Hyacinthe perched
between Egbert and Augustus, who took his brother's
place at one end of the table. At the other end, Lord
Leighton bent his attentions on Elizabeth, which seemed
to irk her adorable cousin no end.

Jeremy Vane sat silently between Elizabeth and Lord
Augustus, making no attempt to engage either young
woman in conversation, although he stared frequently at
Hyacinthe.

It was truly amazing, considering the lengths Hyacinthe had gone to be here so she might assure herself
of Elizabeth's health, that not once had she actually inquired about it. Oh, there had been that touching display
when Hyacinthe arrived. But Elizabeth hoped that at least

David would see through her beautiful cousin's machinations.

"I fancy you will find the roast to your liking," David said as he gestured to a laden platter. "Even if the little cabbage is a bit strong."

Elizabeth smiled. He understood, bless him.

The meal had proceeded nicely, she thought later, as Sidthorp offered the sweets—burned pudding and a nut torte.

Hyacinthe eagerly consumed her portion of torte. Elizabeth accepted a dab of the same, but spent her time watching Egbert with a narrow gaze.

When they left the gentlemen to their port, Elizabeth steered her cousin to the drawing room, urging her to take one of the chairs by the fire.

"You seem quite at home here." Hyacinthe pouted, not quite as charming as when the men were around.

"One can quickly accustom oneself to almost anything. It was most unwise of you to come dashing over here. I fear Lord Leighton now considers you a harumscarum sort of girl. It is not well done to behave so. And I thought better of you. Indeed, Aunt Bel has been constantly reminding me of your propriety ever since I arrived at Montmorcy Hall."

"Truth be known, I felt it incumbent upon me to rescue you from what must be an intolerable situation. Imagine being cooped up in this house with all these men." Hyacinthe gave a dainty wave of a golden-sheathed arm.

Elizabeth wondered if her aunt had ever seen this side of Hyacinthe, then decided that even if she had, she'd not pay the least attention to it. It seemed that once Aunt Bel made up her mind about something, it remained set.

"Well, I will be glad enough for your company on the ride home. It has been a trying day." Hyacinthe had not made it any better. It was clear that now Elizabeth would have to leave. There was no excuse for her to remain.

Any reply she might have made was lost when the men strolled along the hall and into the drawing room. Quite familiar with the leisurely consumption of port, while ladies languished in the drawing room, eagerly awaiting the gentlemen, Elizabeth raised an expressive brow at Lord Leighton.

He immediately sought her side, drawing her away from the others. "We must send your cousin back to your aunt. I shan't allow her to interfere with the progress we have made. Improper little baggage."

Elizabeth struggled to avoid drowning in those hazel eyes, so deep with meaning. "She is curious and a bit willful, but means no harm."

David shook his head, turning his gaze on the young woman.

"As much as I would keep our delightful guest here, I fear her carriage awaits without," he said in a more carrying tone, bestowing a charming, and quite impersonal, smile on Hyacinthe.

As on cue, Sidthorp entered the room, carrying Hyacinthe's lovely purple cloak that had a hood trimmed in ermine. He placed it over her shoulders, then stood waiting to usher her from the room.

Hyacinthe obviously wished to protest, but Lord Leighton inexorably swept her along to the hall, ignoring the complaints from Lord Augustus and Egbert. He ushered Hyacinthe to the coach, fussing over her comfort in a manner that brought pink color to her cheeks. The door clicked shut, and Hyacinthe left long before she intended.

The scene at Montmorcy Hall was as frosty as the weather outside. Aunt Bel proceeded to ring a peal over Hyacinthe.

"I vow that was the strangest dinner I have ever attended," Hyacinthe complained, trying to direct the subject away from herself.

"Actually, you were not invited, so you scarce have cause for grievance," Aunt Bel reminded.

"Well, I think it strange that you permit Elizabeth to remain there." Hyacinthe fussed with her gloves, then her reticule. "I do not see why I shouldn't have gone."

"I suggest you retire for the night, Hyacinthe Dancy. We shall discuss this further in the morning."

9

"I KNEW IT! I knew he had overdone," exclaimed Elizabeth upon learning that Lord Leighton was in bed with a slight fever and not feeling at all the thing. She had spent time with Lord Crompton after breakfasting in her room. When Rose had returned from the kitchen with a light meal for the earl—prepared by Rose and Filpot—Elizabeth had been appraised of Lord Leighton's setback.

Not bothering to check her appearance, she marched down the hall. "I had best give him some of the tonic Purvis sent with me. She must have anticipated such a thing, for she sent an ample supply. I knew he ought not have exerted himself. That stubborn man!" Elizabeth muttered as she made her way along the south wing.

Continuing on to the last room, she stopped, then hesitantly rapped on the door to Lord Leighton's room, unsure of what she ought to do.

Hadlow answered her knock, looking very much the melancholy soul. He immediately ushered her inside, gesturing to the bed across the room.

"How is he?" she whispered. The bedroom was utterly dark, the only light from the fire and one candle. It was stifling.

"I fear for him, and that's a fact," Hadlow intoned in a gloomy, sepulchral voice. He gave Elizabeth the shivers.

"Why do you not join Rose for a moment? Perhaps there is something she needs. You would be just the one to tell her how to go on." It had not escaped Elizabeth that Rose much admired Hadlow, and was not the least reluctant to work with the valet. It was highly doubtful that Filpot had been around, or that he would be willing to assist a mere lady's maid.

"Very good, miss." Hadlow bowed, then reluctantly left on silent feet. His mouth had quirked a moment, and she supposed it passed for a smile.

Once he was out the door, Elizabeth charged across the bedroom and quietly opened the draperies. Soft winter light sifted into the room and over to the great four-poster bed where a man lay in utter stillness.

Sick at heart, Elizabeth cautiously approached the bed, carrying the satchel containing the tonic and potions concocted by Purvis.

She placed a tentative hand on his brow, then nearly jumped out of her skin when a husky voice said, "I am not dead yet, my dear."

"You have a slight fever, however," she replied briskly, once she gathered her wits about her.

"You believe I shall survive, do you not?" One hazel eye peered up at her, followed by the second, wincing at the pale light that now flooded the room.

"Of course. Only the good die young." She prudently avoided meeting that hazel gaze.

"I knew there was a reason for my wicked ways."

"Hush. You ought not say a word, especially those," she admonished. Her heart grew lighter at his silly talk, for she absurdly felt that it meant he was far from hopeless when he could still tease her.

"Truth."

"Rubbish. Now, I shall give you some of the tonic Purvis sent along. I daresay it shall be no more nasty-tasting than that posset you urged on me." She poured out a spoonful, then held it to his mouth. Ignoring all the sensations that came from leaning over his bed, practically falling into his arms once again, she played the proper nurse, poking the spoon into his mouth. "Good," she concluded, backing away from the bed with haste.

"Don't bite," he mumbled, then sneezed.

"Perhaps, but I believe you shall sleep, and well."

"Rubbish," he drowsily replied, closing his eyes once again.

Elizabeth perched anxiously on the chair placed by the side of the great carved bed, a holdover from some other house, for it was not in the current style.

Perhaps he merely had a severe cold, she thought with

hope. His arm lay outside the covers, and once he looked to be soundly asleep, she ever so gently pushed up the sleeve of his nightshirt to examine the bandage. Observing that he did not stir, she deftly cut it loose with the scissors she had tucked into the pocket of her enveloping apron.

A smile wreathed her face as she beheld the wound. A sigh of relief escaped her lips as well, for his injury appeared to be healing nicely. It certainly mitigated her feelings of guilt, although precisely why she ought to feel guilty when *he* was the one who had snuck into her room like a thief was beyond her ken.

"Wait until I tell Purvis," she whispered to herself. "How pleased she will be."

She applied the ointment from the jar Purvis had tucked into the satchel, then put a fresh bandage on his arm, smoothing his sleeve down again and tucking the coverlet nicely about him when finished. If he had a fever, it was best to keep him warm.

Purvis had said she found it helpful to listen to a chest, for it seemed to reveal a good deal about the person's health. Taking a deep breath, Elizabeth cautiously bent over the great bed and placed her ear to David's chest after pulling back the coverlet a little. There appeared to be a bit of a wheeze, but no rattle such as Purvis had warned about. The scent of sandalwood permeated his nightshirt, and she felt an overwhelming desire to place her head against his shoulder, to know again the comfort he might offer—when he wasn't teasing her to death.

She straightened, then smoothed his sheets, studying his face with worried eyes as she worked. Pray his ailment was no worse than a raging cold.

Deciding that since Lord Leighton slept she might as well return to her other patient, she quietly left the bedroom. Out in the corridor Hadlow paced back and forth.

"He is resting nicely, Hadlow. Why do you not catch a bit of sleep? I feel certain you must have been awake half the night, looking after him."

After giving her a grateful nod, the valet ambled off to the little room adjacent to David's, while Elizabeth sped down the hall toward Lord Crompton's room.

"Well, well, if it is not the little angel of mercy," Egbert drawled hatefully.

She looked up, then held the door lever firmly in one hand, guarding the earl against intrusion. "If you like to think so."

"How does my esteemed cousin go? Hadlow refuses to say a word. One might think David at death's door." He minced down the hall toward her, wearing extremely smart Hessians that looked to be too small for him.

"Hardly." She wondered if he wished him there and beyond. "Lord Leighton is sleeping nicely at present, but I believe he has nothing more than a nasty cold. No small wonder when you consider the wetting he took."

"You did as well, yet you appear glowing this morning. How fortunate that David manages to find such a charming attendant to nurse him to health. If I did not detest those nostrums, I might consider it as well." The somewhat oily smile he bestowed on Elizabeth did not appeal to her in the least.

She gave him a furious look. "He is not feigning illness, sirrah. And *I* did not have the affliction of a wound. Excuse me, if you will." She flashed him a quelling look, then entered the earl's rooms.

Rose greeted her with relief. "He wants to speak with you, miss."

Instructing Rose to rest in the earl's dressing room, Elizabeth hurried to his lordship's side, tilting her head as she assessed his condition. He looked much improved.

"Well? I have heard you keep busy today."

"Your son is under the impression he is at death's door, no doubt due to Hadlow and his dreary countenance. Poor man."

"And how did you manage to reassure my son?"

"I told him that only the good die young." Her eyes met his lordships in rueful admission of her absurd conduct.

The earl gave a frail bark of laughter, his eyes twinkling in just the manner she had noticed in his son. "I would sit up, I believe. I feel quite in prime twig today."

"Is that so? We shall see." She touched his forehead, then settled him, nicely fussing over his pillows with womanly touches.

"My son is a shrewd man. I approve his betrothal to you. Sensible girl."

Elizabeth almost laughed, recalling her hoydenish ways while in London. She felt as though she had aged years since coming to live with Aunt Bel—especially the last week.

"I should like to explain a few matters for you, since you are to be David's wife," Lord Crompton declared once settled against his pillows.

"What might that be?" She ought to inform him that she most likely would not wed his son, but that was David's responsibility. Elizabeth drew up a chair to the bedside, looking expectantly at the earl, his knitted nightcap sitting jauntily on his head while he fixed on her that gaze so like his son's.

"I went over my will and the estate papers not long ago. As you may know, much of the estate is entailed and would go to my heir, David, as a matter of course. The settlement is set up in a peculiar way, for ordinarily he could arrange leases. My grandfather did not wish to release a whit of control, and so tied the land to himself and the subsequent earls, reserving even the right to grant leases to himself, and those to follow." He coughed slightly.

"Here, sir," she murmured, offering him a glass of barley water and smiling at his grimace of distaste.

"I gave him the income from this estate, for under the terms of the entail he cannot get any other until he takes my place. At the time of his marriage, I shall settle additional income upon him, and when he has a son, if I still live, that income shall be raised. Since you have no father to bargain on your behalf, rest assured that I shall see to it that you are well guarded, my dear. You need have no concern that you or your children will be unprotected. Your children shall inherit David's land." He reached out and gently patted her hand.

"Oh, dear," she murmured. Elizabeth felt sure that she must be as red as a beet root at these candid words. She didn't know what to say to him, for although David had announced the betrothal and the earl approved, with Aunt Bel pushing things all she could, the two central characters in this farce were not of a mind to wed. Or at least one of them felt that way.

"I like a gel that is modest," the earl said with decided approval. "I trust your brother will be home one of these days. David said he is in Portugal. But rest easy that in the event he is delayed and you two wish to wed beforehand, I shall not let you down."

Elizabeth wished to avoid the subject of a wedding. In her heart she well knew that were the matter of the Valentine's Day visit to her room be widely exposed, she would have no choice. But she also knew she longed for a loving relationship with her husband. And David teased.

"I appreciate your caring more than I can say. I miss my own papa very much, and I should like nothing more than to claim you as my substitute father, if I might." There, she had revealed her affection without actually declaring that she would wed David.

"Do you suppose you might read for a time?" he asked wistfully.

"Certainly." She shared a smile with him before picking up the book again. " 'The next day opened a new scene at Longbourn. Mr. Collins made his declaration in form.' "

"Silly chit," muttered the earl. "She will get into a hobble, mark my words."

Elizabeth nodded, then added, "It is very vexing to have a character in the book with my name who is such a silly widgeon, sir."

"Quite." He shifted, then looked expectantly at Elizabeth, waiting for her to continue.

She returned to the world of Jane Bennet and Mr. Darcy, utterly absorbed in their problems, and annoyed with Elizabeth Bennet as only one can be with a character in a book.

She read until her voice began to fade and he looked as though he would welcome a bit of sleep. Placing the book on the beside table, she gave him a fond smile. She eased him back down in the bed, tucking him in as though he truly were her father.

"Perhaps a little nap after all that reading. I vow the morning has sped by far too quickly."

A willing Rose took her place in the room, while Elizabeth sought a pot of tea and perhaps a small nuncheon.

Out in the corridor, she decided to check on David. Assured that he still slept, she marched down to the ground floor to begin her intensified assault. She was determined to find a clue as to who might be the one who used the poison. Both Augustus and Egbert had strong reasons. Filpot might out of stupid spite, or some peculiar grounds. Only Jeremy Vane was free of suspicion, as he had no motivation. He couldn't inherit, could he? So what would his motive be?

Entering the north wing of the house, she found that here the business of the estate was conducted. In the first of the rooms, Jeremy Vane sat behind a desk piled with ledgers and papers. She glanced at the shelves neatly stacked with books, then smiled at him.

"I haven't seen you in some time. You certainly are a busy man." She casually looked about the room, running a finger along a row of books. She might think Mr. Vane to be as innocent as a lamb, but David detested him. Distrust usually had a foundation, even if it were illogical. Although this was one time she had to ignore an intuition.

"Good day, Miss Elizabeth. I trust you are well. That your dip in the icy water left you none the worse? May I say you look in radiant good health?" His face reddened, and he fiddled with the pen in his hands like a schoolboy.

Elizabeth smiled kindly. "I fare well, thank you. And I believe both Lord Leighton and his father improve daily."

Mr. Vane bowed his head. "I hope that is the case. Poor Lord Crompton has had a time of it, what with his wife dying at the birth of their daughter, and then the child as well. The Percy family is not a prolific one, I fear."

"Witness Lord Augustus and his only son." She glanced at the shelves, then added, "Is there a family tree about?"

"I believe there is, but not quite up to date," he replied dryly. "There will need to be changes once you wed David."

Not knowing quite how to evade that subject, for she

was beginning to tire of the matter, Elizabeth murmured
a vague reply, then drifted from the room. If she wanted
to investigate this wing, she would have to do so when
Jeremy Vane was elsewhere. Whereas Mr. Vane seemed
to her eyes all that was amiable, appearances could be
deceiving.

Back in the central hall, she studied the elaborate fireplace surround while pondering motives for murder. She
absently straightened a picture, then adjusted the placement of a chair too close to the wall.

"Out and about again, Miss Elizabeth? I trust that David appreciates your devotion to the family," Egbert said
in a somewhat acid voice. "Of course, I expect there is
a bit of self-interest lurking in your deeds, if truth be
known."

Remarking the contrast between biting language Egbert used and the gentle speech employed by Jeremy
Vane, Elizabeth wondered how the two could manage to
survive in the same house. Perhaps that was why Mr.
Vane retreated to the estate offices in the north wing.

"I am well, sir," she gently replied, ignoring his insulting remarks about her interest in family affairs. "And
your father? He does satisfactorily?"

"You are wandering about the house this morning,"
Egbert said, ignoring her inquiry. "Inspecting your future home, are you?"

"I understand that Lord Crompton requested that you
remove yourself to London, or wherever you chose to
live. Yet you choose to remain. How decidedly odd. One
would think a gentleman would wish to take himself elsewhere were he not wanted." She'd had enough of his
vitriolic words. Time to let him know that she was not
the milk and water miss he might think her. "Unless he
is at point non plus and has no alternative but throw
himself upon the mercy of a relative. In which case, one
would also think he would conduct himself with amiability."

He bowed, as one hit. "True. When illness struck my
uncle, I could not leave. Such callous disregard for the
head of the family would be ill received."

"Ah, yes," she agreed, "Society esteems a *respect*
for family ties."

His mocking inspection served to bring a blush to her cheeks, one she considered slight, thankfully. "If you will excuse me," she said pointedly, wishing him gone, preferably to the ends of the earth.

"Ah, it would be most ill bred of me to permit a guest in the house to be at loose ends. Allow me to be your guide, as it were."

There was no David to rescue her from his attentions, unwelcome as they were. Elizabeth bowed to the inevitable, acquiescing to his company. He led her past the library toward the front of the house.

"And this is the study, a small room you've not yet seen, I feel sure."

"Charming." Elizabeth paused in the door to the lovely little room. It would be an ideal place for the woman of the house to keep her accounts. From the desk she could gaze across her beautiful gardens to the forested hills beyond. She also would have an excellent view of the drive that approached the house, thus appraised of company long before the estimable Sidthorp could find her.

"You actually feel you might be able to settle in this house, so far from the delights of the city?" Egbert gave a faint shudder, picking an imaginary piece of lint from his coat sleeve with exaggerated care.

"*You* are here, are you not? And you appear to be surviving nicely. Besides, one could arrange picnics at Box Hill, and Brighton is not all that far away—nor is London, for that matter. It is not the ends of the earth, sirrah." Her derisory glance pinned him in his place for a moment before she swept past him along the hall back to the central portion of the house. He followed close behind her.

"My, my, the little angel has a forked tongue," he whispered in that sarcastic way he had.

"I do not speak with such. However, I cannot say the same for others."

At that moment Lord Augustus ambled toward them, corsets creaking louder than usual. "Ah, Miss Elizabeth. How goes my brother this day?"

She opened her mouth to suggest that he visit his brother, when the realization that Lord Augustus might well have a motive for wishing his brother in the grave. It could no be agreeable for him to be a charity guest at his brother's home. Aunt Bel had breezily informed Elizabeth that Lord Augustus Percy had not a feather to fly with. How Egbert managed to finance his foppish attire on such meager expectations provided additional suspicion.

"I assure you that your brother improves daily," Elizabeth managed to say at last.

"Good, good. Tolerates me now, you know. Were once the best of friends," he reminded. He sighed gustily, his corset sounding perilously like it neared the breaking point.

Not wishing to become involved in family wrangling and intrigues, she merely nodded, looking about her for a means of escape.

"Would you excuse me, gentlemen? Mr. Vane promised to find some papers for me." With that vague pretext, and pleasant murmurs of regret, she slipped away from them, drifting down the hall to where she suspected Mr. Vane still lurked in his little den, much like a spider spinning his plans for the estate.

" 'Tis time for nuncheon, Mr. Vane. Do you not join us? I vow, I shall be quite displeased if I must bear the company of Lord Augustus and Mr. Percy alone." She grinned at him, feeling quite in charity with the unassuming young gentleman.

He turned a pleased pink, nodding. "I shall be there." When she lingered, he went on, "Is there anything else?"

"That family tree. I should like to see it, if I may." She hoped her voice sounded sufficiently wistful to prod him to action. How provoking if he again kept her from seeing so simple a thing. Although what it would accomplish, she was not sure.

He said nothing about not knowing where it was this time, but went directly to a drawer from which he extracted a large, much folded sheet of paper. It almost seemed as though he had anticipated her return and had hunted it up for her.

"The details are written in those books up there on the shelf. This is the illustrative drawing representing the various lines of the family. The Percys may lay claim to an extraordinary and illustrious background." He smiled, but she noted that it did not reach his eyes.

He lovingly unfolded the paper, then began to point out the diverse lines of the family, how they were linked by marriage to many of the great houses in the land. It made her very aware that a Dancy, not withstanding she was the daughter of a baron, had scarcely the noble background to become the wife of the future Earl of Crompton. Not when one studied the lineage of past Percys.

Elizabeth stood at Jeremy Vane's side, studying the paper while beginning to appreciate all that had gone into creating her rake. Small wonder he carried himself like a lord of the land. He was one.

"I am exceedingly impressed, Mr. Vane. Most of the Percys did produce large families—until the present generation, that is," she said, reminding him of his earlier words regarding the dearth of Percys and heirs.

"I should think that both David and Egbert would be starting their nurseries instead of dashing about London and worrying about the cut of their coats."

Surprised at his bitterness, she spoke without due thought. "You sound as though you resent them, or at least their behavior. Is it the costs involved? Your concern for the estate?" From what Aunt Bel had said, Elizabeth believed the estate to be in fine shape, which made Mr. Vane's antagonism all the more confusing.

"Yes," he finally said. "I have a deep concern for the estates, its future. However, if *you* are to come here, I fancy that might ease my worries some. From what I have seen, you appear to be a woman of uncommon good sense."

"What a charming thing of you to say, sir. I am flattered, indeed." She beamed a smile of goodwill at him, backing toward the door with the family tree still in her hands. The sound of a monstrous sneeze halted her retreat. Spinning about, she clutched the paper to her breast, exclaiming with dismay, "Lord Leighton! You ought not to be down here."

"I suspect I had better not be in bed, at least not alone." Giving Jeremy Vane a wrathful glare, David availed himself of Elizabeth's arm. Leaning upon her just

enough so she could not scold him for an impropriety,
he guided her from the office.

"What are you doing out of your bed?" she hissed at
him in an angry undertone.

"Good thing I came down," he declared righteously
after blowing his nose. "Found you most improperly
closeted with that blasted cousin of mine."

"When I left your room, you were sleeping like an
angel." She stopped at the end of the corridor as it
opened onto the central hall. In the distance she could
hear the querulous voice of Lord Augustus railing at his
son.

"Pity I had to miss your presence. I am almost reconciled to this notion of marriage, if it means having you
in my bed," he teased.

Elizabeth could feel the heat that flamed in her face.
Without doubt it spread down her entire body, most likely
making her look like a giant strawberry. Those wicked
eyes of his danced with glee when he saw her discomfort.
Oh, how she would love to put him in his place, just for
once. And to get the better of him in one of their contests
of wits suddenly became her utmost ambition.

"Sirrah, I protest," she snapped.

He blew his nose again, then surprisingly agreed. "As
do I. You are too lovely a girl to be involved in this mess.
However," he added as he appropriated her arm again
and began to walk toward the dining room, "I have need
of your intelligence at the moment."

Irritation fought with another, deeper emotion. "I have
not uncovered a clue. Have you thought of anything?
Even though your father improves daily, you must be on
your guard lest you become a victim. After all, as his
heir, would you not be the next target?"

David paused just inside the dining room, glancing
back to make sure they were alone. "I had considered
that gruesome thought. I appreciate your concern. I believe you have actually come to care for me a trifle?"

Elizabeth blushed, to her annoyance, and refused to
respond to that sally. Rather, she veered to another matter.

"I suggest we study your family tree. Your father has
been threatened, you as well. Who is to say but what

your Uncle Augustus and Cousin Egbert might not be future victims too? Who would be the next in line for the title?''

Elizabeth spread out the paper on the dining table for him to peruse, pointing out how meticulous additions to the various families had been made.

"I do not know. It would take a clever investigation by one trained in that sort of thing. It would involve a third cousin and the like, you know." He studied the large paper again, looking at the names printed so neatly.

"There are a lot of us, are there not? Would you mind joining such a motley crew?''

"Motley, indeed," she said, seizing on that word as a means of evasion. "You well know that you are anything but.''

The timely arrival of Lord Augustus, Egbert and Jeremy prevented the exploration of that dangerous subject. She hastily folded up the family tree, tucking it under her arm as the others moved into the room.

"Hear, hear! Out of your bed? Think that wise?'' Lord Augustus plodded over to peer at his nephew.

"I am flattered, cuz. I rightly suspect that dearest David did not trust me with his betrothed.''

"What utter nonsense," Elizabeth roundly declared, not wishing to hear David say the same. "Why do we not sit down so Sidthorp may get on with the serving?''

At Aunt Bel's home, nuncheon was a casual affair. Late sleepers might stray into the dining room to pick at the spread of food as they pleased. It seemed that at Penhurst Place the gentlemen met at the table for a repast, perhaps to discuss the day's plans.

Feeling that she inhibited this, Elizabeth nonetheless was loath to depart to her room. How dreary to contemplate eating from a tray all by herself.

Once the meal drew to a tedious close, for the men spent their time conversing about masculine interests, Elizabeth escaped to the library.

She was followed closely by Lord Leighton. Curiously enough, Mr. Percy watched without making an effort to join them. Instead he agreed to a game of billiards with his father.

David closed the door snugly behind them, surveying

Elizabeth as she sauntered about the room nervously, still hoping to find a copy of a good herbal. ''Why are you here?''

''Why, indeed. Because, my little temptress, I cannot stay away.''

Then he sneezed, and Elizabeth rang for Sidthorp.

''I have just the thing for you, my lord.''

''I was afraid of that,'' David muttered.

10

WATER DRIPPED FROM the eaves. Beyond the house the snow dwindled into little splotches of white in the heavy shade under the hedges. The late February sun filtered through the bare branches of the trees about Penhurst Place, touching on swelling buds with a gentle caress. The cold spell had broken.

Off across the meadow a plump duck paddled its solitary way along the shore of the once frozen pond, although pieces of ice still lingered near the center of the shallow water. A slight breeze ruffled budding shrubs and last summer's grasses. In sheltered meadows crocus sent forth hesitant blooms, and clusters of snowdrops boldly sought the sun.

Elizabeth ignored the beginnings of spring.

In the library she wandered about, wondering why the herbal Lord Crompton had said ought to be on the shelf was not there. Did the same person who had hidden the book on poisons in the middle of a library shelf remove the herbal for nefarious purposes? She shivered at the thought that such a person might be beneath this roof.

"Ka-choo."

Without turning about, she absently said, "God bless you."

"I am feeling neglected," Lord Leighton said from the doorway, sounding a bit like a petulant schoolboy. "Everyone avoids me today. The least you might do is talk to me."

"You persist in teasing me, sir. I vow I become tired of it." She gave him a cross look, for she was indeed tired of everything this morning. The previous evening had been tedious in the extreme. Lord Augustus and Egbert had persisted in claiming her company until she went up to bed. They perpetually wrangled, until she decided she ought to take up billiards, for then they remained silent.

"You're blue-deviled," David announced with gentle derision. He strolled to the French window that looked out on the rolling expanse of green across to the woods on the far side. "That warm wind and brighter sun may have banished the snow, but it has done nothing to better your mood. We need to get out of the house."

"Your father improves, but you, sir, have a wretched cold." Elizabeth was suddenly reminded of Victoria's attempt to solve the difficult cipher, and how she had said it was imperative to get away from the problem at times, else she would go mad.

"On the other hand, perhaps you are right," Elizabeth said slowly. "I could see if I might persuade the coachman to take me back to Aunt Bel's."

"I need you here to keep your eyes open," he said hastily. "With you at my side, I may be less inclined to succumb to poison." He assumed a vulnerable look and gazed at her with the saddest expression she had ever seen.

"You accept you are in danger?" With a worried flash of turquoise eyes at the gentleman who lounged against the window surround, Elizabeth said, "I had not expected to find hunting for missing, er, books to be so trying."

"Ah, yes, discretion," he whispered, glancing at the open door. "Very wise. Now, where shall we go?" he mused, quite ignoring her statement in regard to the coachman and returning to Aunt Bel's.

"You may stick your head in a bucket for all I care," Elizabeth muttered, gathering her reticule and shawl in her hands.

"Now, now, mustn't get tetchy. Sign of old age," he teased.

"I am beginning to feel a hundred, what with catering to you, worrying about your father, and wondering if there is anything to be salvaged from my poor reputation."

"Fine time to begin fretting about that." His eyes seemed to dance with amusement at her belated show of discretion. "Besides, your respectable Aunt Bel is agreeable, most likely to ensnare me good and proper."

In fairness, she nodded regretfully. "I daresay you have the right of it." Elizabeth had no desire to ensnare anybody. She ought to have had more concern before, but her wits appeared to have gone begging.

He straightened, leaving the window to walk to her side. Elizabeth paused on her way to the door, wondering what was up his sleeve now.

"You are not to brood over that. I have a plan to take care of the matter." He reached out to gently touch her cheek, which quite undid her.

Blinking back a threatening tear, she said in a constricted voice, "Filpot would not allow me in to see your father this morning. I just know something is amiss. Tell me that he is not worse."

"I am not a doctor, Elizabeth. I cannot say. I confess he is not the same as yesterday, however."

"I knew it. The dear man. And he had so enjoyed my reading *Pride and Prejudice* to him." She hunted in her reticule for a handkerchief, then dabbed the moisture in her eyes. "I believe I shall return to Montmorcy Hall to persuade Purvis to attend your father." She blew her nose, a dainty sound compared to the great noise when Leighton followed suit.

"We, sir, are a pair of watering pots." Her giggle was distinctly quavery.

"Precisely. I suggest we take ourselves out of here for the nonce." He gallantly offered his arm.

Suddenly wanting to be away from the house, the problems that seemed so threatening, Elizabeth nodded her agreement. Placing her hand on his proffered arm, she gave him a tentative smile. "Where?"

He urged her along the corridor toward the front hall. "Have you ever been to the grotto? My father had it constructed for my mother before I was born. It was her great delight—after me, of course."

"Naturally," Elizabeth replied, chuckling at the mischievous lilt to his grin. "What a pity your mama could not have seen what a scamp you have become."

The look he gave her was most peculiar, unfathomable, and Elizabeth feared she had overstepped that line betwixt friendly banter and polite social chitchat. However, he did not say anything more, which left her totally at sea.

When they reached the hall, he spoke again, relieving her of the worry she had somehow offended him.

"Put on a warm pelisse and stout half-boots, for the caves can be chilly this time of year, and the ground may be quite damp in patches."

"Ought you go there with such a nasty cold?"

"I have a friend who firmly believes that the best way to cure a cold is to take a plunge in an icy pond, then go to bed with a bottle of gin."

"That sounds like a feather-brained notion, if you ask me," Elizabeth said, shaking her head at the image it provoked of a thoroughly soaked Lord Leighton, both inside and out.

"Go," he urged, then stood watching as Elizabeth walked lightly up the stairs.

She wondered what thoughts went skimming through his head. How did the rakish gentleman perceive her now? Then the very idea that she might even care about such brought her to her senses, and she scolded herself all the way to her room.

When she rejoined Lord Leighton, he was also dressed with more care than customary. Even though the day appeared mild, he had wound a scarf about his throat, and his coat was neatly buttoned over his vest. He extended a gloved hand to her, and Elizabeth hesitantly accepted it.

"The grotto?" she sought to confirm.

"Never say you are off to that hideous creation," Egbert sneered from the entry to the hall. "With all due respect to your mama, David, that is a ghastly place, dripping moss and decorated with bizarre statues. Gives me the chills just thinking about it."

"I had not thought you such a poor-spirited creature, cousin." David edged Elizabeth toward the door.

She was relieved that David did not appear angered by his cousin's nasty little barb. Rather, it seemed to her that he sought to avoid conflict with this odious relative. She caught sight of Jeremy Vane hovering in the background, coming from the other wing of the house.

"And do you share Mr. Percy's lack of enthusiasm for the grotto, Mr. Vane?"

The flicker of alarm on his face really was nothing to be concerned about, Elizabeth assured herself.

"Curious spot. I daresay you shall like it. Some might think it romantic." His eyes darted from Elizabeth to David, then back to her again. Suddenly she wondered if she was doing the right thing.

Once outside the house, she turned to Lord Leighton, saying, "I ought to bring Rose along with us. Really, sir, you have drawn me into the most scrambling ways."

"Unquestionably," he smoothly replied. "But then, you must be accustomed to unorthodox conduct, living with your sisters."

"If you mean that we were ostensibly alone after Geoffrey went off to the Peninsula, that is true. But Julia is a highly respectable widow, you know. We were not ever *that* out of bounds, I assure you, and never uncouth, I believe."

"Are you working on a commission at present?" he queried, apparently wishing to change the subject. He assisted her along the rough path, guiding her over a fallen log and around the end of the pond.

"A series of country scenes for Mr. Ackermann. There was but one left to complete when you so precipitously entered my room. I daresay he will accept them, figuring to publish them for next winter. I ought to finish that final one before I forget what winter looks like. Things change so quickly." She gestured to the scene about them, green buds where light snow had blanketed shrubs not long before.

Elizabeth thought the grounds near the house sadly neglected, something Jeremy Vane ought to have tended and obviously had not. Reeds marched thickly along the edge of the water, and pond weed looked to be rampant. Good for the ducks perhaps, but not proper management to her way of thinking. She revised her opinion of the young man as she glanced about her. The gardens ought to have been groomed as carefully as the house or fields, not forgotten.

"Why the frown? Are you having second thoughts about the grotto?"

"Nothing like that." She was loath to reveal her new opinion of the steward and sought a different direction.

"I confess I wonder about this clever person who wishes you and your father ill. We have not inspected the kitchens. If you believe the food suspect, might not the poison be found there?"

He stopped, turning to face Elizabeth, quite serious for once. "I expect you are right. Cannot think why it did not occur to me before this. Perhaps you could snoop about down there, for I dare not consider such—the cook would sense something odd immediately."

"I shall try," she replied, wondering how the cook would accept her presence.

They had reached a cavernous opening some distance from the pond. Large stones buttressed the front and into the entranceway. A forlorn statue of Hera stood guard nearby.

Elizabeth decided that David appeared even more handsome when he became solemn. She matched his mood, standing quietly, waiting for him to conclude his remarks.

"Actually, I suspect that Jeremy Vane is the one we seek." His stark revelation shocked Elizabeth.

"Preposterous," she scoffed. "It seems to me that Egbert takes a far greater dislike of you than poor Mr. Vane. Your own father took him in, trained him," she reminded. "How could Mr. Vane possibly wish his benefactor dead? I think you are wrong. Where does he appear in the line of succession?"

"I confess I had not considered him in that light. He would need to do in the lot of us. Jeremy always presents his best face to others, no one would suspect him but I."

"You are absurd. He is always agreeable to you. Certainly, he has been nothing if not helpful to me." She stepped from David's side, her confusion causing her to withdraw from him in every way.

"Does that mean you shan't help me? Remember, you *are* betrothed to me, and you did shoot me in the arm. You owe me something." That mischievous look had returned to his eyes. Elizabeth did not trust it in the least. She fingered the ring he had given her, presumably for appearances.

"We shall see," she temporized, not wishing to be forced into a decision she might regret later. She looked about her, observing the unusual entrance. "I gather we have arrived at the grotto. I should like to see it now that we are actually here."

He smiled, then took her arm, guiding her along a rugged path that broadened out as they entered a fantastic cavern. It was studded with seashells of every size, shape, and color. Delighted with the beauty concealed beyond the rather grim entrance, Elizabeth clapped her hands with pleasure.

"I gather that you like it?" He stood not far away, watching her as she stared about her, wide-eyed at the unusual scene.

"Yes, indeed. You sent someone ahead to light the torches. How thoughtful of you." Her antagonism began to melt as she slowly turned around to study everything. She observed how the lighting brought out interesting shapes, accenting the beauty of the shells and their delicate colors. From here and there shy cupids and dainty fawns peeped at them, their subtle colorings blending in with the shells rather nicely.

"There originally were small apertures to admit light. Over the years they have become clogged with dirt and debris."

"Mr. Vane ought to have better attended to the care of this charming place," she murmured as she wandered away from David's side to study a particularly lovely shell.

"There are a lot of things Mr. Vane ought to have tended and has not. He has hoodwinked my father, but not me. I see through that mealy-mouthed talk. He is an earwig who tattles tales to my father about me. Fortunately, my father is not about to believe those stories."

"He carries malicious tales? About you?" Elizabeth was shaken. She had believed Jeremy Vane to be a just and righteous man, and had worried that David was not all that was honorable. Could she have been so mistaken? About both of them?

Not wanting to probe further at this moment, she turned to inspect another shell. "Where did these come from?"

"My father had an arrangement with a number of sea captains to bring boxes of shells back from their journeys."

They began to stroll along the irregular wall. The gentle sound of water cascading over rock grew louder until they turned a corner, and the breathtaking view of a dainty waterfall came into sight. Elizabeth stopped short, altogether entranced with the sight.

"This idea is not all that unusual. I have learned of several others who have achieved similar results with their grottos and so-called 'sublime' gardens."

"Well, and I think it very fine. So I shall tell your father when I see him again. If I see him again. I rather suspect there is something you are hiding from me."

He failed to meet her eyes, glancing off to where the icy water tumbled and foamed over the rocks, then bubbled on its way to the pond, not far removed. He began to lead her away from the falls, to where she could hear what he said more clearly. He stepped close to her, tilting up her face so he might search her eyes. "Elizabeth . . ."

She held her breath, looking at David to see if he also heard the click of footsteps on the stone.

"Someone is in here," she whispered, uneasy, suspecting that the grotto had but one entrance, that if another chose to do them harm it would be a simple matter.

A sharp report and a chunk of the ceiling fell next to where David and Elizabeth stood. They stared with shock at the debris near their feet.

Flashing her a warning glance, David cautiously edged forward around the bend. He motioned for Elizabeth to follow him. Inch by inch they made their way along the rough path. Elizabeth stubbed her toe on a rock, and pressed her lips together to keep from crying out in pain.

When they came to the central portion of the grotto, they found it empty. The trickle of water down the walls and around and over the stones was all that could be heard. Elizabeth placed a shaky hand on the head of one of the cupids, feeling stupidly weak.

"Whoever it was has disappeared. I wonder what he planned for us?" David wandered about, studying the floor. He bent over to pick up a small object, dropping it into his pocket without comment.

"I believe I should like to return to the house." She shivered, suddenly aware that she felt very chilled.

David quietly agreed. Outside, they discovered the sun had retreated behind clouds. The wind had picked up and bit cruelly through their coats, tugging at Elizabeth's snug-fitting velvet bonnet with frigid fingers. Many times she found herself stumbling on the path, and was exceedingly grateful for the helping hand extended her. But she remained silent for the most part.

Elizabeth worried over David, although she'd not give him the satisfaction of knowing it. He had insisted upon leaving his bed, and seemed bent on destruction, what with ice skating and now the walk to the grotto. She was sure he ought to have remained quiet, warm, and safe by the fireside, if not in bed.

When they entered the house, she spoke quietly to Sidthorp while he assisted her with her pelisse. Then hesitantly she turned to face David, very much Lord Leighton at the moment, looking down that nose of his at her as though she were no more than his serf.

"I have requested Sidthorp to order you a hot bath. May I suggest you take that bottle of gin along, for surely you are as cold as when you were in the pond."

"What an amazingly selective memory you have."

"Do not sneer at me."

"I can't do it half as well as Egbert, anyway."

Not able to argue this point, Elizabeth walked beside David to the top of the stairs, where she paused. "I believe I shall investigate the kitchen and send for Purvis as well. I should like her to have a look at your father, not to mention tend your ague, which you are sure to develop. She has a way of making a person remain in bed, which is where you ought to stay," she scolded.

"I think you might persuade me," he said with a roguish grin. "I like the way you soothe my fevered brow."

Elizabeth digested this suggestive taunt, vividly recalling the kiss that had followed, then decided to prudently ignore it. "Perhaps Filpot will allow her into your father's bedroom. She does have a way about her." Elizabeth still felt hurt at being excluded from the room where she had spent most of the past days.

"That has a grim sound." He spoiled his frown by a magnificent sneeze.

"Off with you. Now," insisted Elizabeth with a shooing motion as she backed away from him, then turned to hurry along the north corridor to her room.

Rose greeted her with a look of dismay as she saw the wind-tossed appearance of her usually neat mistress.

"Help me tidy up some. I have no desire to have anyone else see me so disheveled." She gave a horrified glance in the looking glass at her rumpled self, then hurriedly divested herself of her pelisse and bonnet.

Elizabeth allowed Rose to straighten her gown and then repair the damage to the arrangement of her curls.

"Filpot will not permit you in the earl's room?" she inquired as Rose brushed Elizabeth's hair.

"No, miss. Said I was not needed. Hadlow, he thinks that Filpot a smarmy sort of fellow." Rose threaded an aqua ribbon through Elizabeth's curls, then stood back to survey her work. "I suspect something havey-cavey is going on."

"Indeed." But then, Rose was given to seeing ghosts and all manner of spectral creatures. "It may be that the earl caught Lord Leighton's cold and has truly taken a turn for the worse." She shared a worried look with her maid.

"I do hope 'tis nothing serious, miss."

Elizabeth did too. Over the days she had grown exceedingly fond of the old gentleman, and did not wish anything to happen to him.

"The food has been handled only by you and Hadlow?" she said with sudden concern, wondering if something had managed to slip past them.

"Yes, miss. The cook don't like it by half, she don't. Muttering something about her special herbs for the earl and the like. I fancy my own cooking to hers, and I'm no cook." She grinned at her mistress.

Once she was restored to a respectable appearance, Elizabeth turned to her maid, studying her open face. "I want to send off a request for Purvis. Could you see that one of the footmen takes it to Montmorcy Hall for me? Then I intend to visit the kitchens."

"Oh, miss, be that wise?" Rose wore a horrified expression on her face at the mere thought of her dear mistress going into such a place.

"I have been in the still room at my aunt's home, and the kitchen as well. Come now," Elizabeth chided.

She wrote a careful note for her aunt, explaining why she needed Purvis to come. Then she gathered a shawl and bravely marched down the stairs to the hall. Sidthorp was nowhere to be seen. The house was as quiet as a tomb.

"Peagoose," she muttered to herself, "you shall be as bad as Rose if you keep this up."

At the door to the kitchen she paused, watching the preparations for the evening meal. Across the stone-flagged floor the kitchen maid bustled about. A high dresser was loaded with platters of all sizes. Several Windsor chairs stood along the wall, and in the center of the room a wide wooden table was littered with vegetables ready for the pot.

A closed range stood on the far wall. The open fire was covered by a hot plate, waiting for the pots and sauce pans. The ovens sent out a welcome heat which would undoubtedly become oppressive by the time dinner rolled around. The pot of soup on the back of the stove smelled dreadful, and Elizabeth did not look forward to dinner if that was the beginning of the meal.

A rusty tin hastener was set in front of the fire, a joint of beef suspended from the dangle spit. One look revealed why the meat was often underdone on one side and overcooked on the other. The bottle jack by which the roast was to revolve worked only sporadically, if at all.

Elizabeth wondered why Mrs. Sidthorp as housekeeper didn't insist that the cook maintain a higher standard of cleanliness—seeing to it that the pots and utensils were polished and things worked properly—when the cook entered from the scullery room.

She was an enormous woman. Her grimy mob cap perched atop frizzled gray hair, her many chins rested on a massive bosom, while a none-too-clean apron was tied around her girth. And she was undoubtedly the meanest, most foul-tempered-looking woman Elizabeth had ever set eyes upon. Little raisin-dark eyes peered suspiciously at Elizabeth, making her hard pressed not to shudder.

Small wonder that meek little Mrs. Sidthorp daren't chastise the cook. Cook would most likely pop her in a pot and be done with it.

"Who be you, and what do you in my kitchen?" Cook demanded, arms akimbo.

Elizabeth stood her ground. "I wished to make a tisane for Lord Leighton. His cold bothers him dreadfully. Where is the still room?" This should have been the province of the housekeeper, and Elizabeth could only hope it proved in better condition than the kitchen.

Before the cook bothered to answer, the scared little kitchen maid tugged at Elizabeth's sleeve. "Please, miss, it be this way."

Ignoring the glare from Cook, Elizabeth gratefully followed the maid into a small room where the smell of herbs and spices scented the air. The herb chest drew Elizabeth's gaze. "Thank you," she murmured to the maid, dismissing the girl.

An inspection of the chest revealed the usual assortment of herbs, from what Elizabeth knew of the matter. Purvis would have a better idea if something was missing, or if there was a substance that ought not be here. The spice chest was locked up, a not unusual occurrence, for spices were expensive and easily purloined. Sugar was kept out and available, a sign of an affluent household, for Elizabeth knew many kept it under lock and key as well.

Up on a shelf, Elizabeth spotted the missing book— the *Family Herbal* by Thornton. She walked back to the kitchen door, watching the cook for several minutes before she observed that there were no cookery books to be seen on the two small shelves next to the dresser. Most households had at least one cookery book, along with the Bible and a few other works for the staff to read, if they were able. All Elizabeth could make out was a dusty copy of the Bible and another book, presumably sermons, from the look of it.

"You cook by memory?" Elizabeth inquired in a gentle voice.

"Cain't read, I cain't," Cook replied in a huff and a

wheeze. It was clear that a cook who could not read would not bother to take a book, conceal it in the scullery, with the intent of using the knowledge therein to poison someone. For that matter, the woman could not read the other book.

"Howere, I can cook with the best of 'em," she asserted, and Elizabeth warranted that there was not a soul who would argue with the intimidating woman, even if the meat was overdone and the soup utterly dreadful.

"But I don't take kindly to people snooping in my kitchen," the cook said, picking up a meat cleaver. "That Hadlow, sneaking about here, says he fixes somethin' fer the earl. Hmpf. I's sp'osed to use my special herbs for him, I am." The cleaver was plunked down with a thump, and the woman began to plop vegetables into a pot.

"Special herbs?" Elizabeth inquired in what she hoped was an encouraging manner. The peculiar taste of much of the food might be discovered if those herbs could be identified—and tossed away.

Cook, seeing the strange miss getting overly curious about the doings of her kitchen, clammed up and turned her back on the guest.

Deciding it was unlikely that she would learn anything more, Elizabeth left the room and proceeded back to her room. She had the foresight to bring a pot of tea with her, along with two cups. She and Rose often shared a pot of tea while at Penhurst Place, for Elizabeth found a household of gentlemen not always to her liking.

"Rose," Elizabeth said with a half laugh as she entered her room, "I quite see why you looked so horrified when I spoke of going to the kitchen. What a dreadful woman. How do you suppose she ever came to be here in the first place?"

Rose poured the tea and they each sipped for a moment before Rose timidly said, "I think she crawled out of the wall one night and has been here ever since."

Elizabeth chuckled at the unlikely tale, then fell silent. If Cook was not involved in poisoning the food, who was?

11

"I DECLARE, this rain has been more tiresome than the snow," Hyacinthe said, an adorable pout on her pretty mouth.

"I believe it looks to clear this morning. John Coachman said his rheumatism is better, which he insists is a reliable sign," Lady Chloe offered in hope of soothing her impetuous cousin. Hyacinthe had paced about the house like a caged animal. No doubt the lack of gentleman callers had something to do with her restlessness.

Aunt Bel ignored them, consulting her collection of superstitions to discover if there was anything to be found regarding rain, other than references to building an ark. "Do you know," she said to no one in particular, "that the superstition regarding red hair goes back for centuries?"

With this she captured Hyacinthe's attention, for she insisted her hair was not the least red, although she did admit her hair might be a bright chestnut.

" 'Twas said that the red-haired Danes who wrought such havoc in our land brought about the feeling that a red head covered a violent disposition."

"Pooh," Hyacinthe snapped, "that was hundreds of years ago. I fail to see what the Danes might have to do with anything." She idly picked at the keys of the pianoforte, playing the same melody she had heard on Elizabeth's music box.

Since Lady Chloe thought the notion about red hair was a deal of nonsense, she said nothing, merely stood by the window and stared at the avenue leading up to the house as though by that means she might conjure up news.

"Well, I will admit," Hyacinthe continued, "if we do

not find something different to amuse us, I might contemplate violence of a kind.'' Her fingers crashed in a discordant sound to reflect her mood.

In her position by the window, Lady Chloe tensed, catching sight of a coach making its careful way up the avenue.

''I believe you are to have your wish, cousin. Visitors are coming.''

Hyacinthe bounced up from the bench, dashing to Chloe's side. ''Who? Can you tell? Oh, I do hope it is Lord Norwood.''

A little smile curved Chloe's lips. While she sympathized with her cousin, she also thought it no bad thing that the exquisite Hyacinthe discover there were men impervious to her charms. She had known far too much success for her tender years. It would do her good to experience a bit of neglect, especially from the man Hyacinthe had made such a dead set at. It seemed to Chloe that her cousin had exhibited a want of good conduct in dealing with the marquess. Norwood was no youth to be dazzled by a lovely face. Hyacinthe needed a lesson.

''I do not think it to be Norwood's coach. There is no crest on the panel.'' Hyacinthe drooped against the window surrounds, then perked up. ''At least it is someone. I wonder who.''

''We shan't troop down to the entry hall to find out,'' cautioned Chloe. ''Even I know that to be bad form.''

''Hyacinthe has such a lovely voice. Why do you not sing up a song while Chloe plays for you? I shall listen, for I am very accomplished at that, you know,'' Aunt Bel suggested with a twinkle in her eyes.

Hyacinthe hastily selected, then began to sing a pretty country tune suited to her light soprano.

Gibbons presented himself in the doorway and announced, ''The Viscount Leighton and Miss Elizabeth, my lady.''

Elizabeth entered the drawing room at David's side. She had removed her outer things, wishing to change while here. David looked complete to a shade in a dark blue coat, white marcella waistcoat, and gray pantaloons tucked into his boots.

''How is everything at Penhurst Place?'' Aunt Bel

begged to know. "Your father? Is he any better? I have prayed he would improve with Purvis to attend him."

"About the same," he replied. "She says even less than Filpot, and that is precious little."

"Odd, that," Aunt Bel declared. "I felt certain that Purvis wold have your father on his feet in a trice."

"She is a treasure, make no mistake. My arm is as good as new, and that ague that threatened me completely gone," he politely assured Lady Montmorcy. He turned his attention back to the girls.

"We have come with a proposition. After all this dreadful weather, you must be as anxious for diversion as we are. Why do we not venture down to Dorking? I feel sure there is something one of you ladies must desire from the shops, and it would be a nice change."

Hyacinthe whirled about in delight, facing her aunt with a pleading look. "Please, dearest Aunt Bel?"

Not to be ignored, Lady Chloe added her appeal. "Oh, do say we may go, Mama."

While they discussed the things that might be purchased on such an expedition, David waited at Elizabeth's side.

" 'Tis very kind of you to offer amusement for us," Aunt Bel said most properly. "It has been dreadfully dreary for everyone, especially the girls."

He chuckled. "With Uncle Augustus demanding everyone play billiards with him, and Jeremy quibbling with Egbert over scoring, it is a welcome change for me and Elizabeth as well. I'll wager she is about to take up billiards just to challenge my uncle."

As she had considered that very thing, she chuckled in response. "Indeed. It is either billiards or something quite drastic. Although I have been greatly worried about the earl, they allow me to do nothing and that becomes tedious."

An elusive expression crossed David's handsome face before he replied. "Yes, well, he did seem better, and then he changed. I fear I cannot give you details."

To her utter distraction he captured her hands and tenderly kissed the inner wrist of each. "I shall look forward to a day spent away from all the troubles at Penhurst Place and in your lovely company."

Uncomfortable, Elizabeth tugged her hands free, putting them behind her in an effort of striving for calm.

His lips twitched, almost breaking into a smile, then he said, ''What a blessing it is that I possess unlimited patience.'' With that, he turned away from Elizabeth. He walked to where Aunt Bel perched on a striped satin sofa, fingering her locket watch.

''I have said the gels may go along with you, although I suspect Elizabeth would have gone regardless.'' Lady Montmorcy glanced at her niece, still standing by the door with a bemused expression on her face. ''Mind you, take umbrellas. I shall have Cook send along a packet of food in case there is trouble on the road. I trust your coachman has the sense to bring a spare wheel in the event of disaster? 'Tis wise in such abominable spring weather.''

''All is in order, dear lady. Shall I chat with you while the young ladies fetch pelisses and reticules?''

''Do not forget your pattens, girls. The streets of Dorking are sure to be wretched after this rain,'' Aunt Bel admonished the girls, who were well on their way out of the room.

Elizabeth paused by the door. ''Is there anything you wish, Aunt Bel? Perhaps some thread I may buy for you?''

''Considerate child,'' her aunt replied. ''I do need another packet of needles for my embroidery. I declare, I cannot fathom how they disappear, when I am certain I have them carefully inserted in the fabric.''

''Very well, a packet of needles it shall be,'' Elizabeth said, smiling at her aunt's dismay. The dear lady might be as punctual as a well-sprung clock, but she often forgot where she put things, particularly needles. Elizabeth had lost count of the number of packets she had bought since coming to the Hall.

In her room, Elizabeth slipped into her best turquoise pelisse, then donned a cottage bonnet that was lined with the same fabric and tied with matching riband. Drawing on her gloves, she again studied the diamond ring on her finger before covering it up with turquoise silk.

What to make of David and his puzzling attentions? Why did she have the uncomfortable sensation he was concealing something from her? When she asked questions, he kissed her wrists most intimately. And gave no reply.

Normally a woman did not expose her hands to a man unless he was someone close to her. Elizabeth was pleased with her hands at the moment. There were no stains or scratches from etching to mar them, and they were as soft as even she might wish. But his kisses presented a mystery. Why had he acted so in Aunt Bel's presence? Did he not realize it would show him as the lover? And make it more difficult to break their betrothal?

In the hallway she could hear the excited voices of her cousins as they made their way down the stairs to the entryway. She hastened to join them, unwilling to think about the riddle posed by David any longer. He had been too particular in his attentions, and if he continued to display such an attachment to her, Aunt Bel would be justified in believing the betrothal would lead to matrimony. He used her Christian name as though given that right, which, of course, betrothal offered him. But they were not really betrothed. In spite of the magnificent diamond on her finger.

Whether or not this was desired by Elizabeth was an entirely different matter. That she had been using David's first name for days remained forgotten, or perhaps ignored by her, in her wish to delude herself into thinking that she truly did not long for marriage with him.

David ushered the three young women to his traveling coach. "I daresay you shall not think the trip too tedious when it permits an escape from the house," he said with that twinkle restored to his eyes.

Not voicing an agreement, Elizabeth merely smiled as she entered the coach. Hyacinthe looked about the inside, a pleased expression on her face.

It was most attractive, with an interior of rich brown leather and plush velvet on the seats in a particularly lovely shade of dark blue. In addition to wood blinds that could be let down if one wished, there were pockets in the door panels to hold articles, or books, in the event one wished to attempt reading.

"I shall leave those odious pattens in the coach," Hyacinthe declared. "If a bit of water lingers in the streets, I feel certain someone will assist me." She did not look at Lord Leighton, but rather gazed dreamily off into space.

Lady Chloe followed suit, tucking her despised pattens away in the corner, hoping her mother would not know she had ignored the horrid things, with their rings of steel that clanged on the stone like dull bells.

"And what do you contemplate purchasing on your foray to the shops, Elizabeth?" David inquired in deceptively dulcet tones.

"I, sir, shall make my way to the best bookshop. Having read everything of interest to be found on your shelves, I desire something else." She spoke quietly, hoping to avoid being heard by her cousins. This might be possible, for they prattled away, discussing what they hoped to find.

"You left Miss Brunton's book unfinished? Or perhaps you have had you fill of *Self-Control?*"

She knew that note of teasing far too well to be surprised at his words. Self-control, indeed. Ignoring his taunt, she said, "I left my copy of *Pride and Prejudice* in London. It is a delightful book, and I believe I shall buy a copy to leave here, for my aunt has never read it. Your father seemed to enjoy it very much."

She darted a look that told him she clearly understood he was trying to discompose her. She'd not have that. She clasped her gloved hands in her lap and gazed from the window, allowing Lady Chloe and Hyacinthe to chatter away, inquiring about the shops, wondering if they might see anyone they knew, and in general monopolizing Lord Leighton.

It was to his credit that he exhibited great patience with the two girls, for away from Lady Montmorcy they forgot to be prim and proper.

"I shall arrange for a repast at the White Horse. Should we somehow become separated, meet there," David suggested.

Elizabeth exclaimed in delight as a deer bounded along the road, then darted off into the woods of beech and oak, soon disappearing from view. After they were gone from her sight, she turned to David. "That is kind of you, but we do have Aunt's packet of food."

Hyacinthe sniffed in disgust. "As if it would compare to the White Horse. All due apologies to your mama, Chloe," she added, not wishing to hurt her cousin's feelings.

The road wound down into the town west of Box Hill. Lady Chloe leaned forward to tap Elizabeth on her knee. "Later on there are simply masses and masses of bluebells along this road. Quite lovely, actually."

"Decidedly," Elizabeth replied, sitting straighter as they neared the center of town. She intended to separate herself from the others, find the needles for her aunt, then enjoy some time in the bookshop without Hyacinthe and Lady Chloe driving her mad with their chatter.

"Do you know," Hyacinthe whispered, although why, Elizabeth couldn't see, "that 'tis said Lord Nelson took leave of Lady Hamilton at the Hare and Hounds before he went off to the Battle of Trafalgar?" She peered out of the window at the building as they passed, quite as though she expected one of the people involved to step from the doorway.

Elizabeth couldn't resist a glance at David, nearly laughing when she met his amused grimace. It was lovely to have someone to share a bit of humor with on occasion.

Lady Chloe and Hyacinthe were enchanted when they discovered that others they knew had also decided to enjoy the respite from the rain. Lady Chloe spotted John Harlowe, dimpling a smile at him when he strode to her side.

Hyacinthe displayed more subtlety when she espied Lord Norwood across the busy street from the inn where they had stopped. She simply allowed her scarf to wave in the breeze, as though unable to capture it. The flutter of ivory silk caught his eye, and he sauntered to the party, bringing along his friends, Peregrine Forsythe and George Barr.

"My, what a lovely day," trilled Hyacinthe, sure of her charms, not to mention looks in a periwinkle pelisse trimmed in cream velvet. She tilted her head, becomingly demure in her smart bonnet cap of cream satin and double borders of scalloped lace. With a dainty hand she coyly toyed with the cream ribands that firmly anchored the bonnet beneath her chin. 'Sirs, what a pleasant surprise. Do you come to shop?''

"Like you," the elegantly attired Norwood said, looking down his aristocratic nose as he spoke, "we are come to town for diversion."

John Harlowe, not appreciating the other tonnish gentlemen in the least, drew Lady Chloe apart, persuading her, with frequent glances at the others, to permit him to escort her to the shops. When they drifted away along the street, Hyacinthe seized the opportunity to snare Lord Norwood, Mr. Forsythe, and Mr. Barr as her escorts.

Elizabeth thought her cousin in fine fettle, and barely suppressed a grin. Lady Chloe ought to have had a maid along, but in this small town it was unlikely to be remarked upon if she was escorted by a neighbor boy, especially one as well liked as John Harlowe.

"And now for you, Elizabeth," David murmured from a point shockingly close to her ear. "What was it you desired?"

She turned her head, finding him close, indeed. Although he was exceptionally tall, he had inclined his head so that his eyes were near the level of her own, and for a moment she found herself lost in those hazel depths. The golden lights in his eyes sparkled with humor, and Elizabeth found herself shaken to her core when she took a step away from him, saying, "Sir?"

"Your desires, Elizabeth. What are they?" That rich voice stroked her senses, teased her with yearning.

Heavens, she knew she must be blushing, for at that moment the notion of a kiss appealed to her more than anything in the world, much less the Dorking shops.

He chuckled, seeming satisfied, even though she had not answered him. He tucked her hand close to his side, guiding her across the cobbled street to the far side, then along the walk. "It is here somewhere, I recall."

Quite stupidly, she said, "What is?"

"Why, the bookshop, to be sure."

Elizabeth wished the ground would open up and swallow her. Never had she felt such a silly miss, not even at the Fenwick ball, where he had teased her with that first kiss. She had never told him that he was the first and only man to kiss her, but perhaps he had known, for she was indeed an innocent and inexperienced in things like kisses.

"Ah, here we are." He ushered her into the bookshop with great polish.

Elizabeth found she rather liked being escorted as though she were fragile china. In the past she had dashed about, not caring in the least for such. Memory of her previous confrontations with Lord Leighton while in London burned in her memory. What he must have thought of her.

"You hunt for that copy of *Pride and Prejudice* you want while I look over their stock of other books. I've a notion to see if they have something on landscaping. Father said my mother wished to have a white garden and formal landscaping out to the grotto. He expressed a desire to fix things up as she would have liked. What do you think about such a thing? Do you agree?" He appeared touchingly eager for her reply.

"It seems most admirable to me. I trust your father will be able to oversee the work himself." If she had hoped for further revelations about his father's health, she was to be disappointed, for David said nothing.

He evaded her searching look, turning to inspect the little penciled markers that gave one a clue as to what books were where.

Elizabeth paused a few moments before slowly wandering off to find the novels. Her mind seethed with the strangest notions. He was being less than truthful with her. No, not that precisely, but secretive. Still, it was none of her affair. With that reminder she persisted until she found what she wished. Knowing her aunt did not possess either of the books, she also bought a copy of *Sense and Sensibility*, and picked up a Minerva novel in the hope that it might prove diverting.

When she returned to the front of the shop, she found David waiting with a stack of books he had purchased. A quick glance at the titles revealed that he had found not only a work on landscaping by Repton, but a number of other volumes as well. A novel, a new history of

Greece, and several other works were being wrapped by the flustered clerk.

She paid for her books, then allowed David to lead her from the shop. Although she wondered, there was no proper way she could question him about his choices. Hyacinthe would have. But Elizabeth had achieved more dignity, unfortunately. It was not deemed fitting for a young woman to ask too many questions.

From the top of the street it was easy to discover where the others were. Hyacinthe waltzed along the way, peeking into the shops, disappearing into one that stocked pretty ribands and lace.

"Have you ever replaced that becoming pelisse that was ruined in the pond?"

"I've not had time, more's the pity," Elizabeth replied, vividly recalling that dreadful accident.

"I feel I ought to buy you a new one. It was most attractive."

"That would be highly improper," she said primly.

He laughed at her. "But I am your betrothed. I am allowed to do things like that. Come, I see a mantua maker up ahead. Permit me my whim."

Distressed, but somehow finding herself swept along to the shop, Elizabeth discovered that when David wanted his way, he attained it. In surprisingly short order the pleasant woman who kept the shop had Elizabeth measured, the fabric selected—by David, to match Elizabeth's eyes—and paid for. Arrangements were made for delivery of the fine wool garment, and they departed, no doubt leaving the mantua maker thinking she had taken a very quick order.

Once again outside the shop, Elizabeth turned to remonstrate with him. "You ought not have done that, sir."

"I am David, my dear girl. And, actually, I cannot lay claim to the idea as my own. My father was distressed to find you had suffered such a loss. He requested I replace your garment."

Surprised, Elizabeth could say no more, other than to issue a proper thank-you. She walked close to him, for he persisted in bringing her arm to his side in a highly familiar way. When she gave him a questioning look, he merely smiled.

"This walkway is narrow, and I would not lose you."

With that, Elizabeth had to be content. Indeed, the proximity of David, Lord Leighton, would have been quite enough to send her into transports if she had been a silly girl, which she wasn't. Not in the least.

It was a gay, almost frivolous group that met at the White Horse for the satisfying repast David has ordered.

Lord Norwood unbent sufficiently to talk to David most knowingly about planning gardens. It seemed that Norwood had rather grandiose plans for his own estate, not far from Oxford. He had consulted several landscape specialists, and brought forth a piece of paper upon which he sketched the final design that would be implemented once the weather proved more amenable.

While the two gentlemen had their heads together over the gardening discussion, Lady Chloe and John Harlowe, Hyacinthe and Peregrine Forsythe—George Barr having found it necessary to take his leave—chattered away with great amiability. Although, as Hyacinthe confided to Elizabeth when they retired to wash their hands and check their hair and bonnets, she could never be serious about Peregrine.

"Fancy being Hyacinthe Forsythe, if you please!"

Elizabeth chuckled, seeing how amusing it would sound. She wished she could share the silly whimsy with David, but when they joined the gentlemen, he still discussed gardening with Lord Norwood.

Oddly enough, Lord Norwood became quite animated when he found something that deeply interested him. He lost that rather stuffy mien, and his eyes crinkled up in a pleasant way. He really was attractive, with his hair tousled by a distracted hand that he thrust through it while pointing out the importance of proper fertilizer.

Hyacinthe was in a miff. "I vow," she whispered, "he is excessively tedious." There was little doubt as to whom she referred.

Only the entrance of the serving maids and the innkeeper with the platters of food prevented Hyacinthe from making a cake of herself. She darted annoyed glances at Norwood, then bent her attentions on Mr. Forsythe with devastating results. The poor man was overwhelmed.

Elizabeth could have swatted her cousin with very little encouragement.

"I beg your forgiveness, Elizabeth," David said quietly while the others began eating the excellent meal. "I do not usually neglect my lady when I can have the pleasure of her company."

"Fertilizer is by far the more important, I suspect."

"What, are you piqued too?"

"Not really," she replied, grinning when he glanced at Hyacinthe. "I wonder that I was ever that young, although we are only a year apart in age."

"May I say the time sits well on your shoulders?"

"You may say anything, sir. Whether I shall believe it is another matter."

"We ought to find a bonnet to go with that pelisse," he said, throwing Elizabeth completely into a dither.

"I'll have you know that it is bad enough for you to order that pelisse for me. To buy a bonnet would be totally beyond the pale."

"At least you did not call me sir," he grumbled.

Elizabeth thought it quite good that he failed to get his way. To her thinking, any gentleman who got his way too often became so spoiled as to be hopeless. Not that she wouldn't pamper a husband with loving care. Thankful the talk was loud and that no one seemed the least noticing of her, she nibbled her food. Finding it surprisingly delicious, she ate a disgustingly hearty meal. So much for the theory that lovelorn maidens wasted away on sighs. Not but what she couldn't sigh. That she might do very well without any doubt.

The happy party broke up shortly after that. Lord Norwood and Mr. Forsythe promised to join them for a small party at Montmorcy Hall two evenings hence.

Once in the coach, Hyacinthe bubbled and bounced until Elizabeth longed to tie her in the corner.

"I trust you have found the trip to your liking, Miss Hyacinthe," David inquired.

"Oh, yes," she replied, batting her lashes at him in her delight. With Hyacinthe flirting seemed to come as naturally as breathing.

Lady Chloe giggled, as young girls do when encountering something vastly amusing.

"What a good thing we left those horrid pattens in the carriage. We had not the least need for them," Hyacinthe declared as they entered the avenue to the Hall.

When the coach pulled up before the Montmorcy house, Lady Chloe and Hyacinthe got out, then bobbed proper curtsies and expressed their pleasure as well-reared girls ought.

Elizabeth was detained by the simple expedient of being kept in the coach awaiting David's help. At last he turned to assist her down the steps.

At her cool look he gave her an amused grin. "I want to see you at Penhurst Place on the morrow. Shall I send my carriage for you?"

"Odious man, to take it for granted I shall come at your bidding. I planned to stay here and not return."

"But you will," he replied with confidence.

"Very well, but only because I care about your father and wish to see how he goes on," she added truthfully.

He smiled a wry acceptance of her words, entered the coach, then waved farewell to her.

She stood by the front door, watching as his coach disappeared down the avenue. Something was up. She could feel it in her bones. But what?

12

"Oh, drat and botheration!" Elizabeth exclaimed.

A wheel of the coach slid into a particularly deep rut, and she found herself tossed about, nearly landing on the floor. She wondered if she had been wise to attempt the trip to Penhurst Place. Righting herself, she glanced at Rose, who sat in wide-eyed silence as they jounced along the country road.

"It looks to rain again," Elizabeth commented.

"Yes, miss," Rose replied dutifully.

Deciding that she preferred peace to attempting a conversation with the taciturn maid, Elizabeth fell to contemplation of her trip to Dorking. David had been all that was amiable, seeing to their every need, especially hers. She had enjoyed their time in the bookshop. Aunt Bel had exclaimed with delight over the novels, declaring they were just the thing to ward off the green melancholy in this dismal spring weather. She had not found a superstition to cover the rain, but she still searched.

Elizabeth ought not have permitted him to buy her the pelisse. Yet when confronting Aunt Bel with the matter, that most proper lady shrugged it off, reminding Elizabeth that not only was it a very nice gesture from Lord Crompton to replace the ruined garment, but that since Elizabeth was practically married to Lord Leighton, there was nothing inappropriate in the purchase.

Chloe and Hyacinthe were no better. Of course, their interest was captured by the coming party to be held at Montmorcy Hall. Elizabeth could not truly be surprised at their dismissal of her concerns.

So she was essentially alone, with no one in whom she might confide her fears. For every instinct in her body told her that danger lurked somewhere nearby. Bizarre, but there it was. Something in David's face had given her the clue. That and an intuitive sense within. Logic as well. For if there was someone who wanted the earldom badly enough to find a way to poison the present earl—supposing that to be true—surely that same person would do away with any other who stood in his way? A man had to be utterly mad to think he might get away with such a scheme. Yet it was terribly difficult to detect a smidgen of poison artfully concealed.

If Lord Crompton was intended for elimination, would his son not be next? Why could they not figure out what substance was being used? And from where it came? She knew that poison was extremely difficult to detect. Even doctors found it difficult. But still . . . It had to be someone in the house.

But Jeremy Vane? That mild-mannered, unassuming man who was politeness itself to Elizabeth? She couldn't accept him as a reasonable suspect. Egbert Percy was the likely one.

Actually, no part of the situation made sense, real sense, to her in the least. But then, murder was a frightening, stupid act and poisoning the grimmest. Victoria had dealt with murder, but Elizabeth had been more sheltered, as had most young women her age.

Further speculation ceased when the coach drew to a halt before Penhurst Place. Even on a cloudy day, the house wore a welcoming look. What a pity that strange circumstances brought her here, for she found the house, and its occupants—excepting Egbert Percy—charming.

The door opened wide and Sidthorp watched her walk up the steps, waiting to usher her inside. "Good day, Miss Elizabeth."

"Where shall I find Lord Leighton, please?" She removed her gray cloak, handing it to the butler, but left her bonnet on, as was proper. It was a small, rather neat bonnet of warm gray velvet, its narrow brim trimmed with a bunch of coquelicot feathers. Her gloved hands nervously played with the cords of her reticule.

"Come to hold my cousin's hand?" Egbert sauntered from the drawing room wing into the central hall, a superior sneer on his face as he observed her start.

"Not really. I do wish to see how your uncle goes on."

"Ha! They won't let you see him. Not even m'father sees him. I think the old chap is dead, and they are keeping it a secret until whatever my dear cousin seeks is found."

At her look of alarm he smiled, a particularly snide smirk, then continued, "I am not deaf or blind, you know." His gesture encompassed the library and drawing room wing, for he had drawn her along with him down the corridor, out of Sidthorp's hearing.

"You had best ask David," Elizabeth said discreetly.

"Do you really think you have truly captured him? He shows no inclination to marry, in spite of the ring you wear for the moment. I expect you are merely a ruse to help hunt for whatever it is he seeks. Recall, my dear girl, that David is a king among rakes. Whatever would he do with an innocent like you?" He drew back to peer at her with an exaggerated leer. "Do not tell me you really believe him to be in love with you? That is too, too amusing. Remember, David adores being amused, dear girl."

"People change," she said, her voice stiff with anger.

"I doubt that he will. But I daresay you have provided him with no end of *amusement*. Country life can be so deadly dull. A chap needs a bit of excitement to liven things up. I shouldn't be surprised if the betrothal is all a hum just to have you here." He strolled away from her side, down the hall, turning partly to add, "But then, some women think they can reform a rake. I say, once a rake, always a rake. He could have his pick of the cream in London. Do you really think you could satisfy him?"

Elizabeth watched Egbert disappear around the corner toward the billiards room. Most likely he would meet Lord Augustus there to commence their tedious rounds of play.

She turned in the opposite direction to walk slowly into the library. A look out of the window revealed that the rain had begun again. If it kept up, they most definitely would need that ark. Or a boat of some sort. Water stood along the roads, fields looked more like ponds.

And she was avoiding her dilemma. David.

How lowering to have to face the truth.

"Elizabeth. Sidthorp sent word you had arrived. Good to see you, my dear." David entered the room, then stopped. Something in her expression must have warned him that all was not as it should be.

She studied his face. Did Egbert have a basis for his words? Would David honor Aunt Bel's insistence the he and Elizabeth marry? Or did he merely toy with her affections?

"David? Kiss me."

She had clearly startled him, not to mention herself. Whatever she intended to say to him, it was not these words. But she did want to discover his real feelings for her. The words hung in the air between them. They had been spoken.

He took a step toward her, then halted, looking exceedingly uncomfortable. "Elizabeth, be serious. You know full well I dare not kiss you."

It hadn't stopped him before, she reminded herself. Her inner mind had been correct, as had Egbert. David had his own reasons for involving her in his scheme, but it did not include love. Perhaps not even regard.

She thought she saw regret on his face, a hint of something else as well. Whatever it was, it was an emotion she didn't recognize.

Pride rushing to her rescue, Elizabeth pinned a polite smile on her face. This was the prime rake of London. She had best remember that. He was not to be *her* rake after all.

"Good morning, my lord. Forget those silly words. I cannot think why I said them." Her laugh was a trifle forced, but she managed it. "Now, what do you hope to do today?"

She crossed to the desk, studying the house floor plan that lay spread out there. "Is there a room we have forgotten, some attic or cellar?" She glanced back over her shoulder to give him a bland, politely inquiring look.

"Elizabeth, for pity's sake, what is going on?"

"Nothing, my lord. Not one thing." She turned to face him, noting the confused look on his handsome face. He was no more bewildered than she. "How long do you wish me to wear this ring? I worry about it. I shall not feel easy until it is safely returned to you.''

She extended her hand toward him after slipping off her glove. ''As it is, I am very careful always to wear my gloves. Chloe laughed when I came to breakfast with them on. I shall take no chances, my lord.''

He approached her with a wary look on his face, as though expecting her to do something extraordinary. Like bite. He took her slim hand in his strong, capable one, glancing at the beautiful diamond, then turning that remarkable hazel gaze on her face.

She stiffened her spine, and her resolve as well. There was only one phrase he could say that would alter matters now, and she strongly doubted he would utter those words.

He didn't.

Elizabeth found herself in his arms, with his lips seeking hers in a hungry, searching kiss. Did he think to uncover her very soul this way? For one mad moment she yielded, for she knew this would be the last of his kisses for her. Then she tensed.

His hands were not idle. From cradling her head just so, they had slipped over her body in a most familiar way, and now compelled her intimately close to him.

She broke free. Somehow her arms had found their own way around him, and the fingers of her ungloved hand had thrust up into those tumbled brown locks, twining possessively in them as though she had that right. ''Forgive me. I feel quite foolish,'' she said in a strangled voice most unlike her normal tone.

Her hands slid down to his shoulders, but neither of them moved away from the embrace.

He shook his head, as though to clear it. ''I ought to be asking your forgiveness. Elizabeth—''

''Well, well,'' Egbert said from the doorway in his most insinuating voice, ''what have we here? The rogue's seduction? The rake's ravishment? Dalliance with an innocent is so sweet.''

Elizabeth stepped away, in her mind echoing the soft swearing Lord Leighton made under his breath. She might have learned something, perhaps heard those words she longed to hear, had Egbert not made his unwelcome entry.

Then again, perhaps his intrusion kept her from facing the truth again. That she would not have heard the words she longed to hear, rather the teasing of a seasoned rake, that dashing man about London who captivated more hearts than could be numbered.

What a silly little fool she was, to think she actually had seized his interest.

"I had something in my eye, and Lord Leighton was merely getting it out for me. The roads are so utterly dreadful in these rains." Elizabeth fumbled in her reticule for a handkerchief, finding it in the very bottom. Dabbing her eye, she turned away so neither man could see the very real tears that now fell.

"Dusty too," Egbert observed in malicious tones.

David assumed an amused look, then strolled across the room to confront his cousin. "I say, old boy, can you not think of something else to do but spoil my fun? May I remind you that my father strongly suggested you take off for London, or anywhere but here. I repeat his request."

"I would not dream of leaving here with my uncle so seriously ill that no one, not even your soon-to-be-bride, can see him. What is it, David? Why the secrecy? Perhaps you grow tired of waiting for the earldom?"

"Egbert, that is quite enough," David insisted in a firm but quiet tone.

"Really?" With his familiar contemptuous sneer tilting his mouth, Egbert sauntered from the room, leaving the door open behind him.

By the time David had collected himself, Elizabeth had dried her tears and composed her emotions.

"That was unforgivable," he declared angrily.

"He is a very bitter man. Do you see now why I feel he might be responsible for the threat?" That David had called that precious kiss mere fun cut her deeply.

She might be inexperienced, but she knew better than to believe a rascal like David could change. No, she would finish what she had promised to do, then go away, with fond memories of the dashing Corinthian, her very own rake, even if but for a brief time.

A loose shutter banged against the house as the wind picked up. Rain slashed against the window panes of the French doors, and they began to rattle and shake as though an angry giant wreaked vengeance upon the house.

Elizabeth looked out in alarm. Once she might have been willing, even eager, to remain in this house overnight. Now she knew she must return to Montmorcy Hall, come what may.

"Surely you do not believe his spiteful words?"

She swung her gaze back to him, then dropped it to study the elegant carpet. "I scarcely know what to think, do I? As he said, I am a little innocent. Hardly the sort to appeal to a rogue like you. It is intelligent to face reality, my lord. And I believe I am quite sensible."

A stir at the door brought her gaze up again. Filpot stood there, an apologetic expression on his thin face.

"Excuse me, milord. Your father requests your presence." He bowed most properly, then left the room.

"You had best go. And I as well. This was a hare-brained scheme to have me here today. Ask Sidthorp to summon a carriage, please."

"Elizabeth, nothing is as you believe. Nothing."

He gave her a frustrated look quite as though he wished to say more, then tore himself from the room, marching down the hall, then up the stairs with impatient steps.

She glanced about the room, wondering if she would see it again. She noted a patch of damp beside the fireplace, and her thoughts turned to Jeremy Vane. At first she had believed him to be a fine steward. But now she wondered.

She had heard of dishonest stewards, men who lined their pockets with vast amounts of money while their masters, absent in London or the continent, believed them tending their jobs. Indeed, Victoria had worried about the management of their father's estate once he was gone. The girls knew nothing of estate administration, and Victoria had done her best. But who knew if the steward was honest, or if he embezzled sums here and there, difficult to detect.

Elizabeth resolved to ask her sister's new husband to look into the matter, if Victoria had not already done so.

She walked over to the fireplace to touch the spot of damp plaster. Odd.

"Miss Elizabeth, your coach awaits you."

She turned away, then swiftly joined Rose, walking along the corridor as though she could not leave fast enough.

Sidthorp looked puzzled, but naturally said not a word. He held an umbrella over her while she entered the carriage, then he disappeared into the house before the coach had gone a few yards.

"A fool's errand, that's what it was, Rose. I ought to have stayed at home." Elizabeth pulled the handkerchief from her reticule, blew her nose, then resolutely faced the wretched trip back to Montmorcy Hall.

Gibbons met her with the large red umbrella kept for such inclement weather.

Once inside the house, Elizabeth ignored questioning looks from her cousins. Instead she threw herself into planning the party.

"Do you think the rain will stop long enough for our guests to come?" Chloe asked with a dismayed look out the window.

"If I could travel on these roads, anyone could. Especially if they are as tired of being confined indoors as we have been. Mark my words, they shall be here."

Hyacinthe had not missed the grim inflection Elizabeth had not been able to keep from her voice.

"And what about Lord Leighton? Will he join us?"

"When I left the house, he had been called to his father's room. I cannot say whether he will be able to come or not."

"I would think if he had any tender sensibilities, he would stay home," Chloe said. She inspected a vase she had filled with blooms from the greenhouse, turning it this way and that to see which angle proved the best.

"He is different," snapped Elizabeth. "Do not expect the more tender sentiments from Lord Leighton. Recall that he is among the premier rakes of London."

"I detect a bitter note in your voice, cousin," Hyacinthe said thoughtfully. "Am I to gather that the course of true love does not flow smoothly?"

Elizabeth gave a wavery chuckle, then plumped herself

down on the sofa, proceeding to mangle a pillow while she spoke. "I believe that might be an accurate assessment of the situation. Except there has been no love from the beginning. It all stemmed from that silly superstition of Aunt Bel's that I must marry the first man I saw on Valentine's Day."

Hyacinthe sank onto a chair not far away from Elizabeth, looking at her with concern. "But if he was in your bedchamber in the middle of the night, what other conclusion can there be? 'Tis not your fault the silly man climbed in your window because he knew you'd not see him otherwise."

Chloe drifted over to join them, leaving her bouquet on a low table. "You had been in that room earlier, Hyacinthe. Perhaps he intended to see you!"

Elizabeth shook her head. "No, he claimed he knew I occupied the room, for he heard me singing, and you all know what a frightful voice I have."

"How did he know?" Chloe demanded, her eyes wide and pretty mouth ajar.

"He had heard me sing whilst on our way back from target practice while in London. With that nasty spy sneaking into the house, Victoria decided we had better prepare for the worst. That is when I got in the habit of sleeping with my pistol beneath my pillow. I heartily wish I had never thought of the notion. If I had not shot the blasted man on Valentine's night, I'd not be in this pickle now."

"Are you in a pickle?" Chloe blurted out, fascinated by this glimpse of the older, most sophisticated girls' lives. "What sort?"

"Ninny," scolded Hyacinthe. "Elizabeth is disappointed in Lord Leighton and being compelled to wed him." She turned to look at Elizabeth, adding, "Although I should think it not so bad. He is most attentive to you whenever I have seen you together. If Lord Norwood paid me that much consideration, I should be in alt, not crying in my soup. I fear all is lost with that man, for he is more concerned with his gardens."

"Who says I cry in my soup!" Elizabeth jumped to her feet and marched to the door. "I intend to do what I can to make the party an enormous success."

"I wonder if John Harlowe will manage to come," Chloe said as Elizabeth strode away.

Far from her cousins and their comments, Elizabeth paused by a window that just happened to face in the direction of Penhurst Place. What went on over there? She thought she could see smoke spiraling up from the chimneys.

Lord Augustus would have his fireplace in a roar, if he wasn't nagging Egbert to play billiards with him. And David? Oh, she did hope that his father was all right.

A carriage appeared on the avenue, but rather than stop in the front of the house, clip-clopped around to the back. Curious, Elizabeth slipped down the servants' stairs and out to the back hall.

Purvis stamped into the hall, shaking her umbrella with care, then setting it aside to remove her patterns.

"What happened? Why are you back home?"

Purvis straightened, giving Elizabeth a narrow look. "So you listened to the earwig, eh? I came back because there was nothing more I could do."

She snapped her mouth closed and Elizabeth suspected that she would not say another word on the subject, come what may.

However, Elizabeth tried. "Is Lord Crompton dead?"

"What's it to you if he is, missy?" the abigail snapped pertly. Then seeing the distress in Elizabeth's eyes, she added, "No, not at this point, he isn't."

Once Purvis had returned to her quarters next to Aunt Bel's room, Elizabeth wandered about, adding finishing touches to the rooms when she remembered where she was and what needed to be done.

By the following evening, the house stood in readiness. Chloe was all flutters and giggles, as might be expected in a young girl barely out of the schoolroom. Hyacinthe worried about her looks, sure her gown was not quite right. Elizabeth was a bundle of sensibilities.

Acceptances had been received from all invited. Aunt Bel had expanded the original group to include the Harlowe family, Emma Fenwick and her family, plus a goodly number of other local notables. As far as Hyacinthe was concerned, the only notable of importance was her marquess, Lord Norwood. All looked forward to a break in the tedium caused by miserable weather.

Elizabeth wondered if Lord Leighton would dare show his face.

"Your betrothed accepted, but I expect you knew he would be here," her aunt informed her.

"Actually, I had no idea," Elizabeth replied, tugging the neckline of her gown. She looked like a frump. The dress was dreadfully proper. Insipid French gauze over a turquoise silk slip decorated with a row of dainty silk roses about the hem looked horridly prim, what with the little puffed sleeves above her gloves. She tapped her sandaled foot impatiently, anxious for the evening to be over.

Since they were in the country, country hours would be observed. Dinner was to be at five of the clock, and all knew Lady Montmorcy's insistence regarding time. None would dare to be late to one of her parties.

Hence, the carriages began to roll up before the house, laughing, chattering guests hurrying in to escape the light drizzle. Gibbons ushered each party inside with remarkable speed, then returned for the next group, holding his huge red umbrella aloft like a torch.

Only Lord Leighton was late.

Aunt Bel was very annoyed. "Ain't like the boy to be late. He is usually most considerate. Cannot think what has happened," she fretted softly to Elizabeth.

"I fear I know nothing about his plans, Aunt. The last I saw him we were not precisely in good footing with each other."

"I did not realize you quarreled."

Disregarding her aunt's exasperated look, Elizabeth calmly, for she had practiced for hours at this, shook her head.

"Not quarreled, precisely. A mere difference of opinion." How could she confess that she had been such a goosecap as to fall head over toes for a polished Corinthian from London who saw her as a delightful girl to tease?

"Well, that is all right, then," Aunt Bel said, relieved.

They proceeded to dinner, Lady Montmorcy unable to tolerate lateness even in her dear Lord Leighton. Midway through the meal, a disturbance in the front hall brought

Aunt Bel's gaze to Elizabeth. A faint nod of her head, and Elizabeth excused herself from the table, hurrying out of the dining room.

Lord Leighton stood in the process of being brushed off by a horrified Gibbons.

"What on earth happened to you? You look as though you crawled through a hedge backward, my lord." Elizabeth added the words of respect as an afterthought, being dumbfounded at David's less than perfect appearance.

"Carriage overturned. Road's a damn quagmire. Ought to know better than to have a party in miserable weather," he grumbled.

"None of the others assembled seemed to have any difficulty."

"None?" He gave her an arrested look, then turned to Gibbons with a softly spoken request. The butler nodded, then bustled off in the direction of the kitchen.

"I suppose your aunt will never forgive me for being late."

Elizabeth allowed a prim smile. "You are a favorite of hers. Like Lady Jersey, she has a soft spot for rascals. Given the circumstances, I would wager you can slip into your place without any difficulty. Come."

Why she was being so nice to the blasted man was beyond her. Yet he winced as he moved, and limped slightly as he walked along with her to the dining room.

Aunt Bel was properly horrified at the accident. At Elizabeth's side, Lord Leighton managed a wicked grin under the cover of his napkin.

She ignored him the best she could, given the fact he sat next to her and frequently brushed up against her, thanks to Aunt Bel cramming so many people at the table.

Before long Lady Montmorcy gave the signal for the ladies to withdraw. Elizabeth gratefully left the table, aware that a speculative gaze followed her all the way to the door.

Rather than join the other women in the drawing room, she went directly to the rooms Aunt Bel had ordered prepared for dancing. The musicians were tuning up, the chairs in place, flowers arranged perfectly, and all in readiness.

How would she manage to survive the evening? Just seeing the dratted man tied her insides in double knots.

"Elizabeth? Here you are. Somehow I suspected you would sneak away from the others."

"David! That is, Lord Leighton. What may I do for you?"

He pulled her along with him until they were safely concealed from any chance view. Then he kissed her with all the expertise at his command.

All those exhilarating sensations charged through her like bolts of lightning in a summer storm. Elizabeth forgot to push him away, much to her disgust when he at last released her. She desperately tried her "serene" look that she had practiced so diligently. "That was not well done of you, my lord." The set-down proved difficult when he still clasped her in his arms, clinging to her as though she were a haven in a storm.

"You will never know how much I needed you." At her raised and skeptical brows, he went on. "I just learned the accident was deliberate. The coach had been tampered with before we left."

"Then someone does wish you ill!" she cried softly. "I suspected it was but a matter of time. After all, if a madman plans to murder your father, would he not also want to do away with you?"

"Dear god," he whispered. "I cannot risk you coming back to the house, even if I could manage to convince Egbert to leave. Yet I want you there."

"So you agree with me that he is the more likely one!"

"Although he is not precisely penniless, for his father does well enough, Egbert has exceedingly expensive tastes, else he could manage nicely on the allowance he receives. He may well wish to step into my shoes," David concluded with a grim twist of his mouth.

People began filtering into the rooms, and Elizabeth saw David and she must end their earnest discussion. Placing her gloved hand most properly on his arm, her earlier resolutions evaporated, she guided him from the room and down the hall. With the strains of music in the background, she turned to him for further talk.

"It is a good thing we are officially betrothed. Otherwise I should put paid to a respectable marriage. As it is, I most likely will have to take myself off to a far corner of the country where they have never heard of me before. I wonder if I have a relative there.''

"Elizabeth, cease this nonsense at once," he muttered in her hair.

"It is all very well for you, my lord, but I have a life after this, I should hope. And you as well. Think of London.'' She had sought to tease him, but he ignored her efforts.

"It might not be Egbert. He may be taking advantage of the situation to be his nasty self."

"Surely you do not hark back to poor Jeremy Vane," Elizabeth scoffed.

"Promise me that you will not listen to the evil words from either of them, or my uncle, for that matter. Just return to the house. I do need you, Elizabeth."

What was a girl to do when the most handsome man she had ever known, or seen in her life, pleaded with her to help him? Begged her to join him? Implored her to lend her intelligence to solve his mystery, looking at her with those melting hazel eyes? Violate propriety and invite possible kisses . . . or worse?

"Of course. I shall come tomorrow."

13

It was a great pity that Elizabeth had so much time to think. Upon reflection, she could find more holes in David's highly persuasive talk than in a yard of lace netting.

For one thing, why had he refused to kiss her when she had asked him—most foolishly, she admitted—and then when he wished to turn her up sweet, kissed her, and most thoroughly? Devious creature. If she didn't love the dratted man so dearly, she would most assuredly plot some cunning means of revenge.

It must be the nature of men, she decided. They—at least the handsome, charming ones—used their attractiveness as a means of securing what they wanted. She ignored the basic truth that women had been doing the same thing for centuries.

"You will be careful, will you not?" Aunt Bel quietly demanded. "I have an odd notion that things are not what they seem at Penhurst Place in spite of your reassurances. I suspect you have been less than forthcoming with me, my dear niece." Her eyes held a hint of speculation.

"Oh, I think it positively thrilling that you are going to Penhurst Place to help Lord Leighton," Chloe cried, clasping her hands before her.

Elizabeth paused in the act of drawing on her aqua gloves that matched her ensemble, wondering if Lady Chloe could possibly be as naive as she appeared. Another look, and Elizabeth decided that dear Lady Chloe had a goodly amount of growing up to do before she was ready to cope with the gentlemen of this world. John Harlowe might be good enough for a beginning, but she had better forego Lord Norwood until she had learned a thing or two, and practiced her feminine wiles a bit more.

Elizabeth could testify to the need for a great deal of exposure to the flirtations offered by Society gentlemen to be able to tell the genuine from the false.

"Indeed," she murmured. She turned to check the portmanteaus Rose carried out of the door, to ascertain all she wished was along. Gibbons bustled about, chatting with Rose, admonishing the coachman from Penhurst Place to take good care of Miss Elizabeth.

The door swung shut. Elizabeth found herself once again alone in the entry with her relatives. Odd, how Montmorcy Hall was a mostly female residence, while Penhurst Place remained essentially male—other than a few maids and that utterly dreadful cook, who rarely presented a decent meal. With a well-equipped kitchen, it must be the cook's face that curdled the puddings. A great deal of food at Penhurst Place was ruined, causing Elizabeth to wonder if perhaps the cook embraced a pagan religion that required burnt offerings three times a day.

"Mind you, send me a message regarding Lord Crompton," Aunt Bel urged. "I would come myself, only the dratted man would most likely bar me from his room." Her feeling of ill usage was most likely mitigated by the knowledge that she really did not do well at nursing the ill. A woman of her sensibilities left that sort of thing to a servant.

"Remember, before I left, I was banished as well," Elizabeth said in reply. That was another point that Lord Leighton had failed to address. Why, after caring for his father for days and days, was she suddenly not allowed to enter his room? It seemed to her that something dashed havey-cavey was going on at Penhurst Place. But what?

Aunt Bel checked her locket watch. "You must leave us now. We will keep you in our thoughts, dear girl." She enfolded Elizabeth in a scented hug, then stepped back to study her face, as though searching for something.

Elizabeth tried to conceal the exhilaration that welled up within her when she considered being close to Lord Leighton. Her aunt had that foxy, I-know-something-you-don't-know gleam in her eyes again. It would almost be worth the coming separation to puncture that balloon of

Aunt's when Elizabeth rejected the connection with Lord Leighton. For the break most assuredly would happen, the betrothal must be ended. After all, who would countenance a marriage based on a silly Valentine's Day superstition?

"We shall entertain Lord Norwood, Forsythe, and the others in your absence the best we may." At a nudge from Lady Chloe, Hyacinthe added, "and John Harlowe as well. I *do* wish you were going to be here, for although you are a quiet girl, we always seem to have a far better time when you are around. You always know just the game to play, or the entertainment sure to please." Hyacinthe wore a puzzled expression for a few moments as she reflected on that curious reality. "I only hope that they will take to a game of cranbo when you are not here to lead us. You think of the silliest words to use." She chuckled, as though remembering a particularly absurd word.

"Well, I feel certain you shall do very nicely. You are both lovely girls and should manage very well, indeed." Elizabeth gave them a bland smile, then marched out of the door to the coach sent from Penhurst Place. It seemed that Lord Leighton wished to take no chances that she might back out of her promise to him.

The road had not improved in the last few days. The coachman tried to avoid the worst of the ruts. Although it did seem, as they drew closer to Penhurst Place, that his lordship or Jeremy Vane had dispatched a number of men to fill up the deepest holes.

Yet she suffered a jouncing drive. Rose looked likely to cast up her accounts if they did not arrive shortly. When the coach drew to a halt before the Penhurst Place entry, Elizabeth exited the coach with a feeling of profound relief. Even Rose was heard to give a great sigh.

"Sidthorp, how is everyone? Does Lord Crompton improve?" Elizabeth inquired upon entering the house. The entry hall was deserted but for the butler. She heard voices coming from the south wing of the house. Evidently Lord Augustus had induced the others into a game of billiards, for the talk was loud and argumentative.

"His lordship passed a tolerable night, I am told,"

Sidthorp replied. He took her warm cloak, then joined
Rose to remove Elizabeth's things to her room.

It left Elizabeth alone in the entry hall, looking about
her while wondering what she was supposed to do.

Jeremy Vane came from the north wing, papers in
hand, reminding her of a rabbit on a serious errand. She
half expected his nose to twitch. "Good morning, Mr.
Vane," she said, speaking up a trifle to catch his ear. He
looked as though he might be hunting Lord Leighton, and
if he was, she wanted to make her presence known.

He gave her a startled glance. "Ah, good morning,
Miss Elizabeth. I trust you are well?"

His timid remark and obvious desire to be gone amused
her. How could David suspect this person of treachery?

"Are you off to find Lord Leighton? Would you be so
kind as to tell him I am here?" Her cordial smile became
fixed as she observed him. Had she not been watching
him carefully, she might had missed that flash of resentment that crossed his face so briefly. She was taken
somewhat aback by this reaction, for if he was the steward here, he must be accustomed to carrying a message
now and again.

"Of course." He bowed just enough to be respectful,
then hurried off as though Elizabeth carried the plague.
Something elusive niggled at the back of her mind.

Sidthorp came down the stairs from supervising the
disposal of her belongings, and Rose as well. It seemed
that quiet Rose was a favorite among the staffs of both
houses, for they all fussed over her. She was one of those
rare treasures, a maid who did her job well, never gos-
siped, and liked everyone, particularly Hadlow.

"When you see him, please inform Lord Leighton that
I shall wait for him in the library." She gave Sidthorp
her warm, gracious smile, earning her a look of devotion
from the butler.

Then Elizabeth drifted off across the hall and along the
corridor to the library.

Across the courtyard, the gentlemen could be glimpsed
through the windows as they moved about in the billiards
room, for that door was wide open. She stopped, watching as Lord Augustus stood waiting to play, cue in hand.

There was something about his stance, his attitude. He stared at David.

Drat the glass. If it were not for a bit of reflection, she might see more clearly. But it seemed to her that the genial Lord Augustus eyed his nephew with less than cordiality. More like hatred.

She retreated to the shadows of the corridor. It must be a distortion. Why, after all these years, would Lord Augustus turn against his brother? Or his brother's son? But she knew stranger things had happened.

Pity, that, for she rather liked the old gentleman with his creaking corset and brusque speech. His indulgent attitude toward his son could be excused on the grounds that Egbert was an only son. Yet . . . what would Lord Augustus be willing to do to insure that his heir inherited more than was his rightful lot? More than one man had murdered for money, and this involved far more than that.

Rain began to fall again, obscuring her view of the billiards room, with streaks of water cascading down the panes. The scene became a blur of black and cream, shadow and light.

Realizing that anyone could stumble across her in the corridor, she continued on her way to the library, mulling over the twist in the mystery of who might be behind the poisoning attempt. Lord Augustus joined Jeremy Vane as somewhat plausible suspects. Her money was on Egbert Percy, the cousin who stood to gain the most.

The curious snippet of knowledge that had teased her memory returned, and she eagerly awaited David's arrival so she might share it with him. He would undoubtedly tell her it was not significant, and she was not all that certain, but it was curious. Most curious.

Then her eyes focused on what she was looking at, and she walked to the fireplace. No fire warmed the hearth or the chilly room. And just above, slightly to the left of where she stood, was a patch of damp plaster above the surround.

"Really," she muttered, "Mr. Vane is most careless."

"What are you nattering about, my dear Elizabeth?" David silently entered the library, strolling over to join her. He was dressed for his day at home in his usual impeccable style: fawn pantaloons under a cream waist-coat and corbeau coat. Hadlow must have used champagne in the blacking, for those Hessians had a shine to rival the sun.

David was about to ring for a footman to arrange a fire when Elizabeth stopped him.

"Do you not think this odd, my lord?" She pointed to the suspicious spot inches from the mantel. Then she frowned. "Although I do remember seeing it the other day, come to think of it. It slipped my mind."

" 'Tis this blasted rain. And Vane is not quite the wonderful manager you think him," David said sourly.

"I confess," she said slowly, "I begin to believe you. At first when we came, I thought everything so noteworthy. It seemed to me that he did a fine job of it." She turned to meet David's gaze with troubled eyes.

"I suspect you were rather seeing the results of my father's management, teaching Jeremy, as it were." David returned her concerned look with one of his own. "As long as Father was out and about, things were well done around here, at least that is what Sidthorp reported to me when I came."

"I just recalled something curious. When I studied your family tree, I noticed Jeremy's name was *not* to be found anywhere. I searched very carefully. Is that not peculiar? For he has claimed to be a cousin."

David rubbed his jaw while she spoke, nodding thoughtfully. "I would think so, but it is not conclusive. Some of our relatives are frightful correspondents. Yet, as you say, it is peculiar. You would think he'd have corrected the omission once he came here."

"David." She reached out a tentative finger to touch the sizable patch, and her nerves tensed as they did when she was working on something critical. "I have this feeling." Her eyes flashed when she caught sight of his handsome face alight with amusement. "You may well laugh at me. I do not mind. Be so good as to fetch me that knife you use for sharpening your quill." She gestured to the desk, then resumed picking at the patch of damp plaster. "I feel a point of something here."

"Your obedient servant, ma'am," he said, mincing over to his desk in a parody of the perfect footman. He returned with the small tray upon which rested the long silver knife, a pot of sand, a stick of red sealing wax, a gray feathered quill pen, and in a chamber at the end of the tray, a full bottle of black ink.

"Foolish man," she chided indulgently, unable to be annoyed with him. "I merely needed the knife."

"I thought you intended to write a reminder to my dear cousin that he ought to tidy the place up a bit, or at the very least manage some repairs to the roof, or chimney, or whatever is the problem."

He proffered the contents of the tray with a slight bow, his eyes brimming with mischief.

Elizabeth ignored that tantalizing face, picking up the knife instead. She commenced to scrape the plaster.

"Here now, what *are* you doing?"

"I have a hunch, a feeling if you like, about this plaster. True, it has rained, but not that much. The roof at Montmorcy Hall is old, and perhaps not in the best repair, but if there is seepage, it comes out around the ceiling, especially in the attics. Not in a patch near a mantel on the ground floor. There is something concealed within. Do you not want to know what it is? It could be jewels or secret documents or something exciting."

"I suppose it is possible, love."

She tossed him a confused glance, then turned her concentration to the patch. "I suspect the plaster is much newer than that surrounding it. Of course, it is possible that it is wet due to all the moisture about, and the chill in the room. Have you never noticed how an unheated room seems much damper than others where there is a fire?" she murmured, concentrating on the curious patch.

"True," he murmured, coming closer to watch what she was doing, after setting the tray on a nearby table.

"However, I believe that in this case there is a different cause." She dug some more with interesting results.

A chunk of plaster fell to the hearth, then another. Elizabeth tried to catch them but failed. At any rate, she did observe there was a peculiar lump protruding. Her heart accelerating its beat, she dug more deeply, ignoring the bits and pieces that flew in every direction.

"Do you see what I see?" she whispered. "A wad of

papers wrapped up in oiled silk. What a peculiar place to put papers, my lord. At least it appears to be a pack of papers. One would think that whoever placed them there was trying to conceal them. If *I* had papers I wished not to be seen, I'd burn them.''

"Indeed. May I?" He pried out the packet with the knife, also ignoring the pieces of plaster that bombarded his fine corbeau coat. Once he had the packet free, he walked to the desk, Elizabeth at his side.

"Best keep this to ourselves." She darted a glance at the door, then stole softly over to close it. She felt it better they would be warned if someone intended to enter the room. The rattle of the door lever ought to be sufficient to alert them.

David had the oiled silk unfolded and spread open on the desk when she rejoined him.

"Well?" She was simply dying of curiosity. Was he not going to say a word to her?

He studied the first of the papers, then the second. There was a third letter in the packet, and this too he scrutinized. He was absorbed in his thoughts. At last he seemed to realize she had asked a question and said, "What did you say?"

"What did you find?" She generously ignored the fact she had made the discovery and he had but pried it out.

"Will you excuse me, Elizabeth? I must take these upstairs immediately." Then he glanced at the ragged hole in the wall and grimaced. "Would you take care of that mess?"

With that request, he hurried from the room. Elizabeth stared at the empty door with exasperation. How like a man to dump the mundane details in a woman's lap. *He* was to have the satisfaction of presenting the intriguing papers to his father, while *she* mended the wall. She sighed with acceptance of a situation that was not likely to change.

The room must not be left unattended. Anyone might stroll in here. The gaping hole to one side of the mantel could scarce be missed. Then she caught sight of the key dangling on the inside of the door, as though it was locked on occasion. While it might excite curiosity, she would secure the room while she sought help. It was the only way.

She locked the library door, then dropped the key into her reticule. In the entry hall she found Sidthorp crossing from the dining room to the stairs.

"Please, a moment of your time, Sidthorp. I need someone who can patch a bit of damage to the library wall, and be discreet about it. It *must* be someone who can be as mute as a fish." She gave him an expectant look, but offered no explanation as to the cause for the hole in the wall. She hoped he might think it due to the excessive rain, which in a way it was. He paused in thought, then nodded. "I believe I have just the man for the job." Never would the butler satisfy his curiosity to inquire how the damage came about. That would not be proper.

"I shall await him in there. Tell him to knock, for the door will be locked."

Even then the stately butler did not stoop to question. He nodded in his dignified way, then started for the office wing of the house. Elizabeth did not bother to tell him to remain silent, for she knew that no one would have torn that information from him, given her secretive attitude when she'd made the request.

She paced about the library after securing the door once again, pausing to stare out of the window from time to time, then resuming her restless walk. What kept the workman, anyway? And what was David discussing with his father upstairs all this time? And why was she not allowed to poke her head into Lord Crompton's room? Was he better or worse? Questions she had asked herself ran through her mind over and over, with not a solution being offered.

A soft, hesitant rap on the door brought her dashing over to grasp the key. "Who is it?" she asked in the softest voice that would still carry to whoever might be on the other side.

" 'Tis Ben, miss. To patch . . ."

She used the key, opening the door just enough to permit the workman to enter, then quickly locked it again.

Ben hardly needed her to point out what needed repair. He had mixed up some plaster, bringing it along in a small bucket. With surprising speed he had filled the hole and smoothed the place over so it looked much as it had before.

While he worked, Elizabeth set about building a fire that would help dry the plaster. Once she had it lit, she stepped back to study the restoration. The workman busied himself cleaning up the hearth.

"That looks very good, Ben. You did a fine job. Lord Leighton will be ever so pleased."

The man was overcome at this high praise, and bobbed his head on his way to the door. Here he paused, waiting.

Elizabeth swiftly walked to free the man, whispering her thanks. She knew she need not remind Ben to keep silent. The very manner in which this all had been done might arouse his curiosity, but if his job depended upon his being as silent as the grave, he would never say a word.

She relocked the door, then returned to tend the fire. Since it was such a dreary day, she found a book to read. With nothing to do, her mind became far too active, dancing off in too many directions. It was a novel she'd read before, but no matter. Her other choices appeared less appealing.

Some time later, after she had replenished the fire several times and read a good deal of the book, another rap came on the door. Placing her book carefully on the table, she glanced at the plaster, noting it still showed a bit of dampness. Shrugging her shoulders, she went to turn the key.

"Oh, David, I am ever so glad it is you. Hurry." She tugged him inside the room, then turned the key again.

He chuckled, causing her to frown at him.

"It is very well for you to be amused. I have been in here tending the fire, watching over this dratted plaster, while you have been doing far more interesting things."

"True." He sobered at once. "I took the papers to my father. They are important documents. And they throw a new light on the threat to Father. Dashed spot for concealment, if you ask me." As to what that threat constituted, he didn't say.

"Perhaps whoever wants to become the next earl is the one who hid the papers. But it seems to me that Egbert would be more creative than this." Elizabeth gestured to the still damp patch on the wall. "As I said before, I should think the papers would have been burned rather than holed up in the wall. What a curious thing to do. Why, do you suppose? And who?"

"I am not convinced that it is my odious Cousin Egbert." David wandered back and forth before the fireplace, while Elizabeth quietly tossed on another scoop of coal over the flames.

"I saw your uncle watching you while you were playing billiards," she said. "It was when I first arrived today, before the rains began. I realize I was seeing him through two pieces of glass, but he gave you a most peculiar look, as though he hated you." Elizabeth was loath to tell David about what she had seen. It surely would distress him.

"Well, I was trouncing him rather roundly, which might have accounted for that look you saw. But hate? That seems a bit strong."

"Not if he wants to lay his hands on the money and the estates, secure it all for his son," she argued.

"Somehow old Uncle Augustus does not seem the sort of man to want to poison his brother, or do in his nephew. If you follow my thoughts." David put his hands behind his back, tapping his foot on the hearth before the fireplace. Elizabeth knelt before the flames, trying to remove the chill that had settled over her at this discussion of premeditated death.

"What do you intend to do?"

She watched as he walked over to the bookshelves, where he commenced to hunt for a book. Upon finding it, he tucked it beneath his arm, then gave her an absent smile. "I shall take this upstairs, then discuss the problem with Father. Unless," he added suddenly, "he is not feeling up to it."

"I fancy I ought to return to Montmorcy Hall. You appear to have solved your mystery." And wouldn't tell her. Elizabeth rose from the hearth and waited for him to tell her to depart from his life.

"What! On no account. It has been pouring rain for hours. Can you imagine what that stretch of road will be like now? No, far too dangerous. Besides,"—he gave her a curious, unreadable look—"do you not want to see how this all turns out?"

"You believe it will be resolved so quickly?" She walked across to join him by the door. Closer up, his face revealed no more to her searching eyes.

"I should say within the week at the outside."

"You are very confident, my lord."

"I thought you agreed to call me David," he complained, leaning against the frame of the door to give her what she considered a highly flirtatious leer.

"That was for the benefit for the others. We have no need to dissemble, do we? I was under the impression that you were eager to conclude this sham betrothal."

He drew himself away from the door, a frown briefly crossing his face. "There is nothing sham about that ring on your finger. Just because I did not get down on bended knee to make some flowery declaration of undying love does not mean I am reluctant to do the proper."

"How vastly condescending of you, my lord," she snapped at him, her temper flaring beyond control. "What makes you think I wish to wed a reluctant man?"

He glanced at his pocket watch, then tucked it back into place. Giving her a hasty kiss, he hurried off down the hall, tossing a few words behind him. "We shall discuss this later, my love."

His love, indeed! Elizabeth spun about, her hands clenching into fists that would have enjoyed pounding the arrogant Lord Leighton.

Unfortunately, he was correct in one thing. With the roads truly horrid, she could not, dare not leave now. Perhaps by tomorrow, if the rains ceased, she might leave this house of torment.

When she joined the gentlemen for dinner, it was to be presented with the same dreary food. How could they tolerate it?

"I see Cook is in a bad mood again," Lord Augustus muttered.

"Is she ever in a good mood?" Egbert snapped.

"I trust you might find a replacement," Elizabeth ventured to offer.

"Father feels sorry for the woman, no one would hire

her without a recommendation, and he could not in good conscience give her one.''

Elizabeth flashed him a look of disbelief. What he said was inconsistent with the concept of good management of an estate. One rewarded a good servant, punished an unsatisfactory one. She nibbled her food, trying to find something edible.

When it came time for the men to have their port, she rose promptly. Never had she left a table with such gratitude for release.

The evening passed very slowly. Egbert begged her to play or sing.

It was the one moment of humor in a dreary evening. Elizabeth chuckled. "I could not carry a tune in a bucket, I am sorry to say. And I have no skill at the pianoforte, either." She held up her hands in mock dismay, and Egbert smiled in return.

"She has other, more fascinating talents," David added with a curve of his mouth.

"I shan't be so rude as to inquire what they might be," Egbert began, a devilish look on his face.

Elizabeth inserted, "I believe he means my etchings, Mr. Percy." With that little comment, she added, rising as she spoke, "I believe I shall retire for the night."

Alone in her room in the unoccupied north wing of the house, she reflected that David had deliberately led Egbert to think ill of her. What a wretched thing of him to do . . . unless he was trying to make her angry with him.

The house was oddly still come morning. Even Rose tiptoed about, although there seemed no need for her to do so.

Elizabeth dressed rather than eat in her room, and quietly went down to the dining room. There was an array of food on the sideboard. Wonder of wonders, the toast was not burnt, nor the eggs cooked to a crusted lump. The ham looked succulent and tender. Had the cook changed her religion?

Egbert entered the room, glanced at the food, then helped himself to a small portion. He sat down without greeting her or saying a word, just sipped a cup of coffee, deep in thought.

Accustomed to a home where everyone chattered with one another, Elizabeth politely said, "Good morning."

"Not so good, I fear. The earl took a turn for the worse in the night."

Her plate clattered on the table. "Oh, I am so sorry."

"David is up there now. He's been with the old man most nights, and last night he slept in his own room. Wouldn't you know it was the night when my uncle elected to get worse?"

"He must feel utterly wretched. Poor David."

"Yes," Egbert murmured, with none of his usual nastiness.

At that moment David entered the room, dressed in somber black. His face looked gravely strained.

Fearing the worst, Elizabeth rose from where she had so abruptly sat down. "Your father . . . ?"

"I am sorry to say he has gone aloft."

14

"DEAD!" Elizabeth exclaimed in horror. She leaned back against the table, thankful for its support. "But he cannot be."

Egbert rose from his chair. "Sorry, old chap. Your father was a fine man." His normally caustic tongue refrained from any nasty barb. Rather, he walked around the table and placed a hand on David's shoulder in sympathy before leaving the room.

Had it not been for the suspicions Elizabeth harbored regarding Egbert, she'd have thought his sorrow genuine. She stared after his retreating figure, then went to David's side. "Is it really true? I would have sworn he was getting better."

"True." His reply was excessively strained, and he turned his head away from her to stare out of the window.

"So you are now the earl."

"And with all the more reason to marry and produce an heir," he said without intonation. "Father wished that Egbert not be permitted to inherit the title." He gave her a curious look, one that confused her. "So it would seem that our accidental Valentine's Day betrothal is most fortunate."

Elizabeth kept a firm clamp on her reactions. "So it would seem," she replied, hoping her voice was as colorless as his.

"I shall need a wife, and as I said once before, I could do far worse than marry you. You'll not hand me the mitten, will you, Elizabeth?" At her startled denial, he went on, "You have been denied a courtship. I shall try to make that up to you." The earnest look on his face surprised her for some reason. It was as though he truly wished that things could be otherwise, and that their betrothal might be as any normal one.

Surprised by his concern over something like a courtship in the midst of what must be a painful time for him, Elizabeth placed her slim hand on his arm, turning his face toward her with her other. "Do not trouble yourself over such a trivial matter now." She lightly touched his arm, then dropped her hand to her side.

"Oh, Elizabeth," he murmured, enfolding her in his arms, as though to draw strength from her slender form. He leaned his head on hers and stood quietly, just holding her.

After a few minutes he withdrew, then began to slowly pace back and forth. "There are a great many details to work out. I have sent for our solicitor. Dr. Dibble was here during the night, thank goodness. He has supervised the laying out. Poor Mrs. Sidthorp was not up to the task, for she had served my father since girlhood."

"The house was so silent this morning. It seems the very wood and brick knew your loss." She waited a moment, then offered, "Is there anything I may do for you?"

This restless ambling about the room was unlike David, she thought. Somehow she had expected him to be more resolute. But people handled grief in so many ways. She recalled how devastated she had been when news of her parents' death had reached her and her sisters. Each of them had shown their heartache in a different way.

David paused by the fireplace. "Pour me some coffee, would you?"

Taken aback, she obeyed his request, handing him a steaming cup while watching his expression carefully.

He continued to deliberate a few moments, then gestured to the table. "Sit with me. Perhaps together we could plan the next few days. Please," he added politely as he moved toward the table.

The absurd thought crossed her mind that she was glad she had donned her coffee-colored mull this morning. Although it had a soft cream lace collar, it was near enough to the acceptable mourning color so as to not be objectionable. Odd, how a little thing like that could bother a person.

"When do you wish to have the funeral?" It was a

sensitive subject that must be dealt with. Notice must be sent out immediately to those in the surrounding area. London was too far away, even though it was sufficiently cold enough to preserve the body for longer than several days. It would take time to send the announcement to London—too long for people to be able to journey to Penhurst Place for the funeral service.

He turned his head to look out of the window at the falling rain. "The heavens mourn the passing of a good man," he said in a soft voice.

"David," she reminded gently. "We must notify the vicar, send notices to the papers in London, and what about the family?"

"I have a list in the study. There is paper in there, everything you could need. If you will take the trouble, I would rather you write them out than Jeremy."

She quailed at the black look that settled on David's face. "Surely you do not cling to *his* having something to do with your father's death?"

"I cannot reveal all yet, even to you." The sadness in David's eyes tore at her heart. How bleak, how utterly grim his countenance had become.

"Of course, I shall do whatever I can."

He rose, then paused, standing over her. While he stared at her with that unreadable expression on his face, he said, "You will not leave me here alone, will you? You *will* stay, will you not, Elizabeth?"

Confused by his words, and the stress he had placed on her remaining in the house when he had his uncle and cousin to keep him company, she reluctantly nodded. Her reputation was likely in tiny shreds by this point. What did it matter? She wanted nothing more than to help her dear rake at his time of sadness. How she missed that teasing look in his eyes, which now were dark with grief and a sort of anger.

"I shall stay. When is the funeral to be?" she repeated, reminding him of the necessary details to be worked out.

"The day after tomorrow." He glanced at the window again, then added, "With this never ending rain, his interment may be postponed. There is a family mausoleum on our principal estate, Crompton Vale, but that is some miles away to the north. I shall have to consider what will be best.''

Confused, but not wishing to pester him for explanations at the moment, Elizabeth rose from her chair, then walked to the door, where she encountered Lord Augustus.

Corset creaking more than usual, the older man paused in the doorway, then studied his nephew with a shake of the head. ''I'd not expected Crompton to go before me. Thought he'd live to a ripe old age. Who'd have believed it? I'm sorry, my boy.'' Tears brimmed in his light brown eyes. He walked over to join his nephew with ponderous steps.

To Elizabeth it seemed as though Lord Augustus had aged ten years overnight. She murmured words of sympathy, then slipped from the room, leaving the two to discuss the matter of the former earl's passing in privacy.

Once in the study, she discovered a neat stack of stiff cream paper, bordered in black. The thought crossed her mind that it was odd David should be prepared to the extent of having the proper paper at hand. Perhaps he'd had a premonition it would be needed. But he had fought the idea so strongly, she was surprised that he'd willingly admit the approaching death to that extent.

Her first task was to write a note to Aunt Bel. It would be a shock for her; Elizabeth suspected that her aunt had nursed a fondness for the earl. Elizabeth also requested that her aunt send over a suitable black gown. Even though Elizabeth was not an actual member of the family, she had been fond of the old earl.

If David was to be believed, she would in six months time—providing they observed proper mourning—be his wife. That she found difficult to accept. In fact, there was something about this entire arrangement of his wishing to marry her that seemed distinctly unreal.

She chalked it up to her shattered sensibilities, and wrote out a note to be taken to the vicar, requesting his presence.

She rang for a footman to deliver the first two notes, the ones she considered most urgent. He assured her that he would ride immediately to deliver them, pointing out that the rain had dwindled to a mere mist. He then took himself off in a rush to be gone, looking gratified to be the bearer of such important missives.

All of the servants wore black armbands, and the maids wore their most somber dresses beneath their aprons. Already a lozenge-shaped hatchment had been hung on the front of the house near the door. The late earl's armorial bearings were beautifully carved in bold relief.

Elizabeth returned to the list on the desk, a surprisingly short one in view of the earl's age and station in life. Perhaps David felt that the information would be obtainable in the newspapers.

But still, it seemed decidedly peculiar. When she completed her task, she stacked the letters in a neat pile to be franked by David.

Around noon she drifted to the dining room. She hadn't expected to see any formal, set meal, and there was none. Rather, the sideboard had an arrangement of dishes. There were beef and vegetable soup in the *bane-marie,* cold meats, rolls, pickles alongside it, and a dish of fruit in the center of the table.

Elizabeth picked a few things, selecting fruit and a roll, for although far from hungry, she knew she needed to keep her strength if only for David's sake.

"Good afternoon, Miss Elizabeth," Jeremy Vane said as he entered the dining room. Gone was his habitual rabbity demeanor. Rather, he stood taller, looked more assured. Could it be that he felt the responsibility of his office more keenly with Lord Crompton gone and a new earl stepping into his shoes, as it were?

She made note of the alteration of character in the back of her mind, then turned to her slight meal.

Lord Augustus joined them, his jowls drooping more than usual in his unhappy state.

"Shall miss him, y'know. Quarreled often, but never really meant it. Suppose everyone thinks he would like to do things differently if given the chance. I do." Lord Augustus dipped out a bowl of soup, then took a crusty roll. With a sigh he joined them at the table.

"Too late, I fear," Mr. Vane inserted, his voice polite.

He appeared somewhat hostile to Elizabeth's eyes. She

had watched him rather than Lord Augustus, recalling
David's unreasonable antagonism toward the steward.

"M'brother was always good to you, you scamp,"
Lord Augustus grumbled, throwing Jeremy a look of dislike.

"I fancy you will be moving along now, sir. With your
brother gone and a new earl taking his place, you shall
wish to be elsewhere, I daresay," Jeremy replied with a
thinly veiled note of contempt in his voice.

Elizabeth barely stifled a gasp of dismay. How bold
the steward had become suddenly. It was scarcely his
place to suggest anything of the sort to the late earl's
brother.

"Eh? Getting above yourself, are you not?" Lord Augustus bristled with anger at the presumptions of the
lowly steward, even if he was a relative.

Mr. Vane shrugged, then said, "It is true nonetheless."

A silence fell over the room which none of them cared
to break, it seemed. When Egbert entered to seek a bit
of nourishment, he was disinclined to disturb the quiet.
He ate his food without saying a word, other than softly
worded comments that didn't reach beyond his father.

As soon as she could escape the dreadful atmosphere
of the dining room, Elizabeth hurried across the central
hall to the corridor leading to the study. Halfway there
she heard a rap on the door.

Sidthorp bustled to open it, while Elizabeth paused,
wondering if it was the vicar, or if the solicitor would
appear. Nothing would surprise her now, not even the
arrival of a man who would not receive word of the earl's
death until tomorrow.

"Oh, Sidthorp, where is my dear niece? I must see her
at once."

Aunt Bel caught sight of Elizabeth across the entry hall
and walked to her, arms outstretched. "My dear girl,
what a tragedy to occur. But then, I knew something was
to come, for the cock crowed three times last night, and
you know that means a death to follow."

Tears rushed to Elizabeth's eyes as she greeted her
aunt. In spite of her eccentricities and superstitions, she
was the closest person to being a mother to Elizabeth,

and the truth of one's mortality had been brought home to her in the past hours.

"Now, explain to me what has happened, and what has been done. I have come to help you, for you were too young when your mother and father were killed to remember the details and what the proper order of things must be."

Elizabeth led her along to the study, all the while explaining what David had requested.

Behind them, the knocker sounded again, and the gruff voice of the vicar could be heard in conversation with Sidthorp.

"Funerals are such sad occasions," Aunt Bel remarked. "You must prepare for the expenses. There will be the sums for the mourners in the village. Will the late earl be buried here, or is Lord Leighton removing his body to Crompton Vale in the north?"

"David had not decided when I last spoke with him." Elizabeth debated a few moments, then seated her aunt on one of the armchairs, while seating herself at the desk. "There is something decidedly odd in all of this."

Her aunt looked up in surprise. She had been surveying the stack of paper on the desk, absently glancing at the list of people to be notified.

"Do you think it singular that David had the blackbordered paper to hand this morning? He had the list of names all drawn up for me as well."

"I doubt that anything unusual is going on," her aunt replied thoughtfully. "It may be that he suspected that his father would not live long and anticipated the need."

"Aunt Bel, it takes time to get that paper, although I know most stationery shops carry such all the time. Yet I do not recall a recent trip to the village, or any servant being sent off on such an errand."

"But then, you are not privy to everything his lordship does, are you?" her aunt reminded.

"True," Elizabeth admitted. Of course Aunt Bel was right. Elizabeth was being foolish about the entire matter. Pushing her feeling of unease aside—for after all, why would David behave in such a bizarre manner when *he* had not murdered his father?—she set to work on the remainder of the letters.

To say that dinner was subdued was to say that a funeral is a jolly occasion. Lord Augustus mumbled mo-
rosely all through the meal. Egbert, oddly enough, had
great patience with his father, rather than arguing as was
his wont.

Jeremy Vane sat quietly at his place, watching the others with that strange look on his face that Elizabeth had
observed earlier. No one else seemed to question his behavior, so she said nothing, deciding that David had
enough on his plate without her silly observations.

When Elizabeth and her aunt elected to go upstairs to
their rooms in the north wing, the men left the table,
each for their own unstated destination.

At the top of the stairs, Lady Montgomery paused,
catching sight of Filpot.

"My good man, we would like to pay our respects.
Would you please show us to his late lordship's room?"

The valet looked stunned, and hemmed and hawed
without giving her an answer. Finally he replied, "I cannot do that, ma'am, until I 'ave a talk with Lord Leighton."

Aunt Bel sniffed and marched down the corridor to her
room with her nose tilted in the air.

A thoughtful Elizabeth followed her.

"I believe I shall take to my bed at once. This has
been a shocking day," Aunt Bel announced in aggrieved
tones.

Purvis waited for her inside the bedroom, which was
immediately next to Elizabeth's room. Across the bed lay
three black gowns.

"Ah, Elizabeth, I found these in the attic," Aunt Bel
declared, perking up when she saw the work to be done,
which she intended to supervise. "They are relatively
recent, for I had them made only last year. One never
knows when one will require mourning. Hold them up to
her, Purvis. See which can be made to fit."

The following hour saw two of the gowns made pre-
sentable, and one which could do only after considerable
taking in. Elizabeth declined this, suggesting that her
Aunt had rather keep the dress for her own use.

Aunt Bel fussed about, urging Elizabeth to take a
sleeping potion, for that was what she intended to do.

"Sleeping with a dead person in a house is so depressing, you know," she said with a sigh. "But then, few have my tender sensibilities."

Elizabeth escaped to her room before she gave way to the ridiculous urge to laugh. Aunt hadn't meant it to sound as though she actually slept *with* the deceased, but it had sounded frightfully like that. Elizabeth decided she was on the verge of hysteria, and accepted the hot milk from Rose as an aid to sleep.

Tomorrow would be another hectic day.

But as she drifted off to sleep, she recalled Filpot. Now, she might not like the man in the least, but even taking this into account, she thought his behavior was most peculiar. Her intuition told her that something was distinctly havcy-cavcy. The problem was to figure out what it might be.

In the morning, Elizabeth rose with a feeling of apprehension hanging over her. A look at the black gown that Rose held out for her to put on brought everything back in force.

David now held the title of Earl of Crompton, with a second title of Viscount Leighton, and head of the Percy family. Such an awesome responsibility for one so young.

And curiously he insisted that she marry him. Elizabeth took comfort that in the six months required for mourning, anything might happen. He might even learn to love her, she thought, as Rose adjusted the black gown of lightweight bombazine. Turning about before the looking glass, Elizabeth could see that the judicious tucks and stitches that Purvis had taken proved rather nice.

While a depressing color, the gown strangely enough flattered Elizabeth to a surprising degree. The bodice was very low in the front and back, but there was a sheer scarf to wear around her neck, so she needn't feel indecent. The short sleeves were quite full, and a pretty little bow tied in the front, directly below the bodice.

With that comforting thought hugged to her ample bosom, she went down the stairs to the dining room.

The only occupant turned out to be David. Elizabeth paused on the threshold, wondering what she ought to say. He wore the deepest black, and the thought crossed her mind that it was fortunate he possessed the proper clothes. But then, men as dashing and restrained in their dress as he would be apt to own a black tailcoat and breeches. Black hose and shoes, the black waistcoat, all could be found in his wardrobe, couldn't they? She suspected they could, yet was she being overly suspicious again because she wondered about it? Foolish, silly, addlepated, that was what she was.

He glanced up from his plate to meet her concerned gaze. "I understand your aunt wished to see my father last evening. Inform her, unless I chance to see her first, that she may see him today if she likes. She flustered Filpot, for he wasn't prepared for such a request."

Elizabeth wondered why not. It was a common occasion after a death for friends and relatives to view the deceased. While this was normally confined to the funeral service, it was not that unusual.

She said nothing of her feelings, for they were so absurd as to be outrageous. "I shall, my lord."

"There is another matter I wish to speak to you about. My father declared he wished that we be married as soon as possible. I have sent off an express to Doctor's Commons for a special license. When the vicar was here yesterday, he indicated he would respect my father's wishes. No one will think a thing about our marriage if we do not wait for six months, for we have been betrothed for weeks."

Elizabeth groped for a chair, then sank down upon it, feeling as though she had stepped into a fantasy world where wishes came true in the most unlikely fashion. What could she say? She had promised only the day before that she would not hand David the mitten. Actually, she had provocation to jilt him, for he certainly had displayed none of the loverlike manners one expected. Perhaps rakes did things differently? She certainly did not know.

"I, er, this is indeed a surprise," she said shortly.

He relaxed a trifle, she noted. Had he expected her to reject him?

"I suppose your aunt will feel it unseemly, such haste. But since she caused the betrothal in the beginning, it is only fitting she see it through."

Whatever he meant by those words, Elizabeth had no chance to ask, for Egbert wandered into the room.

"Elizabeth and I have decided to marry immediately, as soon as the special license arrives from London." David studied his cousin as he made this statement. Elizabeth also watched keenly.

"That makes sense, I suppose. Best fill the nursery as soon as possible." He walked to the sideboard to select buttered eggs, ham, toast, and coffee.

Elizabeth would have blushed had it not been for his prosaic attitude, as though their action was logical and proper under the circumstances.

The nursery had to be filled. That was the reason for their marriage. And was that not common? No profession of love was required, just a willing body, she thought bitterly. Oh, that her aunt had never moved her to the pink bedchamber on Valentine's eve. She would not be in this predicament now. Hyacinthe would. At that thought, Elizabeth realized she did not like the notion of Hyacinthe being married to David in the least.

When her heart was engaged and David was indifferent to her—or whatever he was feeling—marriage became a less than joyous future. But she was not about to let anyone else have the chance.

Then Uncle Augustus entered, corsets creaking. He grumbled a "good morning" to them all, then selected an amazingly hearty meal to begin the day. "Need sustenance, y'know. Dashed hard to get through the day otherwise."

Before Elizabeth could think of a reply, Jeremy Vane walked in, neatly garbed in black, a superior look on his face that she found revolting under the circumstances.

What had happened to the rabbity, meek, and mild man she had first known when coming here? He had been such a delight. This man was a stranger.

"Good morning, all. Pity the rain must continue. However, it does fit the occasion." Jeremy strolled to the sideboard to survey the offerings.

"David and Elizabeth are getting married as soon as the special license arrives from London," Egbert announced somewhat baldly. His words fell into a silence that Jeremy did not immediately break.

He had tensed upon hearing the news. Elizabeth could
see his shoulders stiffen as though receiving a blow. Then
he relaxed a trifle and assumed a polite mask—for that
is what it appeared to her.

"Fine, fine," he declared slowly with patently false
enthusiasm, then compressed his lips a moment before
continuing. "Understandable, considering the circumstances. How fortunate for David that he found a willing
partner in the wilds of Surrey."

"We knew each other while in London, you know,"
Elizabeth said in excuse of she knew not what. She did
not care for Jeremy's insinuation that David had to snatch
at just anyone, or that she was willing to participate in
something faintly underhanded, for that is what he made
it seem.

"Oh, so you did. How providential for you, David.
Things just seem to fall into your lap." With that snide
observation he took his plate with him from the room,
along with a large cup of coffee.

Elizabeth surmised that Jeremy found their company
not to his liking, and she decided those remaining felt
the same about him.

"Dashed loose screw, if you ask me," Egbert commented.

"No one did, but for once I agree with you," David
replied. He finished his meal, then rose from the table.
"There are a few things to discuss, Elizabeth. I shall
wait for you in the study."

She dawdled a bit, wondering what it was he wanted
to talk to her about. Perhaps he would tell her what was
really going on. No, she dare not hint at anything like
that, for he'd think her bird-witted for sure.

Deciding the best way to find out what he wanted was
to go to the study, she left the remains of her breakfast
behind and walked across the entry hall. As had happened the day before, a rap at the door brought a guest,
a stranger this time. Elizabeth paused, curious to see who
had come.

"Ah, Sidthorp. I am sorry to learn things have come
to this pass, indeed. I need to speak with the new earl at
once."

Elizabeth spoke up then. "I am on my way to him

now, sir. I trust you are the solicitor, Mr. Fynes?'' He must have immediately surmised the death from the hatchments. He was a pleasantly rotund man, slightly balding, and possessed of a pair of snapping blue eyes.

"I have that pleasure. I need not ask if you are Miss Elizabeth Dancy, for you match the description I was given to a tee." He gave her a cordial look.

"Come with me." She wondered what had been said about her, like any vain young creature, then scolded herself for being foolish. She escorted Mr. Fynes to the study.

"David, I am sorry this day had to come so soon." The solicitor reached out to clasp David's hand.

"Indeed. I am pleased you could arrive with such speed." To Elizabeth he said, "Does Jeremy know he has come?"

"I chanced to cross the entry hall when Mr. Fynes arrived. Jeremy had removed himself with his breakfast to the office wing before that. I doubt if he knows aught, unless Sidthorp reveals it, and that is unlikely."

David exchanged a look with the solicitor. "Now to business. Have you drawn up the marriage settlement? My father particularly wished to see a goodly jointure arranged for Elizabeth. You contacted her family solicitor?"

Mr. Fynes nodded. "By chance he is a friend of mine and was able and willing to reveal such provision for a dowry as has been made for Miss Elizabeth."

She reeled with shock at the revelations being made, one after another. All this talk of marriage settlement and jointure and arrangements that took a great amount of time to make was almost more than she could absorb.

David's suggestion that they marry immediately had not been precipitous. Their coming marriage had been carefully planned and for some time. Why?

The amount of her pin money, her future jointure, the arrangement for their first son, was discussed and settled. From time to time David glanced to where she sat, but did not ask her to comment. Indeed, she couldn't have said a word, so great was her surprise. A woman did not normally take part on these discussions, anyway.

Since Elizabeth had no father and her brother was on the continent, Mr. Fynes appeared to act on her behalf.

When they concluded the settlement, they turned to other matters, Jeremy Vane, for one.

"What shall you do about him?" Mr. Fynes inquired.

David glanced at Elizabeth, then said, "One moment. Will you inform Mrs. Sidthorp that Mr. Fynes will remain several nights with us?"

"Of course." She rose in a flurry of black bombazine and left the room. Her bosom rose and fell in great agitation as she marched to the rear of the house. He had sent her from the room because he did not wish her to learn what he planned for Jeremy. Just what was going on?

15

"THEY ALL BELIEVE you to be dead."

"Do they, by Jove?" The earl turned from the window, where he had been staring out across the gentle vale to the woods in the distance. The scene presented a misty view at best, but it appeared to offer goodly satisfaction to him.

"You look well enough, I must say," replied a disgruntled son. David dropped onto a chair not far from where his father stood. "I have had to go about with a hangdog face and test my acting abilities to the limit."

"Yes, well, when one ceases to imbibe poison, it does have a beneficial effect on one." The earl joined his son, taking a chair that faced him, and smiled wryly. "Tell me, how do my dear relatives accept the news of my demise?" He gestured toward the bed, where a bust of the earl was placed on the pillow, sheets and a cover arranged so it bore an uncanny resemblance to the real person, what with a few pillows strategically placed to form a body.

"Your brother looks to have aged ten years, expresses sorrow that you quarreled. Whatever did you argue about all those years ago, if I may ask?" David picked at the arms of his chair while watching his dear father grope for words.

"A woman. Suffice it to say that neither of us really cared a scrap for the gel. Egbert?"

"I was surprised there. He has actually been rather civil to Elizabeth and I, conveying words of deep sympathy—for Egbert. However, Jeremy has turned into a toad of the first water. He is cocksure, impertinent, almost patronizing, especially to Elizabeth, as though he pitied her in her betrothal to me."

"Hmm. Of course, that does not mean what we think it might, for whoever it is must be a dissembler of considerable ability. Why the gloomy face?" The earl steepled his fingers while resting his elbows on the arms of his chair, studying his son with a shrewd gaze.

"I cannot like deceiving Elizabeth in all this. You do not know how many times I have come close to confiding in her." David shifted, as though uncomfortable.

"I can see where that might present a difficulty. You are reconciled to the match?" His lordship permitted a smile to hover over his mouth.

"More than reconciled, sir. I have grown to love that aggravating young woman very much. She is such a delight. However, I am not certain if she feels the same about me."

"You arranged the settlements as I suggested?" The earl tilted his head to listen carefully to what was said, and perhaps to what was unspoken.

"She appears quite satisfied with them. And you were exceedingly generous. I thank you for that." David flashed his endearing grin at his father.

"Nonsense. It will all come to you one day, eventually. Although not for some time, I hope. I shall be glad to have this thing over and done with, for I grow restless being cooped in this room. I have read all these books you brought up. Perhaps you will be so good as to exchange them for another selection?"

David chuckled. "Elizabeth saw me with books in my arms. I feel sure she wondered about my wishing to read at a time like this."

"Quite so." The two men exchanged amused glances. Filpot entered the room on tiptoe, carrying a tray he had prepared for the earl while the cook was absent from the kitchen.

"Difficult, milord. Very tricky, indeed. But I find it curious that the quality of the food has improved so greatly since your supposed death." The valet fussed over the tray, placing it on a table close to his master, seeing to it that the dishes and cutlery were just so, the food to his lordship's liking.

Again the earl's eyes sought David, and this time the looks they exchanged were not amused in the least.

* * *

Several hours later, Elizabeth found her aunt relaxing on a chaise lounge in her bedchamber. "The settlement is complete. I daresay my jointure is excessively generous, Aunt Bel," Elizabeth said, referring to the monetary provision for a widow. She paced back and forth in the charming room while her aunt look on in shrewd assessment.

"I was not aware that so many factors had to be considered," Elizabeth continued. "Our first son, should we be blessed with one, is well settled, and the amount of pin money I am to have is wildly handsome." She gestured expansively, while pausing in her walk to look at her aunt.

"The dowry my parents arranged for me is more than I expected. The solicitor was vastly pleased with it, and murmured something about the marriage being a good contract and highly advantageous, as my dowry was so substantial. It appears to me that women are sold into marriage, much like slaves."

"Rubbish," Aunt Bel denied. "It is the way of our society, my love. Without our families to watch over our interests, we could be left without a roof over our heads, utterly penniless. Our children might be denied their rightful share of an inheritance by unscrupulous relatives and conniving solicitors." She paused to reflect, as though she recalled instances where this had occurred. "Whether or not you love the man you wed is immaterial in the long run. Through the settlement, your future is assured by careful planning. Lord Crompton is being extremely considerate, and you are a very fortunate girl," her ladyship gently scolded.

Elizabeth considered this information at length, then paused by the fireplace, exchanging a puzzled look with her aunt.

"I do not reject marriage, not even to a man who has never said he cares for me. I am a silly, romantic girl and would dearly like to have my future husband say other than he could do worse than marry me." She flounced into a chair, propped her chin on her fist, and glared at an inoffensive vase full of snowdrops.

"He said no such thing. Or did he?" Aunt Bel inquired in faintly horrified tones.

Elizabeth nodded, then roundly declared, "When it came to the discussion about Jeremy, I was requested—ever so politely—to inform Mrs. Sidthorp that Mr. Fynes will be staying several nights. As though Sidthorp had not already done that. It was merely a ruse to remove me from the room. David might have saved himself the trouble of inventing an excuse and just told me to run along, like a child of six."

"My, my, such a feeling of ill usage," Aunt Bel said dryly.

Elizabeth smiled acknowledgment of her infantile anger. "I know. I am being a peagoose. I suppose I long for a chivalrous knight to sweep me into his arms, rather than a prosaic melding of my dowry to David's estate, with a ceremony to mark the event. He said something about his not having courted me, almost sounding sorry about it. Do you suppose he intends to woo me properly later on?" Elizabeth gave her aunt a wistful look.

Aunt Bel smiled at her romantic niece. "Stranger things have happened."

"There is a funeral service tomorrow morning. I thought he would wait until he took his father by hearse to the main estate up north. Apparently he has decided to hold two services, with the interment up there where the family vault is located. That will be an enormous undertaking. I recall seeing a procession once. With six horses for the hearse and six for the mourning coach, plus all the outriders, it was an impressive sight. When they come to the town near the home estate, a great many people assemble along the road. The mourners require such an outlay. Funerals are expensive." Elizabeth sighed, lost in reflection.

"I believe I shall venture forth to the other wing and pay my respects to the deceased. That valet, Filpot, has said we might." Lady Montmorcy rose from her chair, then walked to the door. Here she paused, turning to study her niece. "Will you join me?"

Reluctant to admit how depressing she found the entire viewing, Elizabeth obediently rose to join her aunt, knowing this was expected of her as David's future wife.

Her coming wedding seemed unreal, like a fantasy, or something she read about as happening to another. She well knew it was inevitable, and she truly did not hate the idea. She longed for it to be a love match, however. And it seemed to her that David was not very loverlike for a rake.

As the two ladies walked across the central area to the south wing, she glanced down at the hall below. Sidthorp could be seen crossing on some errand. Egbert entered, obviously having come from a ride in the morning mist. He shook his hat and coat to shed the moisture from it.

Would it ever turn warm and sunshiny again? This was undoubtedly the longest winter she could ever recall.

Filpot met them at the door when they knocked. At the sight of Lady Montmorcy, he opened the door a little wider, enough to permit them to enter. He coughed discreetly, then said, "My Lady Montmorcy and Miss Elizabeth," as though announcing them to the body on the bed.

Elizabeth did not quite believe her ears and followed her aunt into the room with considerable reluctance.

The room was as dark as night, with but two flickering candles some distance from the bed. Draperies were drawn tightly over the windows. Filpot muttered something about it being like Lord Nelson's viewing, when there were but two candles lit.

The earl's face looked handsome, carved in high relief as though in stone. Although she had to admit it was difficult to see very much, for he was in deep shadow. Not having been at a similar scene, for she had never viewed her parents after they died, Elizabeth couldn't say if the sight was typical. Burning incense produced a heavy, spicy odor, not unpleasant but slightly overwhelming after a time. Had it been any other situation, she would have sworn she smelled food as well, but surely Filpot would not eat in this room!

"Hmph," Aunt Bel murmured to Elizabeth. "One would think there was a heavy tax on candles, as dark as it is in here."

"It presents a mood, Aunt." Elizabeth agreed that the room possessed an odd appearance, but what did she know?

"I shall miss him. I thought I might have a chance to renew our acquaintance, for he was always a darling boy to me. Oh pride, how foolish it can be. I loved him deeply before my parents compelled me to wed Giles. I could not even tell Herold that I cared, for I was whisked to London to be married there. Years later, when I returned after Giles had died, Herold did not call on me. I trust he had forgotten all about our youthful attachment. And now it is too late for me to tell him. I am merely a silly old woman," Aunt Bel concluded softly, mindless of Filpot and Elizabeth. She accepted the sprig of rosemary from Filpot to place on the bed, then stepped away, a handkerchief to her eyes, her head bowed.

Elizabeth felt her aunt's murmured words were more to herself than to her niece, and so remained silent. But she was filled with sadness at what she had heard. How tragic to allow foolish pride to come between two people who had once loved each other.

When they at last returned to Elizabeth's sitting room, her aunt rang for tea, declaring she needed restoration. She blew her nose a number of times, but had composed herself when the maid entered bearing the tea tray.

Elizabeth drifted over to the window, wondering what was going on in the study, where David again was meeting with his solicitor after a break. Did she dare intrude? She had taken his request to Mrs. Sidthorp, who had indeed known all about the solicitor's visit.

Something simply did not feel right. Was she becoming as superstitious as her aunt? To rely on hunches, feelings?

"Join me, my dear. We shall drink to a fine man with a good cup of Bohea."

"Better that than port, I suppose." Elizabeth left the window, after noting that the mist continued to fall outside. She returned to the chair she had occupied earlier and accepted a steaming cup of Bohea from her aunt.

"What shall you do, my girl? If David proceeds with the wedding?"

"What can I do but agree? Everyone around knows we have been betrothed ever since Valentine's Day. I did not write of it to Victoria and Julia, thinking it useless, for I had intended to hand him the mitten long before this."

"Did you, now?" Aunt Bel peered at Elizabeth over the rim of her teacup, her brows rising.

"I feel it wrong to compel two people to marry merely because of a superstition. But somewhere along the line things got out of hand. I should like to let my sisters know. Victoria has returned from the continent, and is in the family way, according to her latest letter. Julia is off up north, and I doubt if she can be here, either. I am excessively glad I have you, Aunt Bel," Elizabeth added with a fond look at her slightly eccentric but much loved aunt. "Chloe and Hyacinthe shall stand up for me in place of my sisters."

"Sensible, for you do not know precisely when the wedding is to be, do you?" Aunt Bel took another dainty sip of tea.

"He keeps remarkably quiet about that," Elizabeth replied thoughtfully. "I believe I shall approach the matter now. A girl likes to plan for things. Especially a wedding. Although I realize that many people do not make a great fuss. When the sixth Duchess of Devonshire married, only her parents, her grandmother, and the duke's sister were present. And Lady Harriet Cavendish had no one but her father and stepmother and Lord Granville's sister attend her wedding. David said he had written for a special license, and I suspect he wants no fuss, particularly so close to his father's death. It would be unseemly."

With her aunt's permission to discuss the matter with David, Elizabeth left her rooms, walking down the corridor with an anxious heart.

A hush hung over the house when she ran lightly down the stairs. Sidthorp was not to be seen. Egbert could be heard chatting with his father in the billiards room. She could see them standing near the billiards table, cues in hand while they discussed something.

Her footsteps lagged. There had been a distant alteration of the attitude of both of them since the earl's death. She stopped, watching the two, who carried on as though nothing had occurred. Surely that was not the way to behave? While she did not actually know, not having been around a house where there was a death for years—and then being quite young, it seemed callous to just go on as usual, playing game after game of billiards.

As she neared the study, she discovered the door stood ajar. Not wishing to intrude, she slowed her steps again. Mr. Fynes's deep voice could be clearly heard. In spite of her resolve not to listen in to another's conversation, she could not help herself.

"Marrying her is the best way out, my boy. You may rest assured, that is one area settled. Her dowry is respectable, and even if she is a trifle young, that is not so very bad. She is a lovely girl. Remember, a wife cannot testify against her husband." He chuckled at this bit of wit.

Elizabeth froze, waiting to hear David's reply.

"It was not what I had wanted."

"Is anything in this life?"

Not wishing to hear another word—for she had certainly heard no good of herself, as she supposed was only just—she fled. A silent skimming across the hall brought her to the stairs, then up to her room. Fortunately, Aunt Bel had returned to her own quarters, and Elizabeth was quite alone.

Now she knew why David insisted they wed. The only feeling he possessed toward her was gratitude that she was so conveniently at hand. Confused and hurt, she paced about the room, threading a hand through her curls.

What a pity her parents had left such an acceptable dowry. Mr. Fynes might have counseled David to look elsewhere for a more eligible wife.

She wouldn't do it. She would run away. Somewhere there must be a place she could hide. Perhaps Victoria and Edward would allow her sanctuary?

Then her common sense returned. She had shared lovely kisses with David, they had laughed together, and he did possess a sense of humor—something she felt important. Could she not take the risk of marriage with him, and try to build on the shaky foundation to achieve something more solid?

Then another thought occurred to her. Since she cared so deeply for David, could she not do this for him? Marry him to protect him from whatever he and his solicitor feared? She did not know what circumstances might be that she could testify against David. She did know she would never do anything to harm him. Not willingly.

"That is what I shall do. I shan't say a word about what I have heard," she declared to the vase of snow-drops. "I will proceed with the wedding just as he wishes, when he wishes. It will be my gift to him."

Chin up, resolve quite firmed, she slowly strolled back downstairs, as though she had not just stormed back to her room in hurt anger minutes past.

"Elizabeth, there you are," David exclaimed as he strode across the hall to her side.

She gave him a wary look, wondering what he would say. "Yes?"

"I have finished with the solicitor. I thought perhaps you and I could discuss the details of the wedding."

She forced a brave smile to her lips. "That is precisely what I hoped to do now, why I was coming to look for you."

Was that a sigh of relief from David? she wondered.

At the entrance to the office wing, Jeremy Vane watched the two lovers stroll arm in arm toward the drawing room. They ought not be alone, even though betrothed. But then, propriety had not been strictly ob-served in this house for a long time.

If he had the running of the place, things would be different.

On the other side of the courtyard, Egbert also watched David and Elizabeth walk to the drawing room, deep in discussion. Did his cousin know how lucky he was? What a treasure Elizabeth Dancy had proved to be. Egbert felt that his dear cousin did not fully appreciate his good fortune.

If he were in charge of affairs, things would be differ-ent.

"What are you doing, lad?" Lord Augustus spoke with unusual sharpness to his only son.

"Watching the betrothed couple head for the privacy of the drawing room. I fancy they want to plan the wed-ding. Shall we join them?" He gave a faintly malicious smile at the thought of disrupting a lover's tryst.

"Someone ought to be there. Can't think what that totty-headed Isobel is thinking of, to leave her niece alone with a rake like Leighton. Even if they are to wed. Were I in charge of things around here, they would be a good deal different, I can tell you that.''

With a nod to his son, the two men set off to the drawing room, virtuous condescension in their faces.

Elizabeth looked up in startled alarm when Lord Augustus entered the room, followed by Egbert, who wore a distinctly gleeful look on his face. She stood by the fireplace, David not far away. They had been about to set the time and place of the marriage when so rudely interrupted.

"Ho, what have we here?" Lord Augustus said with false jollity.

"The lovers, no less. Cannot have this, you know." Egbert wagged a finger at the pair across the room. "Not at all proper. Would never want the servants to spread it about that the new Lord Crompton was less than honorable in his attentions to his future wife, now would we?"

Elizabeth cast about for some means of changing the subject. A glance at Lord Augustus gave her the idea. "Would anyone care for tea?" She had scarce touched the food set out at noon, and would welcome something to nibble.

"Allow me to ring for the footman. I trust a slight repast will be an acceptable way of passing the time?" she begged, hoping that Egbert would not be nasty about it.

"Ain't proper, my boy. Dallying with a young lady don't show respect befitting your station as the new earl," Lord Augustus declared with more than a hint of pomposity.

David raised his brows at this bit of reproach. His uncle had lived a life anything but decorous, according to what Elizabeth had heard.

"Begin as you mean to go on, perhaps?" David reached out to draw a reluctant Elizabeth to his side, for she stood not all that far from him.

"Do not mock, David," Egbert scolded in a serious voice all of a sudden.

"I wasn't."

Not understanding what was afoot, Elizabeth was about to walk away when she found herself firmly held. It was impossible for her to leave without an unseemly struggle. She remained, deciding to add her bit to the scene by snuggling up to David. If he wanted to make a particular impression, it behooved her to cooperate. Besides, she rather enjoyed it. Oh, what a wicked girl she was, to even think of her desires when the poor earl lay dead upstairs.

The footman who answered the summons could not fail to take note of the proximity of the betrothed couple. She was all but enfolded in David's arms, for pity's sake.

Feeling distinctly at a disadvantage, Elizabeth requested a tea tray, with a substantial repast included. She was curious to see if the cook repeated the accident of unburnt food.

With Lord Augustus and Egbert playing chaperone, it was impossible to discuss the coming wedding in a way they would like. When Aunt Bel strolled into the drawing room, it made the group complete, for immediately behind her came Jeremy Vane.

"The funeral is tomorrow morning," observed Aunt Bel. "Do you intend to have your wedding before you go to Crompton Vale?" she added with a delicate reference to the trip north with the corpse.

"That would be the following day, I believe. How do you feel about it, Elizabeth?"

"Sooner you wed, the better, in my opinion," Lord Augustus inserted, his corsets creaking as he leaned over to select something from the tea tray just delivered by the young footman.

"You ought to know," David replied with dangerous quiet.

Aunt Bel glanced up sharply at this note, and with a horrified look at the footman, who seemed to have turned into stone, she said, "I do hope the rain stops. It would be nice to have sunshine on your wedding day."

Elizabeth settled against David, knowing that somehow her aunt would take matters in hand, and that tempers would not be permitted to flare out of control.

Trapped by the look David sent him, Lord Augustus harrumphed twice, then nodded, as he accepted a cup of tea from Lady Montmorcy. "Dratted stuff," he murmured before taking a tentative sip.

"Well, it seems to me," Egbert said sometime later,

"that one should be prepared for the past to return to haunt him." He was looking at David when he spoke, rather than his father.

Elizabeth suspected what was in his mind, and she said, before David might utter something he'd regret later on, "If you refer to anything my future husband may have done in his past, imagined or real, I daresay there is little I do not know, or have heard about. And if there is something I do not know of, I do not wish to be told." She gave Egbert a cold stare, aware that he could ultimately cause a great deal of unhappiness if she did not make this point crystal clear at the outset.

"Well, well," David murmured at her side. "My little valentine has claws."

"That's not all," she whispered back quite daringly.

The following morning the family, along with Aunt Bel and Elizabeth, assembled in the entry hall. The servants, given the morning to attend the modest service in the village church, joined the procession.

There was a hearse of sorts, more of a dray pressed into service, given the lack of proper notification to the undertaker from the nearest town. This was followed by carriages bearing the relatives, then Aunt Bel and Elizabeth, and last, the vehicle containing Filpot, Hadlow, Rose, and the Sidthorps. The remaining servants drove along in a somewhat antique coach.

The service was blessedly short, and the casket remained closed, much to Elizabeth's surprise, for her aunt had informed her it usually stayed open so that others could pay their respects.

However, she had little time to dwell on this, for the procession was reversed, and they all trouped back to Penhurst Place.

"Most peculiar, I say," Aunt Bel pronounced when she and Elizabeth were once again in Elizabeth's room.

"What does it matter? I must look to the wedding now. I do hope that people will not look too askance at our haste." Elizabeth stared at her aunt from her comfortable chair by the fire. She uneasily twisted the diamond that David had placed on her finger.

"No, no. If there is gossip, something else will come

along to catch their ears. It usually does. I must send a note to Chloe and Hyacinthe. They will think themselves sadly neglected. Poor Hyacinthe has declared Lord Norwood too stuffy. She announced that he can take himself off to his landscaping and fertilizing for all she cares. Not only that. Some fool told her that he is a shocking rake when in London. She is totally undone.''

Elizabeth smiled at that, then said, "Surely they understand the circumstances?''

"True. I would wish them to find suitable gowns to wear to your wedding. Which brings me to another matter. What shall you wear?'' Aunt Bel leaned against her chair, studying her niece with a careful gaze.

"I detest wearing black, for it is so gloomy, but I expect I must.'' Elizabeth sighed, then turned her gaze to meet that of her aunt, who frowned.

"Perhaps not. Pale lavender might be acceptable, or dove gray. I fail to see the haste, my dear. I cannot think why David does not wish to wait the proper six months of mourning before marriage.''

"I do not know, but I have my suspicions.''

Beyond that, Elizabeth refused to confide. There were some things a woman did not share with anyone, not even a favorite aunt. There was something decidedly smoky going on at Penhurst Place. She didn't know what it was, but she would support David in any way she could. It was the least she could do for the man she loved.

"I wonder what will happen at the reading of the will. Mr. Fynes said something about meeting in the library this afternoon. I suppose he is anxious to return to his office.''

Elizabeth also wondered. Would they learn at last who had poisoned the earl? She had the feeling that it was not a stranger, but one known to them all. Which one? Jeremy Vane, Lord Augustus, or the dreadful Egbert Percy?

Or could there be another?

HE HAD TO BE the most provoking man alive. Elizabeth glanced at the man who nearly drove her mad, one way or the other, and sighed with discouragement. He had not sought her out for further discussion regarding their wedding, even though they'd had a bit of time to themselves. Perhaps all he had truly wished to know was that she did not plan to jilt him.

Then Mr. Fynes cleared his throat, gesturing to those assembled in the library to be seated. He had taken a place behind the large desk at the far end of the room. Behind him was the fireplace, the damp patch now reasonably dried out, thanks to Elizabeth's diligent efforts.

Lord Augustus settled on a high-backed chair to the right, amid the usual corset-creaking accompaniment, with Egbert lounging immediately behind him and to the side.

Ranged on the other side were David and Elizabeth, with Aunt Bel sitting discreetly behind them, although neither of the women actually needed to be present. David had requested them to come. Elizabeth wouldn't have missed it for anything, and she suspected that Aunt Bel had itching ears as well.

By the time everyone had gathered, the afternoon was nearly past and the room was dim. Sidthorp supervised the lighting of a good many candles, plus an Argand lamp for Mr. Fynes. This delay was tolerated by all, for each appeared to want to see the others.

Jeremy entered late, taking a chair near the far end of the room, not far from where the Sidthorps and other servants clustered.

While Mr. Fynes shuffled papers on the desk, Elizabeth spent her waiting moments studying the faces of the three men she suspected. Lord Augustus looked uncomfortable, and she wondered if his corset was too tight today, or if he felt guilty. Egbert wore his usual expression of boredom, tinged with curiosity. Knowing more of his relationship with his uncle, she surmised that he really did not have great expectations.

By turning her head a bit, as though to listen to something Aunt Bel might be saying, Elizabeth could see Jeremy Vane. He puzzled her. That newly acquired demeanor of his could not be liked in the least. Whereas he had been so kind and polite before, he now wore a sort of sneer on his face and held himself aloof from the others. Well, she hadn't liked that sort of timid-rabbit expression he'd worn in the past. But surely he should have been able to figure out something halfway between?

Mr. Fynes coughed, then commenced his reading of the will. David, quite naturally, took over the entailed estates, as well as the bulk of the fortune. Elizabeth was impressed at the number of estates that the family owned. In addition to Crompton Vale and Penhurst Place, there was a hunting box in Scotland, a manor house in Oxfordshire, and a house in London that possessed an excellent location.

His brother, Lord Augustus, was to receive a handsome bequest. This would go to his son in the event his father was no longer living at the time of the earl's death. Then Egbert also received a tidy sum in his own right. Not the vast estate that David received, naturally. But nothing to scoff at. She noted that he sat in his chair with a nonplussed expression on his face, from which she reckoned that he had not expected to be remembered quite so generously.

A suitable amount had been designated for the distant relative and steward, Jeremy Vane. An ample amount to permit Sidthorp and his wife to retire was also included, plus other random amounts for various others. The servants filed from the room at a word of dismissal from Mr. Fynes.

Elizabeth sat on her chair, tensed, waiting. What next?

Mr. Fynes cleared his throat once again, then took a sip of water. This was followed by a long look at David.

"There is an unexpected complication. A challenge to

David Percy, Lord Leighton and now Earl of Crompton, has been issued by one claiming to be the rightful earl." There were a number of gasps at this news. Elizabeth glanced at David, suspecting he had been warned in advance, for he looked not the least surprised. "I have had lengthy communications with his solicitor recently. This young man asserts that he is the legal son of the now deceased sixth earl's elder brother, Edward. As such he would have legal claim to the title."

There was a rustling of fabric as everyone looked about them. Elizabeth could not see that any new figure had entered the room.

"Mr. Vane, would you please come forward?"

Aunt Bel gasped. "Of all the . . ."

Lord Augustus mumbled something that sounded like "Presumptuous puppy."

Jeremy Vane strode to where Mr. Fynes considered him with an unsmiling face.

"I have carefully studied the letters from your solicitor. I confess that I do not know why you have waited so long to make your history known." Here he paused to look up at Jeremy from beneath his brows. "Surely, if you felt the title rightfully yours, you would have been most anxious to lay claim to your birthright. Do you have any additional papers to offer? For I must tell you that what has been proffered so far falls considerably short of convincing me. I doubt the House of Lords will accept the claim, either." Mr. Fynes clasped his hands neatly before him on the desk, staring at Jeremy with a hard expression.

Elizabeth decided she would not like to challenge Mr. Fynes at any time, in a court of law or elsewhere.

Jeremy extracted several papers from a folder, then presented them with a flourish to the solicitor. "These bear the signature of my father. I also include papers which prove the validity of his marriage to my mother."

With this done, Jeremy tossed a confident smile at David, then stepped away from the desk. He waited for a moment, then continued. "I daresay that you will wish to study them further, but I assure you that the signature is legitimate. If referred to Committee in the House of Lords, I believe they must support my claim."

"Lord Augustus, will you have a look at this?"

With the customary creaking of his corset, Lord Augustus rose to his feet, then ambled to the desk. He perused the various documents, frequently raising his eyes to look at Jeremy, then David. "I cannot say, in truth. But I am not a one to remember signatures. It appears like it, but I could not swear one way or the other in a court of law." His final look at David was one of apology.

Elizabeth reached out to cover David's hand with her own, trying to offer comfort during what must be a dreadful ordeal. That Jeremy should wait to present his case immediately after the earl died was highly suspicious to her. He must be responsible for the earl's death. But . . . how could they prove such a thing? She would like to institute an inspection of his room. It might be well to check the estate books, come to think on it. Anyone who guilty of murder could be guilty of embezzlement as well.

"Pity you did not think to demand a hearing before my brother died," Lord Augustus mused. "He was the one who knew Edward best, y'know. There ought to be a number of letters with his writing on them. He was not much to correspond. Like me, there. Hated to put pen to paper. But Herold kept what few he sent. Where are they? We can compare the writing on them."

"Papers?" Jeremy queried with seeming innocence. "I have seen no papers as you describe among the late Lord Crompton's correspondence."

"What did you see, cousin Jeremy? Or more to the point, what did you do?" David had risen to face his defiant relative with a surprisingly cool demeanor. He stood with crossed arms, looking rakishly handsome but most assuredly determined.

Elizabeth watched the two intently, a worried frown pleating her brow. How could David be so cool? He said those papers she'd found had been important. If so, how?

"I did all the tedious little jobs no one else wanted to do," Jeremy snapped, glaring at David. "And I learned far more about this estate, as well as the other places, than you will ever have a chance to know."

"Dashed odd, seems to me," grumbled Lord Augustus. "I smell a rat."

Egbert rose from his chair, then sauntered between David and Jeremy. He looked at one, then the other. To Mr. Fynes he said, "Choose David, please. I could not bear to think of the family being represented by this rabbit."

Jeremy tensed, clenching his fists. "Should I be declared the new earl, you will be out of here in a flea's leap."

Egbert shrugged. "Ta-lol. With you in residence as the earl, I scarce believe I should want to stay, old chap." After this shot Egbert strolled back to stand behind his father. Although his bequest had been read, he was not about to leave the field of battle, as it were.

"I fancy you have done your job well enough," David inserted smoothly. "I am told you even took to doing minor repairs. Like plastering?"

At this thrust Jeremy paled, but stood firm.

David strolled to the desk, picked up the quill knife, examining it as he walked to the fireplace. He glanced at Jeremy, then began scraping the wall where the recent plaster had been applied. As might be expected, it had not hardened to match the old, but was still somewhat fresh, although not moist.

Jeremy strode to the fireplace, his face mottled with anger. "Here, what are you doing? I demand you stop at once!" He reached out a hand to wrest the knife from David's hand, only to be pushed away while David easily kept the knife out of his reach.

"Problems, Jeremy? What difference could it make to you if I dig at this plaster?" David's eyes flashed with menace as he stared at his cousin.

"I do not want my property damaged," Jeremy declared in a shaking voice. "And why do you want to dig there, anyway? Seems a dashed fool thing to do." He shrugged off David's detaining hand, but did not make another attempt to take the knife away from him.

"Almost as foolish as concealing papers in the wall, eh?" Another chunk of plaster fell to the floor. David raised the knife again. It glittered in the light from the Argand lamp.

The former steward winced when the piece clicked on the hearth. He stared at it, then looked back to David.

"What do you mean?" Jeremy said, looking distinctly taken aback and not a little worried.

"What he means is that you hid some papers in the wall." Elizabeth rose, crossing the room to join the two by the fireplace. "During that dreadful rain the new plaster stood out, for it was not quite dry. I saw it and wondered. You did not do a very good job of it, or so Ben tells me. With David's help I dug until the packet of papers came to light. I should like to know how you thought you could get away with the deception," she demanded, standing between the two men.

She faced Jeremy, hands on hips, wishing she had the gun that now reposed beneath her pillow at Montmorcy Hall. How she would like to wave it beneath this scoundrel's nose and threaten him for daring to challenge so fine a man as David Percy.

"I should like to know that as well, Jeremy," came a raspy voice from the shadows in the back of the room. The supposedly dead earl stood erect; one hand rested on a chair, the other clasped a cane. At his side the dour Filpot hovered like a sentry on guard.

"Dear heaven! Herold!" Aunt Bel exclaimed, then fainted dead away against her high-backed chair, a heap of black bombazine.

Made of sterner stuff, Elizabeth whispered, "Oh, Lord have mercy," and groped for the nearest chair. Ignoring her aunt, who would regain consciousness eventually anyway, Elizabeth concentrated on the old earl. She slowly sank to the seat, while she watched him come nearer and nearer.

Jeremy froze, looking as though he saw a ghost. "But you can't be . . ."

"Why? Because you poisoned me? The potion was tested, first by Purvis, then the local apothecary, so we know what it was. Opium." The earl drew closer, one step at a time, making his way with determination. "You believed me safely out of the way so you could stake your illegal claim to my title once I was no longer about to refute your dastardly attempt." He waved several papers in the air with his free hand. "I was the only person alive who could identify my late brother's signature, the only one who stood between you and your claim on the title. Or what you hoped to claim.''

Elizabeth recognized the papers the earl carried as the ones that had been concealed. She glanced to see if Jeremy also grasped their import. He had.

''Where did you get those?'' he said, his confidence rapidly seeping away.

''My future daughter-in-law discovered them. David found himself a treasure in that girl. None of your namby-pamby sort, she. A true partner in the best sense.''

Jeremy darted a look at the plaster, now deeply gouged, then back to the earl. ''You cannot prove a thing.''

''No? Mr. Fynes is taking the estate books to have them gone over. After checking a number of pages, David and I both suspect that you have diddled the estate, my lad. I have been remiss there, trusting you too much.'' The earl exchanged a firm look with his solicitor, then continued, ''I am reluctant to take you to court for that out of respect for Edward's memory, but I dare-say I can convince the cook to reveal that you paid her to put certain herbs in my food. Only it was to poison me, was it not? You kept feeding me doses of opium. Then, when I became too weak for regular food, you convinced her to put the poison in the potions my valet brought me. Everyone seemed to suspect Filpot. It was he, however, who discovered the part that Cook played in the entire affair.''

''I refuse to listen to such rubbish,'' Jeremy exclaimed, while looking as though he would dearly like to flee. He took several steps in the direction of the door before Egbert casually moved between Jeremy and his objective.

''Rubbish?'' The earl queried. ''I think not. You see, I have those missing papers in my hand, and it will take but minutes to compare them with the ones you have offered to support your claim.''

The earl suddenly sank onto a chair that Filpot had brought forth. ''I expect, with the tender care of my new daughter, to be as fit as ever.'' With this, he turned to Augustus. ''I apologize for the deception. But do not worry, I shan't turn you out." Then his eyes shifted to Egbert, and he added, "As yet."

Mr. Fynes walked around the table, accepting the papers from the earl. He examined them, then compared them with the ones Jeremy had set forth. Giving Jeremy a narrow look, he then turned to David.

"I believe you have no cause to worry for your future, my lord. Your father is safe as the present earl, and you certainly have your title assured."

"I would wager, although I could not say for certain, that you are indeed my brother's son, for you have the look of him," the earl said to Jeremy. "But your mother was never married to him, of that I am certain. You know, had you made known the whole of your tale, I might have been more generous with you. A good education, good marriage, you might have had so much, although you could never have had the title."

"It is not fair," Jeremy cried, his face blotched red with anger and frustration. "He intended to wed her, she told me so after he died. The title should be mine. Mine, I tell you!"

David exchanged glances with Elizabeth. She stepped closer to him, wishing to be near his protection. She said to the pretender, "You wanted David out of the way so that there would be no chance that he could fight your claim to the title and estate. He would have made a compelling defense before the House of Lords Committee, one they'd not have rejected." She narrowed her gaze. "I rather fancy Egbert would have been next to die. But as for me—I suppose I merely got in your path, an annoyance to you, someone to eliminate. You sir, are no better than a murderer even if the Earl survived, for you had intent to kill."

Mr. Fynes moved to Jeremy's side, taking a firm hold of his arm. "I believe we shall handle you and your false claim immediately. I trust a new life in Canada will be to your liking? Or perhaps transportation to Botany Bay would please you?" He offered the choice in a wry voice, for he, and everyone in the room, knew there actually was not a chance that Jeremy would refuse the ticket to Canada.

"This is outrageous," Jeremy sputtered, but walked

along with the solicitor. His words were brave, but his shoulders drooped in defeat. He knew he had little choice in the matter, for if the earl chose to prosecute, who would take his part against a peer of the realm?

"There is a ship sailing this week. If you are to be a passenger on it, we had best get you on your way immediately." The solicitor turned to Sidthorp, who ushered Jeremy away to his room at once. Packing would commence instantly, and by the following day Jeremy Vane would be an unpleasant memory.

Elizabeth hoped that the former steward would not be allowed to escape with his filched money. Concerned, she spoke up. "The funds he took? Can they be recovered?"

"I shan't take any chances, my dear," the earl replied. "I shall have Fynes check everything, you may be sure. I hope it is not too late for that. Perhaps Filpot will discover useful information when he goes through Jeremy's things. Possibly the money?"

From behind them Aunt Bel spoke up. "Let that be a lesson to all of us, not to put off what needs doing." She moved closer to the earl, fiddling with the scrap of black-bordered cambric in her hands before adding in a hesitant voice, "Herold, I would have a word with you at your earliest convenience." She glanced at the locket watch she always wore.

"Ah, yes, my dear," the earl said, turning in his chair to look at Isobel. "There is a bit of unfinished business between us. It is not too late, my lady," he said with a smile. He rose, offered her his arm, and they began to walk to the door.

Sidthorp returned just then, appearing somewhat flustered. "Sir, if I may have a word?"

"What is it? What is it? I am in a hurry. So much to be done. No time to waste." The earl paused in his walk to stare at his usually calm butler.

"The cook has disappeared, milord. Decamped."

Lord Crompton glanced at Lady Montmorcy, then at his son. "Not surprising, I imagine. It merely proves, in a way, the charge I made regarding her. Had she nothing to fear, she would be here yet."

"I think not," muttered David. "We'd all had enough

of her scorched meals. If you had not sent her packing, I daresay the entire household would have risen in revolt.''

The earl looked chagrined, but said nothing in defense of the cook. He turned to Sidthorp. ''Who prepared the food today, for it seemed good enough to me?''

''Cook had sent word she was indisposed, so the kitchen maid stepped in to do what she could, with Mrs. Sidthorp's supervision. It was not until the kitchen maid sought instructions for the evening meal that the absence was discovered.''

''Gave Cook time to get clean away, eh? Well, carry on, Sidthorp. The kitchen maid is doing fine, until you locate a new cook.''

''Very good, milord.''

''I wondered about breakfast, for the eggs were not crisp, nor the toast burned,'' Egbert said as he passed the others on his way to the drawing room.

Lord Augustus lumbered toward the door, intent on convincing his son to join him in a game of billiards rather than settle for a dull round of cards in the drawing room.

Mr. Fynes gathered his papers, then removed himself to the study to complete his task. If he was put out at having to make the trip under false pretenses, he didn't show it. As it was, he had the problem of the estate books to handle, and that would occupy much time.

The earl and Aunt Bel strolled toward the corridor before glancing back to where David hovered at Elizabeth's side. ''We shall see you later, I trust. David, I cannot begin to tell you how much it has meant to have you at my side for support during this ordeal. I suspect that had it not been for the intrepid Miss Elizabeth, I should be dead by now.'' He gave them a benign smile.

He turned to Aunt Bel and added, ''Your Purvis is indeed a treasure. I hope that she comes with you?''

''Why, whatever do you mean, sirrah?'' Aunt Bel said in a fluttery voice, tapping the earl lightly on his arm.

''Why do we not find some privacy so I may explain it to you in greater detail?'' He chuckled, the twinkle in his eyes matched by her sparkling smile.

''Well, I shall never forgive you for that business of

the body. Dreadful thing it was," Aunt Bel declared as they continued their walk to the other side of the house.

The earl was last heard explaining how they had managed the deception, and why he and David had felt it necessary to conceal the truth from everyone, even his dearest Bel.

Alone in the library, Elizabeth turned to face David, her beloved rake. She wanted everything settled as soon as possible, for in the event she lost him, she wanted to be out of this house as soon as she could.

"I suppose you realize that it is no longer required that you marry me?" Elizabeth began. "With all that has gone on, the announcement that we are not to marry will be virtually ignored. I should think your father's resurrection from the dead, as it were, will have tongues wagging for some time to come."

"You wish to hand me the mitten?" He sounded outraged, or at the very least deeply wounded.

"Well," she blustered, unable to lie outright to him, "not jilt you, precisely. More like a mutual agreement. I would set you free, for I have no wish to marry a gentleman who treats me like a sister"—she ignored the several kisses that had been most decidedly unbrotherly—"and may long to marry someone he truly cares for. Unless . . . you must marry me for some vital reason?" Not waiting for his response, she rushed ahead. "I overheard Mr. Fynes tell you to marry me, for a wife could not testify against her husband. And you"—she cleared a sudden obstruction from her throat—"said that it wasn't what you wanted."

"Go on." He leaned against the desk, arms crossed, staring at Elizabeth with a look that did not make her words any easier.

"If there is trouble afoot, I shall marry you," she declared resolutely, "for I do care about you, David, and I would never wish anything bad to happen to you." She clasped her hands in front of her, willing him to reveal what it was that she could do for him. She had decided that if he wished her to wed him in order to protect him for some strange reason, she would, and gladly. As Rose often said, half a loaf was better than none. And besides, if given time, she might learn to entice him, so as to progress from teasing to something better.

"As to what precipitated the comment from Mr. Fynes. I had told him that there were moments when I could easily throttle Cousin Egbert. That prompted his reply, the one you unfortunately overheard."

"Then you do not *need* to marry me?" She thought she well concealed her disappointment from her voice. "Well, I hope that you will forgive me for shooting you, sir. But," she hastened to add, "you did ask for it, by coming into my room in the middle of the night." She reflected a moment while twisting the handkerchief in her clasp to mangled shreds. "Pity that Aunt Bel dashed in so quickly, or that you were foxed. Else you might have gone back out through the window, and no one would have been the wiser."

"I might have died without your care," he suggested, leaving the desk and walking to her.

"Oh, pooh. You would have found help," she replied, but did not sound convincing, even to her own ears. Then, determined to allow him freedom should he desire it, she said, "It is silly for Aunt Bel to say that we must marry merely because you were in my room on Valentine's Day. I believe that for two people to wed because of a superstition is not at all the thing."

Her resolution slipped when he reached out to bring her closer to him. She could feel the strength of his body as she was slowly drawn up against him.

He drew her closer yet, removing the shreds of cambric from her hands. He tossed the pathetic remains aside, then studied her face. "You care for me?"

She chewed her lower lip, uncertain what to admit. If she confessed her love for him, he might feel constrained to marry her out of pity. If she lied, and said she cared not a jot, he would be free, and she would be forever lost.

Deciding she would acknowledge something, she at last said, "I care for you."

"It is not like you to hedge, Elizabeth. One of the things I love about you is your fearlessness."

She heard only one word of what he said. "Love?" She snuggled closer to him, wondering if what she heard was true. Searching those beautiful hazel eyes, Elizabeth was at a loss on what to do next. What a pity David was merely a tease, not her splendid knight. Chivalry was indeed dead.

"I do *not* think of you as a sister, you know. Haven't for a long, long time." He feathered a finger along the sweet curve of her face, ending up in threading his hand through her curls.

Fascinated by this turn in their conversation, Elizabeth took another tiny step closer to him and said a breathless "Oh?"

"Indeed. I love you, my little one, and I suspect you love me as well, only are too wary to reveal it. Perhaps a bit of persuasion will help?"

With that, any gap between the two was closed completely.

Elizabeth cherished the feel of his strong arms about her, not to mention his powerful physique as she nestled in his embrace. If she had believed his previous kisses teasing, taunting, and quite provoking, this was not. This kiss was all any girl might wish for.

At last he released her, but just enough for her to look up at his face. There was no denying the expression she saw there. He loved her, plain as that aristocratic nose on his face.

"Ah, that look in your lovely aquamarine eyes tells me you do love me. Why is it so difficult to say?"

Honest as ever, Elizabeth said, "I did not wish you to feel compelled to marry me, as you might if I declared myself to you as you seemed to wish. I do love you, very much," she affirmed.

"My Valentine bride may come to me in March, but come she will. Since all in is readiness, I believe we should marry at once. I fear I cannot wait much longer for you, my little love."

As he captured her lips again in another kiss, Elizabeth decided that Aunt Bel's Valentine's Day superstition was not quite as foolish as she had first thought. In fact, it appeared to have considerable merit. Chivalrous knights might be well enough in books; she would happily settle for the man in whose arms she snuggled.